CRONE

A WITCH'S TALE

JAE MAZER

FEATHERED
TENTACLE PRESS

First Published by Feathered Tentacle Press, a division of Corvidae Literary Services, LLC., in 2018.

❀ Created with Vellum

PART I

The oldest and strongest emotion of mankind is fear, and the oldest and strongest kind of fear is fear of the unknown.

— H. P. LOVECRAFT

1

―――――

~

"We're out of rolls."

Rolls. Bread. Harmless carbs, notorious for comfort, for dipping, for stuffing oneself during an already gluttonous feast.

But not these rolls.

"Abbey? Would you?"

These rolls meant descent. Abbey hated it down there.

Abbey toyed with the food on her plate, pushing it with the tip of a fork prong, stabbing individual peas and hearing them scream in her head. She could already feel the abrasive carpet beneath her pink, smooth feet, the transition to the splintered slats at the base of the journey below.

Her dad's voice landed on her like a sledgehammer, a command on a single word.

"Girl."

She shivered and placed her hands on the table, preparing to push back and perform the requested task. A dozen sets of eyes bored into her: her aunt, her uncle, the immediate kin…

But she didn't stand. Her legs refused.

"She's fucking scared."

"Anton! Watch your language, young man," Mother scolded.

Anton was the stereotypical older brother, beefy and pretentious, an angst-riddled jock with a huge frame and an even bigger bravado. Six years Abbey's senior, he acted fifty years her wiser, and twice the cunt. She knew he was an idiot, and his jabs grated no flesh from her confidence, but she still recoiled at his words.

"She's being a fucking pussy, like she believes in the old woman," Anton said, chuckling through a mouthful of roast beef.

The old woman.

The tale Anton had been feeding Abbey since she was old enough to consider the possibility of monsters under beds and trolls under bridges. Now, at twelve years of age, her overt fear subsided, but still hid in the crannies of her mind.

"Anton, quit terrorizing your sister," Father scolded, looking over the top of his plastic Roy Orbison glasses.

"Sweetheart, you know there's no witch under the stairs right?" Mother said, slender hand grasping her daughter's stiffened forearm.

Abbey knew there was no witch under the stairs. She forced herself to know. But she didn't quite believe. So many trips down the stairs, phantom fingers groping at her calves, black eyes peering in the dark. Her brother's incessant reminders of the witch beneath the stairs, waiting to get children who were sent to fetch extra linens from the laundry room or potatoes from the pantry. Dinner rolls from the cold storage room.

"Girl, you ain't bein' told again."

The quiet strength in Father's voice told Abbey that this was the final instruction before she would have to carry out the task with a tanned ass, regardless of the extended family seated around the dining room table. Abbey commanded her limbs to do their duty. She moved back from the table, side-stepping her chair and pushing it beneath her place setting. She hung her head, her hair a veil of protection to hide the terror clearly advertised across her face. The clink of silverware alerted her to continued life in the dining room, but voices remained silent, an awkward recognition of the black sheep leaving the flock. As she passed into the kitchen and away from judging gazes, she heard Anton snicker, and the whispering released like water from a dam.

... that girl ...

... so immature for her age ...

... she acts a fool. Must be on the spectrum ...

... such a strange girl ...

The words didn't hurt. They never did anymore. The same scar slashed over and over again hurts less every time.

Abbey let the door close behind her, shutting her life behind. As she stood on the landing, the journey down seemed longer than ever, additional stairs appearing as she stared down into the black abyss. Her feet iron weights and muscles resisting, she grabbed hold of the rail and started the trek, the damp mustiness soaking into her bones with each step. The wood creaked, slicing the quiet of the dark, announcing her presence to the phantom predator in the space beneath the stairs.

"Oh Abbey," Anton had said once during a rather aggressive bout of teasing. "What if a twister comes? You know the safest place is under the stairs. It's where we'd have to go to survive. Under there. With her."

The laundry room with the noisy sump pump and jumpy old washer also housed the space under the stairs. The fabled nest of the witch. Thankfully, the laundry room had a door, and a weighted door at that. Father had weighted the door ages ago to keep the cold air contained in that room during the winter months. Unless it was propped open, Abbey wouldn't even have to look inside to verify the existence of the thing that wasn't there. Didn't stop her pulse from racing as her feet reached the last step.

Best way to approach the basement?

At a sprint.

Abbey loped across the concrete floor to the storage room door, ignoring the entire area at her left. After she was safely inside the storage room, she trotted to the back, into the cold storage, and fetched a bag of doughy dinner rolls. Without pausing to separate the approximate amount they might need, Abbey tossed the entire haul over her shoulder and turned to flee the basement. Her muscles relinquished their tight hold on her bones as she exited the storage room and saw the light on the stairs highlighting her escape route and the end of her plight. With a new confidence in her step, she walked towards the stairs at a more casual pace, scolding herself for her silliness.

Maybe they're right, Abbey thought. *I'm just a silly girl living in a silly world in her silly little head. Stupid child.*

But then. The light.

The light caught her eye and stilled her heart.

Moonlight, the after-supper glow of a mid-autumn night, shining through the window and cutting through the dusty, yellowed glass like a stained flashlight. Through a window that should have been hidden behind a shut, weighted door.

The laundry room door was wide open, silently screaming at her, a toothless maw waiting to eat her alive.

"Abbey?"

A sliver of light appeared at the top of the steps, casting the shadow of another flavour of monster.

"Coming, Uncle Herman." Abbey's voice went up the stairs, but her eyes remained below, searching the dark beyond the impossibly open door.

Heavy boots clumped down the stairs, slow and steady. Abbey's heart pounded in her ears, and she wasn't sure if she should run up or beneath the stairs for safety.

Maybe a scary old witch isn't so bad after all.

"What's the matter, girl?" Uncle Herman said, his portly figure eclipsing the bald light shining over the stairs.

I'm glad we don't have lights in the main room, Abbey thought. *I wish to see neither witch nor warlock tonight.*

"Comin' up so quick, darling?" Uncle Herman said, propping himself against the wall and leaning in such a way that it would be impossible for Abbey to slip by him and up the stairs.

I mustn't show fear, she thought. *A dog smells fear and reacts in primal ways.*

"Got what I need," Abbey said, puffing her chest and walking towards Uncle Herman as if he didn't make her flesh want to crawl straight off her bones. When she got close, she could smell his breath, a stew of tobacco and onion that made the meager contents of her stomach leap for her gorge.

"No need fer bein' in such a hurry, princess," he said, reaching out a clubbed finger and twirling it through a lock of her hair.

"Father wants the rolls while dinner's still on the table, I imagine," Abbey said.

Fear. He smells it.

"What's the matter, honey?" he asked, taking a step towards her, close enough that she could feel the heat from his body. Instinctively, she backed away, and his boots followed her bare feet until her heels were against the walls and his boots against her toes.

"I…" *leave me alone! I hate you! I hate you! I hate this, you, all of you!*

She thought it, screamed it in her head, but nothing came out. Nothing but wisps of trembling air.

"What's that, sugar?" Uncle Herman said, his voice a greasy whisper.

He wrapped his fingers through her hair until grasped in a fist, and leaned down until their lips brushed together when he spoke. "Somethin' wrong with that tongue of yours?"

When he ran his tongue over the edge of her lips, she dropped the bag of rolls and closed her eyes. Her heart slowed and she held her breath. She felt nothing and everything, and told herself the trick was to just wait.

Just wait a minute, five at most. He hasn't much time before they call down the stairs for us.

But nothing happened. Before it could begin, the laundry room door creaked, the fright of it sending Uncle Herman stumbling backwards, running a guilty hand through his thinning hair.

"Who's that?" he blubbered, a shudder latching to his voice. "I's jus' checkin' on her. Slow simpleton. Jus' a pack o' goddamn rolls —"

His clumsy defense was cut short when he turned and saw the upstairs door was still latched. His eyes trailed to the laundry room door, and the sliver of moonlight that had grown considerably more narrow in the past few seconds.

Abbey held her breath. Uncle Herman held his. But breathing persisted. It wasn't loud — certainly you had to focus to hear it — but it was there. Raspy. Wet. Laboured. A panting...

"Well then," Uncle Herman said, clearing his throat. "Let's get those rolls upstairs. Daddy be waitin' on those. Quit yer dilly-dallying."

He didn't look at her as he hurried across the room and back up the stairs. Didn't check on her even once as he passed through the upstairs door, leaving her behind to the hands of the unimaginable. Abbey stayed put in the dark, relieved and terrified, panicked and curious. She picked the bag of dinner rolls off the floor and walked up the stairs, her eyes searching the moonlit sliver as she passed by the laundry room door.

2

———————

The school bell rang, piercing through the fog in Abbey's head. She was already at her desk—had she still been up, she risked walking by her peers, a herd of judging eyes evaluating her hair, her skin, her every movement. She wasn't unpopular, but not popular either. Or liked. Or even noticed. What she was, however, was uncomfortable in her own skin. The feeling of her flaws pulsed like throbbing blisters, the plainness of her hair and clothing glowing like neon for all to see.

The dawn of puberty had made it infinitely worse.

Abbey had seen her first blood only a month before, and tried to keep it hidden from her family and friends. She didn't want to be a woman. Her breasts were tender, tampons had replaced the toys in her backpack, and she had to use her spending money to buy Midol rather than books and pencils. And now she was self-conscious about getting up in front of her class or walking through the halls, certain that her peers would notice her bloating, her budding breasts, or a sneaky crimson leak through her thick jeans.

The students filed to their desks, papers shuffling and chit chat dying as the teacher pulled out her lesson plan and scrawled chapter numbers on the board. Books opened and pencils lifted.

"Good morning everyone."

"Good morning Mrs. Tyler," chimed a chorus of small voices.

"Did we all bring the stories we wrote?"

Abbey cringed. The story. She loved to write stories. No, stories wrote themselves. All day everyday as she lived in her own head. A fully functioning universe of many worlds and plenty of characters to create the community and family she craved. But the stories in her head and the ones down on paper were very different from ones that needed to be presented to the scrutiny of outside minds.

"Abigail?"

Abbey's stomach lurched.

"Me?" she said, her voice a dampened whisper. "First?"

"Yes, honey," Mrs. Tyler said, more pity in her tone than Abbey cared for.

Abbey grasped her scribbler with clammy fingers and slid out of her chair, suddenly quite conscious of the wrinkles in her dress and the tangles in her hair. As she walked up the aisle towards the chalkboard, she felt little eyes all over her body, on each freckle, each fold of her far-too-baby-ish ensemble.

Then her shoe—that tattered Mary Jane with the scuffed toes and the yellowed bow. That goddamn shoe with the floppy sole caught on the edge of her metal desk, swiping her feet out from beneath her. She fell without grace, smashing straight down and catching herself with her face, knocking a tooth out on the hard, wooden floor.

Abbey lay there, eyes fixed on the chunk of tooth laying on the floor by her face, a puddle of blood-tinged drool pooling beneath her cheek, the sound of whispers and giggles ringing in her ears.

"Oh my goodness, dear," Mrs. Tyler said, clicking her tongue. "You need to be more careful."

Not "are you okay?" or "let me help you".

No hugs, no consolations.

You need to be more careful.

Abbey didn't cry. She picked herself off the floor and scooped up her scribbler as Mrs. Tyler ushered her out of the room towards the nurses station. Abbey walked down the hall, but didn't go see the nurse. She kept walking, out the front doors, into the sunshine and the fresh air and the freedom. She reached the road and sat on the sidewalk, waiting for the bus that would carry her from one prison to another.

~

ABBEY SCRATCHED HER PENCIL AGAINST THE YELLOWED PAPER OF her red journal, sketching lies of happy dreams that she never had in her head. She figured that's what girls her age were supposed to do, draw pictures of kittens and rainbows and happy families holding hands. That's what she did so they wouldn't think she was crazy. Which she was.

Must be, she told herself. *I'm not like others.*

The autumn day was unusually warm and moist, a gentle humidity resting on her skin and fattening her hair. The sun had kissed her nose, leaving a skiff of coppery freckles across her pale complexion. The thin straps of her sundress irritated her shoulders, which had cooked to an uncomfortable shade of pink despite the thick slathering of sunblock she had doused herself in before leaving the house for the day.

Saturdays were the best and the worst. The best because she didn't have to go to school, to be paraded in front of dozens of assessing eyes; she felt so suffocatingly alone while drowning in a sea of bodies. The worst because at home she really was alone, but a bad alone. Alone with a person or two, people more hateful than a hundred generic faces. Hateful, intimate interaction was in no way preferable to general, disconnected apathy.

But at least she had the outdoors. Outside the space was long and high, and the air clean and fresh. The old house was set on an expanse of land, with the nearest neighbours a good distance away on either side. The back border of the yard behind the house touched the edge of a forest thick with birch and pines and littered with deadfall; a terrain rarely traveled by much other than hooves, wings, and paws. Abbey often sat by that forest, leaned up against a tree, scribbling in her journal or nose in a book. She felt safe, lingering on the edge of two worlds, nature and civilization, not immersed in either; no expectations, no consequences. Just balance.

"Abbey, honey, come clean up for lunch!" Mother called from the back porch.

Abbey looked at Mother, standing there on the porch, wiping her hands in her tattered apron, her eyes heavy and face sullen and sagged. Abbey's heart clenched at the sight of the matriarch of her household, defeated and empty, carrying out the duties of life as if moving through a side-scrolling video game.

She gave up long ago, Abbey thought. *I wonder if giving up works. I wonder if it hurts less than trying.*

Mother locked eyes with Abbey for only a moment before looking down at her cheap pedicure and shuffling back into the house. Abbey's eyes were pulled to other movement in the yard. Her brother, sitting on the picnic table, finger dancing wildly across the screen of his cellphone, oblivious to the fresh air, the sunshine, the flora and fauna in his peripheral.

How grey a world his must be, Abbey thought.

And Father and Uncle Herman milled about in the long drive beside the house, covered in grease and sweat, beer seeping from their pores, hearty chortles and heavy hate hanging from their words. *Disgusting jokes, no doubt.* Abbey could see those words oozing like bile from their lips, dribbling down their chins like coagulated, black semen.

"Abbey!"

Anton's eyes had left his phone. They were now pinned on her, his lips pursed into a scowl, arms folded over his barrel of a chest.

"Mom called you, Abbey! Get yer ass in gear!"

Abbey considered scowling back—flipping him the bird, even—but opted to dip her head into a nod. She hadn't the energy to start the day with a battle. Anton rolled his eyes and stood, slipped his phone into his pocket, and made his way into the house for lunch. Abbey did not stand. Not immediately, anyways. She tucked her journal under her arm and placed her palms on the ground. She closed her eyes and felt the cool grass, the earth, and imagined sinking into that clay, the loam filling her mouth and nostrils, taking her away from all of this…

But she opened her eyes and stood, knowing full well a human girl couldn't grow in the ground like a plant; she could not and would not sink into the ground, no matter how hard she wished it. She would need to go back to that house, for food, for shelter, to live out her days until she was old enough to get away.

If she got away.

Abbey started walking towards the house, dragging her feet and taking her time, when her toe caught on a stray root poking up and fell to her knees. Something sharp pierced the skin on her kneecap, and Abbey's hand flew to her mouth to muffle the yelp of pain and surprise. She didn't want to draw attention to herself while the waters were still calm. She rolled onto her bum and hauled up her dress to evaluate the damage. A long, white shard protruded from her skin, a dark trail of blood seeping around the wound.

Abbey panicked, the sight of her blood and bone making her woozy and nauseous. She plucked the white shard, and it slid out with little resistance. She held it up to her face, examining it, seeing the blood caught in the tiny striations. Smooth, wet, so tiny…

Not hers.

Abbey looked at the ground and ran her hands through the soil, sifting through grass and leaves and dirt until she found another chunk of white, smoother and rounder.

More bone.

Not hers.

Abbey rolled onto her knees, favoring the one with the tiny gash, and started raking her fingers through the dirt like a dog digging for, well, bone. She found a piece here and there, the fragments appearing more often as she crawled towards the tree line. She picked each piece like a treasure, setting them aside in a tidy little pile. Didn't take long—just a few moments and a tiny skull—to realize that the bones belonged to forest animals; squirrels, mice, birds and the like. Each bone was bare, picked clean or flesh rotted from a lengthy stay in the ground.

So many bones in such a small area. Odd, that.

Her fingers didn't search further. The trail led into the woods, off the soft grass and into the harsh tangles of the forest floor. Abbey could see the ground was disturbed here and there, perhaps anthills or mole tunnels, perhaps more buried bones. The brush was thick and braided, but beaten in a single track. If Abbey's eyes hadn't been drawn to the disturbed earth, she wouldn't have seen the footpath.

She knew she had to go back. Go to the house, come because she had been beckoned, come because it was lunchtime and her family had commanded her presence. But curiosity clenched her gut, pulling her by the organs, drawing her into the trees. She walked, sandaled feet clumsy over heavy root and brush, following mounds and squirrel-piles of loose dirt. As she passed each one, she upset the piles with her toes, revealing stashes of little bones. She kept walking and the light grew dimmer, the sun filtered through a heavy canopy of trees.

So dark, she thought. *So still. So quiet.*

No wind.

It was breezy out. Surely she should have heard leaves rustling and branches creaking.

No birds.

No chirping, no falling flora from where talon and claw met branch.

Something is wrong.

She felt it, like ice cold water stabbing her flesh, the feeling of absolute solitude in the presence of a predator.

And then a hiss, a gurgling rattle, moist air expelled from thick lungs.

A grunt.

A throaty giggle in the woods, crawling up from the tree roots, through the soles of her feet and up her spine like icy, brittle fingers.

Abbey ran.

She ran fast as she could, straight out of those glittery pink flip flops she hated so much, straight through the branches and brambles that snapped her and cut her like razor blades on fishing poles. Dark warmed into the brightness of noon, and Abbey burst from the trees, careening at full tilt towards the house, the safe familiarity of abuse.

3

———

*A*bbey's belly was full of pasta, so that was good.

She tried with all her might to enjoy the minutiae of life, the little things that tugged at the corners of her mouth. Food, fresh air, smiles from strangers.

Happiness was sparse, but it was there.

And the day was pert near over, so that was good too. Sleep was an amazing, involuntary respite from reality. Abbey felt most at home under her covers, closed off from the outside world. Oh, how she wished she could hole up there, in that Fortress of Solitude and Blankets with her many books and the occasional meal delivered by faeries.

Unfortunately, it was only a short break the length of the moon's nightly performance, then life would begin again. Another day, more eyes, more loneliness, more hurt.

But it was a break, and Abbey relished it. She tried to stay awake as long as she could, flashlight, journal, and pencil in hand, concocting prose and art to release her inner demons. Her eyes betrayed her, though, heavy as lead curtains until the sliver of torch light became a red glow, and soon all was black and silent in her brain. She breathed deep, the cloak of sleep shrouding her, keeping her safe and content until her dreams would unsettle her.

Breathing in and out, in and out, heavy, raspy…

Abbey sat up, the intensity of her own exhalations startling her.

Was I snoring?

Abbey had never been woken by the sound of her own breath. The flashlight had gone out, batteries out of juice, and the cloudy night allowed no illumination from the moon. Their small, rural neighborhood had no need for streetlights, and Mother and Father had denied her a nightlight. *Those are for babies*, they'd said.

So there she was, in the dark with the goblins and demons of the night bundled in shadowed corners and huddled in the dark reaches of her closet. She pulled the shield of a blanket down her cheeks and below her eyes, daring to peer at the horror that waited. A shadow here, a shape there. *Did something just move*, she asked herself, every tremble of her lashes drawing her mind to ghosts and demons in her peripheral.

She jumped out of bed and turned on the light.

No scurrying, no hustling of guests or intruders trying to stow away under the furniture or back in hidey-holes. Just a room—books, curtains and furniture. And her, a frail, cowardly girl with a vivid imagination.

Abbey let her finger hover over the light switch for a moment before flicking it, sentencing the room to darkness again. She walked to her bed, the skin on her feet tingling as she approached the bare expanse beneath the box spring. She leapt up onto the mattress and pulled the covers up to her chin, monitoring the life of the room. It was still, but not silent. The house creaked and groaned, the wind caressing the tin eavestroughs outside.

But beneath the regular sounds were scratches that did not belong. Rhythmic, slow, grating.

Screee, screee, screee, screee…

Not the furnace, not the settling of the old structure, not Anton or Mother or Father shifting in their beds. Scratching. Too big and bold to be rodents, too small to be tree branches.

Abbey swung her feet out of bed and turned on her light again, focusing on the sound.

Screee, screee, screee, screee…

Below.

Abbey knelt and pressed her cheek against the hardwood floor, listening to the speech of the house and its levels below. Muffled and garbled, the dripping of pipes and the beating of her own heart. She sat up and listened carefully, cocking her head towards the floor.

The vent.

Abbey crawled to the corner of the room and peered through the slats of the vent. She saw nothing, but the sound reverberated there, bouncing up the tin tunnel from the furnace below.

Screee, screee, screee, screee…

It's just the furnace, Abbey thought, placing her palm against the open vent. *But there's no air…*

This time, Abbey left the light on when she crawled back into bed, her eyes fixed on the vent. The scratching persisted, growing louder in her mind until she feared the noise would claw away her last shred of sanity.

She jumped out of bed, threw her door open, and ran for the basement, knowing that if she moved any slower she would lose both courage and curiosity. A whole night listening to that sound and she would go mad and miss out on the serenity of sleep. She passed through the basement door and descended the concrete steps, tugging the chain to illuminate the naked bulb over the stairs. The mouth of the basement flooded in light, and she stepped no further than the light's reach and listened.

The scratching had stopped.

One minute, two. Abbey stood there, silent and still, until she was certain there was no scratching coming from the basement. When she decided it had been her imagination, she turned and put her hand on the rail, determined to resume her slumber.

SCREEE…

Right on top of her.

The furnace was across the way, adjacent to the cold storage room. The noise wasn't coming from there. She had never suspected it would be. It came from her left, behind that weighted door, from the room under the stairs.

Against every grain of sense she had, she went there, into that room. The floor was cold and damp, the air thick and musty. The washer and dryer were on the wall opposite the door, and a large drying tree was on the left, a makeshift wall for the space under the stairs. Abbey reached out and pulled the chain on the light, illuminating the tiny space and sending shadows pirouetting around the room. But the space under the stairs remained shrouded in black, its secrets hidden in the shadows.

"Hello?" Abbey said, her voice a dry quaver.

Nothing.

No response, no scratching. Nothing.

Abbey took a step forward, a bravery that surprised her, and moved the drying tree out of the way. The space under the stairs wasn't large, but deep enough that the family could cram in there, if need be. She stood on her tippy toes, then ducked down, trying to get a good look at the area from all angles. Piles of old comforters and camping blankets, a few crushed boxes, and an old David Bowie poster. No ghosts, goblins, witches, or other creatures of the dark.

Abbey backed away and pulled the chain, welcoming darkness into the room once again. Moonlight peeped through the small window at the ceiling, glistening off the wall and dripping silver to the floor. Abbey smiled at the beauty of the night seeping through the dusty air. She moved the drying tree back into place with her foot, but it jammed on something. Abbey jiggled it, but it wouldn't budge, and she didn't see what it was caught on. Her eyes focused on the silver, the wet gleam on the wall. She took a step forward and reached out, pressing her fingers into the silver moonlight.

Wet.

She pulled her hand away, fingers glowing white in the dark of the room, and saw the tips were coated in a deep darkness, warm and gritty.

Blood.

The drips of moonlight were reflections off bloody claw marks dragged across the wall. Abbey's eyes dropped to the floor, to the obstruction blocking the drying tree.

A foot, contorted and boney, covered in filth and dirt and rotting flesh, crimson talons protruding from knobby toes.

Abbey's eyes followed the body from foot to knobby knee, to bare hip and exposed, drooping labia. Abbey blushed and gasped, stumbling backwards into the laundry room, and the foot retracted into the mound of camping blankets under the stairs.

I imagined it, Abbey told herself.

It's dark, and I'm a coward. A pussy, like Anton said.

Her self-loathing was answered by a hiss, a raspy whimper, and the scratching.

Squeeeeeeee

Morbid curiosity was a Clydesdale that pulled Abbey forward until she was at the precipice of the space beneath the stairs. The gleaming silver gashes of moonlight had grown, elongated by contorted fingers dragging them downwards, fingertips ground to the bone and then some. Abbey turned to the owner of the hand, at the end of a long and crooked arm, and looked into its white, milky eyes. It turned its head towards her, and its gob opened into a wide, toothless cavern, black saliva oozing over a cracked bottom lip.

Abbey stepped back and stumbled over a balled-up blanket, crashing onto her bottom, sending pain radiating up her back. She scrambled away, but the thing rolled over, bare breasts and bloated belly dragging on the floor as it pulled towards her. Abbey, frozen in fear, responded with feeble kicks towards the beast, only one making contact before it wrapped its skeletal hand around her calf. She desperately sought for air to scream, but found none, remaining silent as the creature yanked her, pulling her close until they were nose to nose.

The creature sniffed her head to toe, flicking its thick, meaty tongue over her in spots here and there. It was massive, at least twice her size—hell, twice the height of Father, and as round as two Mothers combined. It ran its mangled, grey fingers through Abbey's hair, a crooked smile further cracking its already chapped and bleeding lips.

Abbey found her scream. Deep in her belly, finally crawling overtop her fear, the scream reverberated off the walls of the small laundry room, piercing the silence previously occupied by the creature's laboured breathing. It startled, darting back onto its haunches, and brayed like a wolf, black mouth aimed at the sky and eyes wet with tears. Abbey wailed and it howled, a chorus of the dead and damned. And in the painful song, Abbey gathered the fortitude to move, launching forward and shoving the creature back into its hidey-hole before running out the door and up the stairs, screams of terror exploding from her throat the whole time. She reached the opposite side of the kitchen before being greeted by the cavalry.

"Abigail Theresa," Mother scolded, grabbing her by the shoulders. "What in tarnation is all this racket?"

"Why the hell you out of bed, girl?" Father said, his face a harsh scowl.

"It's… it's her," Abbey gasped, her eyes moving frantically between her family and the door to the basement.

"Her?" Mother asked, also looking at the door.

"Oh," Anton said, snickering as he came down the last few steps from their second story. "The fucking witch, is it?"

"Y-yes," Abbey stuttered, her gorge resting high on her stomach. She could still feel the claws on her calf, the tongue on her flesh…

"Pussy," Anton said, shaking his head. "Bullshit. I've been feeding you a steaming pile of bullshit for years, and you bought it like the stupid twat you are."

"Anton!" Mother scolded, as if the torment surprised and horrified her.

"Girl, what is this nonsense?" Father asked, his eyes moving to the open door to the basement.

"I'm telling the truth!" Abbey wailed, her tears now fully liberated, soaking the front of her nightgown. "She's there... I think... she..."

Silence enveloped the kitchen, the family staring in uneasy disbelief at the stairs. For a moment nobody moved, all focus on the lack of sound and movement from the basement. Anton was the first to crack, letting out a nervous chuff before turning to the patriarch for direction. Mother did the same, wringing her hands and looking at her husband.

"Hogwash," Father mumbled as he stomped towards the basement door, descending the stairs without hesitation. Mother fetched a wet cloth from the sink and cleaned up her daughter's face, feeling for the fever that might have caused the ridiculous accusations.

"Unbelievable," Anton muttered, and Mother tossed the wet cloth at him.

"Damn you," she said. "Terrorizing your sister like this. No doubt she's scared, you brat."

"She's thirteen years old, goddamnit!" Anton shouted. "If she don't know better by now she's a fucking idiot!"

"Watch your language young man!" Mother shouted, moving towards her eldest. "You're eighteen, and you don't know your head from your ass half the time!"

Abbey couldn't help but smile, partially from her brother getting chewed out for once, partially from nervous energy. All was silent down below. Father had said nothing yet, despite there being such a small area to explore.

"Daddy?" Abbey said beneath the squabble of Mother and Anton. Abbey stood and walked to the basement door, peering down into the dark, trembling hands clasped at her chest. It took only a moment for Mother to notice, and she darted down the stairs past Abbey, calling for her husband.

"Great job," Anton said, patting Abbey on the back. "Got 'em rattled now. Your ass is gonna be tanned when they find you've worked 'em up over nothing."

Abbey's hands continued to tremble, and the tears flowed freely, but not for the memory of the beast beneath the stairs. Not for the worry that Father may have succumbed and been consumed, and the possibility that Mother was about to share the same fate. She cried because there may actually be nothing; that she was indeed crazy, and just caused herself a whole lot of pain.

"Damn girl," Father snapped, slamming the laundry room door. Mother trailed behind him up the stairs, tugging at his shirt, her placating tones resting upon deaf, determined ears.

By the time Father had reached the top of the stairs, Abbey had retreated to the far side of the kitchen, her back pressed against the icebox and her hands at her collar, ready to protect her face.

"Let me see your hands," Father demanded, grabbing her wrists, her bones groaning under the pressure.

He pulled her hands to his face and examined the tips of her lily-white fingers still coated in blood.

"It's… it's not mine, Daddy."

"Whose, then?"

"Hers."

Abbey yanked her hands out of Father's grasp and examined the blood herself. The crimson globs at the end of her fingers were tacky, smearing dry blotches of brown on the pads of her fingers.

Hers, yes?

"I saw the blood. I mean, I saw the moonlight shining on the wetness on the wall and I—"

"You what?" Father hissed. Mother and Anton were at her side, staring at her fingers.

"I…"

Abbey's eyes were focused on her fingers, the puffy skin, the gnawed-down nails…

"Maybe… no, but… I…"

"Sleepwalking?" Mother offered.

Take it, girl, her eyes said. *Take it, or he'll take you for a round you'll feel for days.*

"Yes," Abbey said, brushing her hands on the front of her night-gown. "I can't remember getting down there. Sleepwalking. I'm so sorry."

Father eyed her from head to toe, then grasped her hands once more, examining them closer. "Sleepwalking, eh?"

"Yes, Daddy. I guess so. Sorry."

He dropped her hands, warily satisfied with the explanation. Or just too angry to care. "Well, you got yourself some problems, then, clawin' up the wall that way." He directed his attention to Mother. "That girl is nothing but trouble. Should've breastfed 'er longer."

"Breastfed my fucking ass, you buffoon," Mother said, striking him on the arm and storming out of the kitchen. "I tell ya, if men had the babies and the tits…"

Father followed Mother, and Anton followed them both, looking back over his shoulder to snicker at Abbey one last time before returning to his room.

He can feel safe wherever he is, whatever he does, wherever he goes. All because of his penis.

Abbey had nowhere to go, and no one to comfort her. She considered going after Father, telling him the witch was real and that she had left the marks, and that Abbey was terrified and wanted to be cuddled and comforted. She was. And she did want that. Maybe Father would beat her, call her names, and they would laugh at her, pity her, scold her. But at least they would be there, touching her, speaking to her. And she wouldn't be so alone and so afraid.

Or so crazy, as it were.

Abbey shuffled up the stairs to her room, managing to close the door behind her before she broke into violent sobs. She ran to her bed and dove under the covers, screaming her anguish into the mass of feather and cotton squeezed against her face. She cried until her eyes were swollen and her throat raw, feeling her tension melt into her mattress. Exhaustion started to take hold, but an ache tickled her senses. A cramp, a slight pain. She curled up into a ball and her hand travelled to her calf, and the five, hard lines of bruising forming in the dark.

Abbey wished the witch had killed her. All the pain would be gone, and she wouldn't have died alone.

4

———

*A*bbey spent a good portion of her lunch hour crying in the girl's locker room. Not on the benches where other girls might console or check on her, but locked in a stall, bottom stuck to the plastic toilet seat, her anguish hidden from the world. The other kids weren't mean to her, but they judged. They all judged. Abbey felt it, so she knew it to be true. She didn't want to feel them. Their eyes, their pity. Worse than that, their indifference pained her.

When Abbey finally emerged from the stall, leaving just enough time to grab a quick bite to eat before her next class, she was not alone. *Odd, that,* she thought, glancing at the clock on the wall. *Never anyone in here towards the end of lunch. The next PE doesn't start until last period—*

"Hey Abbey," Gloria said, eyes focused intently on her mascara application in the warped bathroom mirror. "Whatcha doing in here? Have you had lunch?"

Gloria was beautiful. Calm and happy. With her soft peach smile, precise make-up, lush ringlets of copper hair, and emerald green eyes. And confidence that swelled beyond her to the chest of any passerby. Abbey wanted to be her, if only for a moment.

"Abbey?"

Abbey saw Gloria's eyes flit from her own to Abbey's reflection in the mirror.

I look like a pale, sickly deer in headlights, Abbey thought, and dropped her chin to examine her shoes.

"Hey," Gloria said. "I don't care what you were up to in there. We all have our silly things," she said, waving the mascara wand through the air. "My mama hates me wearing this. Says it's 'conformist' and 'caters to the whims of men'. I just like the glam. I like how it makes me feel. And why shouldn't we feel good, right?"

Abbey nodded, resisting the urge to make eye contact lest Gloria realize that she was a supreme loser. Gloria set her mascara down on the counter and walked to Abbey. She moved the hair away from Abbey's face and grabbed her hand. Abbey lifted her head and looked at Gloria.

"Abbey. Are you okay?"

"Yeah. Fine." Knee-jerk response Abbey had been regurgitating for years.

Gloria's thumb moved up Abbey's forearm to the shadow of a bruise.

"Hey, you wanna hang out after school?" Gloria asked.

Abbey choked on her own breath.

"Yes!" Abbey said, hand flying to her mouth as soon as the over-exuberance had been spewed.

Stupid, stupid, stupid girl, Abbey thought. *Now she thinks you're a desperate loser.*

"Good," Gloria said, giving Abbey's hand a squeeze. "I'm glad. I've been wanting to ask you for quite some time, but don't see you around much after hours. You live on that cool property on the edge of the woods, right? So much land. You like it?"

"I like it well enough," Abbey said. "Lonely, though. Kinda isolated."

"I bet it is," Gloria said, dropping Abbey's hand and returning to her preening. "I like being in town, walking distance to everything.

But sometimes I think it would be awesome to disconnect, be closer to the woods. Town gets monotonous after a while."

"I have no friends," Abbey blurted, again dropping her eyes to the floor as soon as the words had been liberated.

Gloria looked at her, a warm smile on her face. "How could you? There's no one out there! How do you get to and from?"

"School bus."

"Well, tell you what. Why don't we skip the afternoon tomorrow, go get some food and browse town."

Abbey shuffled her feet and clenched her own arm, gnawed nails digging into her flesh. It was a habit she had developed as a very small child. *Focus on the pain from your own fingertips to distract from all other discomforts.*

"C'mon Abbey," Gloria said, her green eyes locking onto Abbey's pale greys. "What's the harm?"

What's the harm, indeed, Abbey thought, the feeling of impending lashes radiating through her body. *Gonna happen anyways. Might as well make it worth my while.*

"Yeah, sure," Abbey said, colour rising in her pale cheeks. "Sounds like fun."

"Settled, then," Gloria said, snapping her makeup caddy closed with a satisfied click. "Grab your stuff and meet me at the corner of Poplar and 91st. You know where that is?"

Abbey nodded.

"See you there in, say, half an hour?"

Another nod.

"Great!"

And with that, Gloria spun on her heels, red ringlets bouncing off her shoulders as she flitted out the door like a hummingbird, boot heels clicking on the floor, audible even after the locker room door closed, leaving Abbey in solitude once again.

～

Gloria's laughter sang in Abbey's ear like the song of a whippoorwill, shrillness and pleasure riding the same note. Abbey couldn't help but chuckle, the ridiculousness of the giggle fit infecting her like a virus.

"And then he just spat it out," Gloria choked through the laughter.

"Spat it?"

"Yes!!!!"

The laughter continued for an extra-long minute before the girls calmed down enough to draw sensible breaths without tears dripping from their eyes and root beer from their noses. Quiet washed over them as the sun hovered high in the sky, their young skin throbbing with the last tint of summer colour. Abbey felt good. Really good.

The girls found a dirt nook to sit in behind the old movie theater, in a brick alleyway devoid of traffic or eyes. They talked of food, of books, of the funny shoes with the reflective flames and neon laces that the football team wore . "Like dirty, stinky peacocks!" Gloria laughed. They sipped on root beer floats they had picked up at the Macs store kitty-corner from the school, and stuffed their faces with coke-bottle gummies Gloria lifted while Abbey payed for their beverages. They played in that alley for hours, gossiping and racing around, braiding each other's hair and painting each other's nails with glittering lavender polish that Gloria stole from her mother's top drawer.

On that long afternoon frozen in time, hidden from the rest of the world, Abbey was at peace. Not really, not deep down, but in a shallow illusion. Abbey thought she might create a home there in that alley, walls of cardboard boxes papered with colorful trash, meals scrounged from the nearby diner. Her own boss, her own rules, a personal space all her own.

"Whatcha thinking about?"

Abbey startled, the voice of her friend—though beautiful—drawing her back into the sadness of a reality without cardboard walls and a mismatched buffet of scraps.

"Nothing," Abbey said, punctuating the lie with a shrug of her shoulder.

"Mhmm," Gloria said, a carefully shaped brow arching over her green eye. "You worried you're gonna get in trouble? For being here? Doing this?"

"No," Abbey said, muscles tensing. "Yes."

Both girls were quiet, Gloria studying her shoes, searching between the laces for something to say.

"I'm afraid and I'm not," Abbey said. "I mean, what's the worst that could happen, right?"

Gloria looked up, her face communicating her lack of belief, but she smiled regardless. "Yeah. Better to have fun now, apologize later. Pretty much sums up being young, right?"

"Yeah," Abbey said, feigning a smile of her own.

"We should shove off, though. Mum's gonna be looking for me at pickup, and you have a bus to catch."

"Suppose so," Abbey said, the lightness of her mood growing fat and thick and heavy once again.

"Hey," Gloria said, putting her hands on Abbey's face. "Besties, right?"

"Besties?"

"Yeah, besties!" Gloria said, leaning in and brushing Abbey's lips with her own. Abbey's mouth tingled where Gloria had pressed her lips, the brief contact sending a jolt through her body and a flush to her cheeks. "To you , my beautiful friend!" Gloria said, raising her plastic cup to cheers with Abbey.

Gloria giggled and flew to her feet, her amber ringlets bouncing off her pink shoulders. She extended her hand to Abbey and Abbey took it, allowing her new friend to pull her to her feet and down the alley, dragging her back to reality.

~

ABBEY SET HER DISHES IN THE SINK, THE CLINK RATTLING THE

thick tension hanging in the air like Beijing smog. She didn't know what was wrong, but she knew something was up. Dinner had been quiet, with barely a word spoken between her folks, Anton, anyone. Anton's eyes remained on his plate the whole meal, and his quips hidden behind a face-wide smirk.

Something's amusing him, Abbey thought.

Abbey, for once, was the chatty one, trying to draw something out of her suddenly reserved family.

Abbey didn't like it.

The calm before the storm.

Is it me? she wondered. *Do they know?*

"Is there dessert?" Abbey asked, her eyes searching Mother's sullen face.

"In a bit," Mother said, without a gram of sugar in her tone.

"Why?" Abbey asked, wondering why they were waiting. Wondering what was coming.

"Excuse me?" Father said. "Because we said so, is why."

Father's eyes were not like Mother's or Anton's. They were not trained on the floor, or his hands, or the dishes in the sink. They were locked on her, boring deep inside her head.

"Yes sir," Abbey said, lowering her eyes to the floor.

Mother cleared her throat and wiped the dish in her hand for the eighth time. "Aunt Petal and Uncle Herman will be here soon. We'll have dessert then."

"They're coming on a weeknight?" Abbey asked.

"Yes," Father snapped. "Now go about your business until they get here. Go do your homework."

"I haven't got any—"

"Go." Father's voice was heavy and stern, more than usual. And, as usual, Abbey obeyed. She trod up the stairs at a clip, skipping every second step on the way. She had no desire to be at the door to greet Aunt Petal and Uncle Herman. In fact, she didn't much care for making an appearance at all, even though Mother's marble cake waited under the dome in the kitchen. No dessert was worth those visitors.

By the time the doorbell rang, Abbey had convinced herself she would stay up in her room, working on phantom homework that had an imminent deadline, thus preventing socialization that evening.

Turned out that wasn't an option.

"Girl!" Father shouted. "Down here!"

Abbey opened her door a crack, and swore she could smell the sweat under Uncle Herman's man-breasts.

"No thanks," she called down, voice barely strong enough to carry her words where they needed to go. "I'm not hungry, and I've got to finish this—"

"Girl. Now."

No bend in Father's voice. Abby closed her journal and slid on her slippers, procrastinating as long as she believably could before making her way downstairs.

The scene on the main floor seemed stuck in molasses, a thick and awkward tension slowing everyone's movements. Uncle Herman sat on the couch, unlit cigarette hanging from his moist lower lip— Mother would kill him if he lit that inside. Aunt Petal stood on the threshold of the kitchen, one foot on the tile and one toe tapping the berber in the living room. Her hands were clenched together, fists held tight to some passive aggression.

"Hi."

Abbey's voice stilled the room. The only movement was Aunt Petal's eyes snapping towards the sound of Abbey's voice the minute it was airborne. Uncle Herman examined the front of Abbey's pajamas briefly before dropping his gaze to the magazine in his lap. Father stared out the window and Mother banged around the kitchen. Anton was nowhere to be found.

No one said hello to her.

"How are you tonight?" Abbey said, reluctant to come down the final step.

"Fine," Aunt Petal said, ice in her words.

A dish dropped into the sink and slipper clogs charged across the kitchen. Mother pushed past Aunt Petal, shoving her out of the way with a firm nudge of her pudgy shoulder, and stood right in front of Abbey at the bottom of the stairs.

"And how was your day, young lady?" Mother said, not a hint of interest in her tone.

Oh shit.

"What do you mean?" Abbey said, her voice soft and steady. "We talked at dinner —"

"You know full well what I mean," Mother said. She stepped to the side and nodded her head towards Aunt Petal. Her eyes never left Abbey's. "Or do I need to hear it from your aunt?"

Abbey looked over at Aunt Petal's face, a combination of judgement and disapproval furling her precisely manicured eyebrows. Abbey craned her neck to look at Uncle Herman on the couch, whose glistening lips had curled into a sinister grin. One more turn of her head gave Abbey a partial view of Father's face, anger carved into stone. Rage. Abbey looked back at Mother, whose face feigned anger, but whose eyes were damp with tears. Tears of fear; anger at what Abbey had done, but not because of the act itself. Because she had gotten caught. Because of the consequences, consequences Mother didn't want.

Abbey loved Mother, and Mother her, so much so that they hated each other for it. Abbey hated Mother for not stopping *it*, and Mother hated Abbey for causing herself trouble.

"Gloria," Abbey said, the word trembling. She picked at her nails, chipping away at the condemning lavender polish. "I skipped and went with Gloria, got some floats and messed around. Like normal girls, Mom."

Mother's lips sealed tight, her eyes far away in a distant youth. Then her eyes dropped to the floor, a resignation that turned Abbey's stomach. When Mother stepped away, Abbey saw that Father had stood, and was looking at her. Right into her. His pants were sagging, his old leather belt grasped in a white-knuckled fist.

"I saw you, Abbey," Aunt Petal said, her voice distant and dampened, like she spoke through a wall of pink insulation. Her voice kept going, but Abbey didn't hear it. All she heard was a humming drone where Aunt Petal's voice should have been, and the creak and strain of the leather belt as Father massaged it in his massive fist.

"I don't have friends," Abbey said, to anyone and everyone in the room. "I don't hang out with anyone, ever. I didn't think it would hurt, and it wasn't a boy, and we didn't do anything bad, well, 'cept cut school, but... "

Nothing changed. Aunt Petal didn't stop talking, though Abbey still didn't hear what she was saying. Uncle Herman still sat, disgusting smile plastered across his pocked face. Father still stood, squeezing that belt. The one thing that changed was Mother.

Mother had left the room. She was in the kitchen, or maybe out back, Abbey wasn't sure. She hadn't noticed Mother's exit from the scene, but she knew what Mother's absence meant.

Father moved towards her, steps casual and calculated.

"N-no, Father, please. Is it so bad?"

Abbey turned to Aunt Petal, who had fallen silent when Father became animated. Aunt Petal left, suddenly remembering she had some sort of business in the kitchen. Uncle Herman, though. His business was there, and intriguing enough for him to shift forward in his seat to the edge of the couch.

It was too late. Once again Abbey would be the outlet for Father's rage. He waited for the most minor infractions to release his irritations and frustrations. He was an angry, hateful man, and she was a weak little girl. The perfect scapegoat.

Abbey's panic turned to calm, her shaking quieted, and her heart softened to a dull pounding in her head. Father was upon her in an instant, his cold, calloused hand tugging the ribbon of her pajama bottoms, loosening the bow in one smooth movement. She felt the fleece pants hit the top of her feet as Father sat on the bottom step, grabbing her around the waist and bending her over his knee in a flawless, uncontested move.

Abbey felt many things. She felt the snap and cut of the leather belt as it struck her backside over and over, welts upon welts. She felt the hateful push of Father's hand holding her against his lap as he struck her like an animal. And she felt Uncle Herman's eyes on her, hot and heavy, watching her, her privates hoisted in the air, covered by thin, white panties, her flesh jiggling with every strike of the belt.

Abbey opened her eyes and turned her head, morbidly curious about the expression on Uncle Herman's face. His grin had widened, exposing yellowed-teeth, and drool glistened on his fat tongue. His hand rested perilously close to his groin, his finger twitching and stroking, inching towards his swollen shaft with every strike of the belt.

And a hand.

Abbey didn't notice Uncle Herman anymore. Or her exposed lady parts, or the lash of the belt.

All she saw was a hand, grey and rotting, fingers long and crooked like tattered tentacles. They clenched the couch, squeezing the upholstery and splitting the thin fabric with hostile strength. Uncle Herman didn't notice the presence creeping towards him, depressing the couch mere centimeters from his shoulder. The fingers seemed to have a sense of smell, quivering and scouring for Uncle Herman's flesh, hungry for his pain. Uncle Herman—finally able to take his eyes off Abbey's delicacies for a moment—caught her eye, and Abbey couldn't help herself. Despite the physical pain, the humiliation, and the terror of the mysterious hand, she smiled, relief and humour tugging at the corners of her mouth like twine.

Uncle Herman shifted uncomfortably in his seat, his head cocked as if to communicate his confusion. His lips parted, ready to scold or tattle, to wipe the grin from Abbey's face, but his words caught in his throat. The hand had stretched and groped its way far enough to drag a sharp, crimson talon down the flab of Uncle Herman's cheek.

Uncle Herman shrieked and flailed like a damsel in a spider's web.

"What the hell—" Father said, springing to his feet, relinquishing his grip on both Abbey and the belt, allowing both to fall to the floor.

"Get it off!" Uncle Herman squealed, brushing at his shoulder and stumbling over the coffee table. He landed on the floor with a boom that made the floor creak, and scrambled back against the wall. Abbey came to her knees, pulling up her pajama bottoms and smoothing her hair. The sound of the room became muted in her ears, Father bellowing at Herman to tell him what was happening and Herman blathering an incoherent reply while shaking a finger at the couch.

There was nothing there to see. Abbey looked at the couch, also watching the scrambling men in her peripheral, and rose to her feet. She walked over and peered into the tiny space that separated couch from wall, and in the dark expanse between the couch and the end table.

Nothing.

Of course there's nothing, she thought. *How could there be? There's no space for anything…*

But her eyes told a different story. And if her eyes were not to be believed, surely Uncle Herman's unashamed screeches were.

"Get away from there!" Father barked, grabbing Abbey's arm and pulling her to the side. "Bloody hell, Herman. Was it a bug, you think? Snake?"

"No blimin' snake, you fool!" Herman snapped. "Up in here? Never seen it. And that would have to be one hell of a bug."

Both Abbey and Father looked at Uncle Herman as if his screws had wiggled loose.

How does it feel, you goat's arse? Abbey thought.

"Right here, on my cheek," Herman said, poking his finger deep into his flesh, punctuating the seriousness of the matter.

Father looked once again, actually pulling the couch out for a better look.

"Girl, fetch me a torch so I can check under this thing. Put minds to rest," he said, glaring at his frenzied Brother-in-Law.

Abbey retrieved the light, of course, but in the end, the search was fruitless; they found no bugs, no snakes, no beasts of any kind. Barely a dirt bunny—Mother kept a tidy space. Shoulders were shrugged and heads were shaken, and Uncle Herman attributed his episode to long hours and little sex. Abbey waited for the commotion to settle before approaching Father.

"Are we done?" she asked, voice forced to be small.

Father looked at her, subsiding anger and rising shame on his face, and gave a curt nod.

'Sorry, Father," Abbey said. "I won't cut class again."

"See that you don't," he said.

Abbey went upstairs, stealing a long glance at the couch and the absence of the hand that never was.

5

———

*A*bbey hovered in the lunch line, tray balanced on flat palms, mind miles away, tangled in grey fingers. The previous night's lashing lingered nowhere in her thoughts, but the monstrous hand was on the forefront of her mind. Its calloused texture, the creeping, disjointed slither of those gangly fingers...

"It's not that exciting. Yams or mash."

"Huh?" Abbey said, turning to the voice.

"Whatcha thinking about?" Gloria asked. "Certainly not pondering the choice of slop," she said, tapping the glass protecting the lunch selections, earning her a scowl from the androgynous lunch server.

Abbey's mouth opened, but nothing came out. What could she say? She didn't even know what to tell herself. She resorted to her classic shoulder shrug, and pointed to the peas and mash. The lunch thug plopped the selection onto a plate, and Abbey shuffled down the line, taking a roll and a pastry before following Gloria to a window seat. Gloria sat, hardly breathing around her tales of the new hair mascara she had found down at the Macs store on Clairmont Street, hand flying through the air as she attempted to act out the swath of colour choices.

Abbey took her time sitting. Though her punishment had been absent from her thoughts for most of the morning, her throbbing backside served as a reminder every time she eased herself down to sit. Her delicate seating did not go unnoticed.

"You okay?" Gloria said, suddenly quiet with hands stilled.

"Fine," Abbey said.

"Fine," Gloria repeated. "Mhmm."

The cafeteria was noisy with the comings and goings of herds of kids, arguing, laughing, chewing and sputtering. But the bubble around the table where Abbey and Gloria sat was drenched in heavy quiet, words hanging in the air unsaid.

"Are you okay?" Gloria asked.

"You already asked that," Abbey said.

"I know, but—"

"I'm fine, I said."

Neither looked at each other. Both kept chewing.

"It's not okay, you know."

Abbey looked up at Gloria, whose face was red and eyes trained on her peas.

"What's not okay?"

"Getting hurt. Them hurting you."

"I don't know what you're—"

"You don't have to tell me," Gloria lifted her eyes and looked deep into Abbey's, "but I know."

The girls remained eye-locked for a moment, uncomfortable and emotionally charged, before Abbey broke free and returned to her meal. Silence ensued. Abbey shifted uncomfortably in her seat, tapping her foot along with the rhythmic, heavy beating of her heart, her face hot and flushed.

"Why should you be embarrassed, Abbey? They're doing it. Not you."

I hate being a helpless little child. Powerless.

Abbey jumped when Gloria's hand covered hers.

"How bad is it?" Gloria asked, her lower lip trembling.

"Never mind," Abbey said, pulling away.

"I do mind!" Gloria said.

Abbey wanted to grab her tray, to pick up and go somewhere else where she could be alone with her thoughts, removed from reality, to a land where phantom hands and witches were the terror lurking in the shadows; terrors that aren't real are far less terrible.

She looked up at Gloria, at the heavy moisture on her big green eyes that threatened to mar that perfect wing-tip of liner that aged her to a card-wielding adult. It was too much. Abbey already felt like a baby. She didn't need to start bawling in front of everyone. She picked up her tray and spun around, heading to the bathroom to eat her lunch in solitude, but Gloria intervened. She grabbed Abbey's forearm, trying to stop her, but Abbey braced herself, wincing from an impending blow that wasn't coming, and the tray came crashing to the ground.

Once the peas and mash had settled, both girls realized that all eyes were on them. Gloria dropped to her knees and started to scoop the mess back on to the tray.

"Oh Abbey," Gloria said. "I didn't mean—"

Abbey left the upset tray and food behind, along with her friend, and headed for the bathroom. She heard whispers—some hidden, some loud and mocking—as she passed through the herd. She quickened her step, eager to get away and forget, forget, forget...

She slammed into the locker room and barred herself behind a shower door, sliding down the wall until her swollen buttocks settled in a lukewarm puddle of water. She clasped her face, covering her mouth and trying to stifle weeks, months, years worth of tears from escaping. She held her mouth even tighter when the bathroom door squealed, announcing someone's entrance. Probably Gloria. She didn't want to talk to her. She was nosey, and was making her uncomfortable.

After a few seconds, Abbey stopped sniffling and held her breath.

After the squawk of the door there had been no sound—no water running, no peeing in the toilets, no spray from the shower. Nothing. If it was Gloria, she would have announced her presence, shoving her prying nose straight through every door and curtain until she found Abbey.

"Hello?" Abbey said in a voice barely above a whisper. "Who's there?"

There was no answer. Abbey listened for footsteps or breath or anything that might allude to another occupant in the locker room, but the room remained silent. Abbey unlocked the stall door and opened it a crack, squeezing her face against the grimy metal, trying to get a look at the room beyond her stall. After not seeing anyone, Abbey got frustrated by the interruption of her private meltdown.

"Hello?" she said, stepping out of the stall and looking around. "I heard you come in."

She cocked her head at a faint rustling sound, finally cluing in that it was the communal shower. Her irritation gave her bravado, and she charged forth, ready to confront the stealthy intruder. She rounded the corner to the showers. The water was running, steam hanging like heavy gossamer in the air, but no one was there.

"Hello?" Abbey said, angry fists loosening to trembling fingers.

Slowly, she walked over to the shower knob to turn it off, but stopped as she approached. The shallow basin under that shower-head was retaining hot water that covered the tops of her shoes. She knelt closer to the drain so she could see through the steam. The drain was clogged. A mass of hair, coppery auburn ringlets clumped in a dense mass covered the holes of the drain, floating in the accumulated water like fingers of orange blood. Abbey reached down and ran her fingers through the hair, pulling it out of the drain in handfuls, massive wads that she tossed to the side.

And it didn't stop.

There was no end to the hair. Abbey kept frantically pulling hair out of the drain, pitching it to the side, but more hair kept coming—a seemingly unending, regenerating growth of hair clogging the entire drainage system. She would have kept going, too, if not for the yelling and commotion outside the locker room door.

Abbey stopped and cocked her head towards the sound. She heard kids, teachers, the principle, maybe?

And above all, she heard Gloria. That sing-song voice cater-wauling like a tortured feline.

Abbey jumped up and ran towards the door, but the reflection in the mirror stopped her dead in her tracks. She was covered in the hair from the drain—her arms, her shirt, even her face. Red hair, curly, clumped with…

Abbey looked closer at her reflection. At the wet hair clinging to her, stains of crimson seeping into her white shirt, clumps of bloody meat attached to the hair…

Abbey ran, screaming and flailing at the hair in a futile attempt to free herself from the webs of gore coating her every surface. She burst from the bathroom, sprinting the few steps between the locker room and the cafeteria. She stopped when she saw a crowd had gathered, their eyes turning from their initial subject to the girl who had just come exploding like a screeching fool from the bathroom.

"Blood!" Abbey screeched at them. "Hair, and…"

There was blood and hair, all right. Abbey snuck a glance through a gap in the bodies, and saw Gloria, sprawled out on the floor, dark crimson trickling down her pale, freckled face, those coppery curls caked in a bloody mass on her forehead.

Abbey stopped screaming. "What…?"

She looked down at her body, her clothing, her arms. All bare, clean, devoid of hair and blood and other undesirable matter.

"What…" she repeated, her lower lip trembling.

"Abbey?" Gloria said, her voice sloppy through snotty tears.

"It's okay, dear," the principle said, wrapping an arm around Abbey and turning her away from the scene. "Gloria slipped on the floor and hit her head on the table. Nasty spill, but she'll be fine."

"But in the locker room…" Abbey trailed off, giving her body a cursory glance before looking back at Gloria, who was still splayed out on the floor, her face a stunned mask of confusion. The way Gloria looked at her, the fear in her eyes.

A fall.

That's all.

But…

Abbey caught a peek at the blood on the corner of the cafeteria table, bits of hair and flesh hanging off in tendrils. Her eyes trailed back to Gloria, who had resumed her wailing, holding her head as blood poured down over her eyes.

And the weathered, grey hand that was clamped around her shoulder.

6

"Terrible thing," Mother said as she wiped the suds off her hands with a dishtowel. "Have you spoken with her? This Gloria girl?"

Abbey was at Mother's side at the sink, drying dishes and putting them away. She looked over at Father, who was leaned back in his chair, newspaper extended in front of him. His eyes were trained on the page, but Abbey knew he was watching her, monitoring her every word.

"I haven't, no," Abbey said. "She went straight home, I think. Didn't see her in class after lunch."

"What caused that, I wonder?"

"Slipped on something, I suppose," Abbey said, voice meek and strewn with suspicion.

The blood, the hair. That hand.

Mother noticed Abbey's apprehension, and cast her a wary gaze.

"Yes, slipped," Mother said. "Or something."

"It wasn't drugs, was it girl?" Father said, bending the newspaper down so Abbey could feel his scowl.

"No, Daddy. I mean, I don't know —"

"You don't know? Seems you and that truant brat are pretty tight."

Abbey knew better than to respond.

Father mumbled something under his breath and raised the newspaper, covering his face once again.

"Well, whatever it might have been, let's hope she gets better quickly," Mother said.

"I'd like to check on her," Abbey said, looking up at Mother.

"And how are you going to do that?" Father chuffed from behind the paper. "We ain't driving you nowhere."

"But it's Friday," Abbey said, then hesitated. "Are we heading into town sometime this weekend?"

"Not unless we have to," Father said. "Waste of time and gas. Got what we need, so we'll stay here. Got chores and such to do, anyways. Flitting about town doesn't get shit done."

Mother clucked her tongue, scolding Father for his language. Abbey nodded and finished drying the dishes before settling down in front of the television. Anton was watching some sort of Redbull sponsored sports nonsense, regarding her with an eye roll when she sat on the floor. She didn't like Anton's shows—she really didn't like shows at all, truth be told—but she actually wanted the noise and the company, as unpleasant as it was. She still felt uneasy after the events of the day, and didn't want solitude to take her mind places it didn't belong. Father retired to the front porch to smoke a half-pack of duMauriers, and Mother sat in the kitchen, rum in hand, phone cradled between ear and shoulder, talking to anyone and everyone who could distract her from the slow-moving evening hours.

Abbey sat a while, tolerating the noise from the television, thinking no less than a hundred times that she was tired enough to head up to bed and the peace of slumber, but she wasn't actually tired. Her thoughts reeled around the fear that encompassed her life; pain, judgement, control, and now phantoms dictated her every move. She felt panic swell and tears well, so she stood and walked through the kitchen, nodding once at Mother who paid her no mind but continued on her eighteenth conversation of the night.

Abbey went through the back door and out into the night where the frogs could sing to her and the owls hoot their lullabies. Barefoot, she swished her way through the blue grass to the base of her tree and sat, back pressed against it's jagged, ragged bark. She closed her eyes and breathed the night, the pine, the moss, the wet and musty dirt. It was humid and chill, and Abbey's arms were exposed. She hugged herself and rubbed her arms, ripe with gooseflesh, and her teeth chattered, a jackhammer in the solace of the rural night.

Abbey didn't mind the cold bite of the night. She would have sat there until the sun rose, oblivious to the world beyond the flora and fauna, if it wasn't for the sudden rush of heat that blew her hair in front of her face. She opened her eyes and looked through the thin, wispy drapes of her hair, contemplating the possibility of a warm gust.

Not unlikely, this time of year. Chinook, maybe?

Her mind shrugged it off, but her heart clenched in her chest. Her senses tuned in to the space around her and beyond, the sound of the leaves in the wind, Father's chair creaking on the porch in the distance, a crackling in the woods.

But the owls were gone. Frogs were, too.

And that crackling.

Abbey parted her hair with shaking fingers, tucking it behind each ear so she could see and hear better in the dead of night, and craned herself to peer around the tree at her back. The woods behind the property appeared still and asleep, the animals having retired suddenly to silence. The crackling sound was faint but there, ampli-fied by the dampening of all the others sounds. Even the wind seemed to fall still, stepping aside to allow the sound to echo through the trees. Abbey stood and walked to the forest's edge, noticing a change in temperature.

Warmer, here.

Abbey held out an open palm, feeling for warmth as if the edge of the woods was a door barring a fire. She wasn't disappointed. A rippling heat radiated from the dark woods, source unsettling in its mystery. Abbey didn't consider the squeaks from the chair and squabbles from the kitchen behind her. She didn't think of Anton rising from the couch for chips and calling attention to her absence. She didn't consider the whipping she would get, or the swollen ass she would suffer through the weekend and all the way to the hard chairs at the school Monday morning. Abbey thought of none of that as her bare feet crossed the border onto the rough underbrush covering the forest floor.

Taking care to avoid snapping twigs and rustling bushes, Abbey walked into the black abyss, the night growing ever darker below the increasingly dense canopy of trees. The deeper she got, the warmer it became, bordering on the edge of hot. The crackling grew louder and louder until it shrieked in her ears like the splintering of bones. Each step was a struggle, the heat and noise straining her every joint and muscle. Abbey dragged feet made of solid concrete, ploughing forward to her unknown destination.

After walking what seemed like an eternity, Abbey could no longer bear the assault on her senses, on her body. She fell to her knees on the unforgiving ground, sticks and thorns and brush piercing the skin on her kneecaps. She covered her ears to silence the crackling, and squeezed her eyes shut for fear of the creature that was making the horrible sound. Her skin grew hotter, sweat beading on her brow until she was sure she could cook an egg on her flesh. The pain was excruciating, a searing heat that scorched the fine hairs on her arms. Abbey screamed, but no sound came out, just fire and hot air from the pit of her belly. She screamed and screamed until her guts hurt and her throat was raw. She was on the precipice of unconsciousness when a cold hand cupped her cheek.

Abbey stopped screaming. The woods were silent again, the crackling ceased as if it had never been, and the chill returned to the air. Abbey swiped her hand across her face, rubbing away tears and sweat, and opened her eyes.

"Oh."

She was surprised, but not scared. She was in a small clearing, lush grass in place of barren loam, with a cozy cottage perched right in the middle. It was a large structure with cobblestone walls and a wooden porch, surrounded by ponds and gardens that glowed in the moonlight. Abbey stood and brushed off her battered knees, looking down to find that she had been kneeling in a line of small bones around the perimeter of the clearing. She looked up again at the oasis and moved forward.

The plants were moist and plump, their leaves all shades of emerald and lavender, magenta flowers dripping silver honeysuckle to the greedy bees below. The ponds glittered in the moonlight, ripples dancing around lily pads, stone waterfalls, and tiny fountains. Abbey stepped up to the water and looked at her reflection, her image distorted by the movement of the creatures below the surface.

Tiny faeries, iridescent wings, long purple hair floating around pale silver shoulders like cloaks, limbs tentacles that gleamed like crystal. Light radiated from their tiny, silver bodies, illuminating the ponds and the gardens. One faerie caught Abbey's eye and flashed a mischievous smile, baring pointed red teeth that sparkled like rubies in the light from its flesh. The faerie sang out to the others, a bubbling warble, and they all turned, red eyes wide and curious, looking at Abbey. They all went mad, giggling and waving, tentacles braiding together as their play ignited into a raging bonfire. Some were in the water, some out, joyous and rambunctious and gorgeous.

Abbey smiled. *So pretty*, she thought, stroking her own hair and imagining it was as full and luscious as the violet manes of the faeries. As they twirled Abbey did too, pirouetting, her face turned to the sky, the faeries' song and laughter filling the air. In the blackness that surrounded the garden moat, Abbey spied a blip and stopped spinning.

And gasped.

The faeries followed her gaze, then stopped their revelry, smiling sheepishly as they settled into the sand and onto the rocks below the water and on the porch. Their light extinguished, leaving the water and the gardens in total darkness, amplifying the white figure that stood on the porch.

Her.

The witch stood before her, propped up on a carved, wooden staff at the top of the steps leading to the cottage. She was large, her head nearly touching the overhang of the porch, shoulders the width of the door. Muscle rippled beneath heavy folds of flesh, writhing and flexing as she shifted her weight from foot to foot. Her skin was pure white, black veins seeping through like a pulsating road map. Her hands and feet were too long, like snakes, her fingernails and toenails red talons like sharpened tongues. The witch opened her mouth, a gawping black hole, and brayed in Abbey's direction. One of those gangly hands lifted from beside the witch's contorted body as she pointed a talon at Abbey, then turned her hand and curled a finger, beckoning Abbey forward.

Abbey felt a warm gush explode between her legs as urine escaped her, soaking her pajama bottoms and seeping into the clean, black dirt of the garden. Curiosity quashed by terror, Abbey started shaking and blubbering, spewing words coated in fear and mucousy sobs. The witch dropped her hand and attempted to straighten her body, leaning on her staff as she descended the stairs. Abbey was paralyzed by fear, but her mind ran, back through the woods, back to the house where she could run to her room and hide under her blankets and wake the next day to find this was all a dream.

But it wasn't. She was there, frozen in place as the witch approached, the faeries floating to the edge of the pond for their front row seats to her execution. The witch hobbled forward until Abbey could smell her breath, rotting and sickly, and feel the heat radiating off her body. Abbey winced as the witch leaned in, her ample breasts and black nipples pressing against Abbey's cheek. She wrapped her arms around Abbey, embracing her in a hug that stole her breath. Abbey was stiff as a board, acutely aware of the areas where the witch's nudity brushed against her flesh, the warmth of the witch's thickness pressing against the soaked spot between Abbey's legs.

The witch started rocking, foot to foot, slowly and rhythmically, humming a haunting ballad deep in her throat. Abbey couldn't help but sway with her, surrendering and melting into her arms.

The faeries rose their light into a gentle glow and the witch pulled back, lacing her fingers through Abbey's and leading her towards the cottage. Abbey didn't resist. She didn't want to. The witch tugged her along, up the steps and through the front door. Once inside, she dropped Abbey's hand and walked away, leaving Abbey alone to absorb her new surroundings.

The cottage was warm and rustic, walls made of old pine, moss and ivy growing and vining up to the ceiling. The main room was large, one side a humble dining room, the other a living area with a large stone fireplace in the wall and a wood stove next to the window. Every surface was covered in knick knacks, talismans, and taxidermed animals. Fabrics of all colours and textures were strewn about the furniture, and candles flickered in sconces lining the walls.

There's no electricity, Abbey thought, scanning the walls for outlets and light switches. There were none, the light in the room coming exclusively from the candles and the roaring fire in the fireplace. The wood crackled hypnotically and heat wafted from the open chimney, blowing her hair back.

I felt this fire?

The sound of dragging footsteps interrupted Abbey's thoughts. She watched as the witch came lumbering back into the room, white tray in her hands. The tray was covered in leaves, berries, and meat of some sort. The witch set the tray down on the table and patted one of the stumps fashioned as a chair. Abbey hesitated. The witch snapped her fingers, scuffling over to the couch and selecting a plush piece of fabric from the pile. She draped the red velvet blanket over the stump, patting it again and giving Abbey a wide, toothless smile.

Abbey forced the corners of her mouth up and took a seat at the table, still scared, but intrigued. She questioned the reality of the cabin, the witch… everything. Though it was oddly beautiful, it simply could not be.

Abbey ate. She was ravenous, having trekked so far into the woods—*how far did I go; how long have I been gone?*— and the meat was tender and berries sweet. The witch disappeared and reappeared several times, each time bringing more for Abbey to consume. Soft bannock and jam, tea, chocolate. When Abbey was finished gorging herself she felt full and recharged, and ready to take on the world. The witch stood in the doorway to the kitchen, smiling, looking like a twisted, wrecked grandmother. Abbey smiled, and decided it was time to exercise her courage. Her voice came out cracked and weak, but it came nonetheless.

"Thank you."

The witch startled at Abbey's words, nearly striking her head on the door frame. Abbey smiled and gave her a thumbs up, a gesture that felt silly and out of place, but the witch smiled and put her hand over her heart. Abbey returned the gesture, placing her hand over her heart as well. The witch's cheeks lit with a rosy glow, a beautiful reprieve from the white-grey porcelain of her body. Abbey tapped her chest, pointing at herself.

"Abbey," she said, sharply articulating the syllables. "Abbey."

The witch cocked her head, then smiled again. She pointed her finger at her own chest, on the ribs protruding between her mammoth breasts. A sound came from her throat, but there were no detectable words that Abbey could decipher.

"I'm sorry, I don't understand," Abbey said, shrugging her shoulders.

The witch made the noise again, this time with more force. Her mouth was moving large and wide, her gums chewing on words that would not form, and all that came from her cavernous throat was a guttural moan. When Abbey didn't understand, the witch furrowed her forehead, bone in place of brow, and huffed. Outside, the light of the faeries grew brighter.

Abbey watched the witch chuffing in frustration, the way her fleshed sagged, the gleaming gash between her legs. Abbey shifted uncomfortably on the stump, then rose and moved to the couch. The witch watched with a wary eye as Abbey selected a large, mustard-coloured silk sari from the pile and brought it over. Still frightened to get too close to the creature, she held out the fabric, and draped it around her own body, modeling how the witch could wear it. Abbey repeated this several times, then handed the garment to the witch. When the fabric was exchanged, the witch ran a talon up Abbey's arm, leaving a small scratch. Abbey yelped. The witch looked at her —into her—and held the fabric in front of her.

"There," Abbey said, confidence and comfort waning. "Put that on. Cover yourself."

The witch looked at the fabric, then down at her body. She seemed to study herself, her drooping black nipples, her heavy muscles and pallid complexion, her crooked bones and mismatched limbs. She looked at Abbey. Abbey stepped back when she saw the witch's eyes, solid black, now seeping crimson tears down her white face. The witch opened her mouth wide, splitting her face in half as she bellowed at Abbey, an angry sound that shook the ornaments off the shelves of the cottage.

The witch brayed and Abbey screamed. Abbey put her hands up to shield herself from the spray of blood coming from the witch's mouth. Several rows of sharp, rotting teeth emerged, and the witch chanted words at Abbey in hateful tones. Abbey backed away until she reached the door, then turned and ran. The faeries quickly extinguished their light when the witch stomped out onto the porch, so Abbey pointed herself blindly into the woods. Once inside a few layers of tree-cover, she turned back to see if she was being pursued. The witch was still on the porch, flailing her arms wildly at the trees, screaming and raging like a feral animal.

Abbey ran. Branches whipped her face and tore out clumps of hair, one cracking her right across the bridge of the nose. Having very little sense of direction, Abbey ran blindly in the direction she felt was away. She didn't care if she got lost. She didn't want to see that monster again, nor did she want to see her home again.

Lost in her thoughts, Abbey stumbled when she burst out into another opening. Down on her hands and knees, she willed herself to look up, bracing herself for the appearance of the cottage in front of her once again, wailing witch and all.

But it wasn't.

It was home.

She was back at the edge of the woods, her tree a mere few meters from where she had landed on the ground. She could hear the squeak of Father's chair and the chatter of Mother's latest conversation.

Not possible, she thought.

She stood, brushed the forest off her pajamas, and walked to the house, checking behind to see if anything was following her. She passed through the screen door, turning her back to Mother as she walked through the kitchen. No need. Mother didn't even look up.

Abbey walked into the living room, where Anton was still watching television. Still the Redbull, testosterone-infused competition.

"What-up, dumbfuck?" Anton said, flipping her the bird.

How long was I gone?

Was *I* gone?

"I've gone mad," Abbey said.

Anton stopped chewing and looked at her, brow raised.

"Uh-huh," he said, contemplating her for only a moment before returning to his program.

"Mad," Abbey repeated before going to have a bath to cleanse her body of the outdoors, and her mind of her insanity.

7

———

Abbey stomped through the house, pacing and pondering. Sleep had not come easy, visions of tentacled faeries and howling witches fresh in her mind. She scolded herself and her foolishness, a wanton belief in the impossible. She was mad not just because she believed, but because it had been magical. Horrifying, yes, but ethereal.

"But she was a jerk," Abbey mumbled, chin tucked into her chest.

"What was that?" Mother asked.

"Nothing," Abbey said.

"Mind your attitude, girl," Father shouted from the front porch.

It was a Saturday morning like all the other Saturday mornings. Anton was out working on his car, Father was sitting on the porch in his rocker, whiskey-touched coffee in his hand, and Mother was in the kitchen, dishtowel over her shoulder, cleaning god-knows-what.

What is she cleaning? Abbey thought. *What is she always cleaning?*

"Better fix your mood, Abigail," Mother said, "or it's going to be a long weekend for all of us. You especially."

Abbey grunted a response, then returned to her pacing, circling the living room, catching glimpses of the back yard but not really looking. After she had nearly paced a trench into the floor, Mother leaned around the corner and smacked the wall with a wooden spoon.

"Stop it!" Mother shouted. "Now! Get yourself outside or start cleaning. Find something to do with yourself before you fray my last nerve."

Abbey gathered her things—her journal, a scarf, and her saggy black toque—and charged out the front door.

"Mind you don't bother your brother and father," Mother called behind her. "They have real work to do."

Of course they do, Abbey thought, sneering at Father as she passed. *Man's work, I suppose. Busy work, all it is.*

"What's up your ass?" Anton said as she dragged her feet down the gravel drive.

"None of your business, that's what," she muttered, never intending for him to hear.

Anton set his torque wrench down and looked up from his metal lover. As soon as the words had left her mouth, she realized she had picked a fight. She braced for impact.

But Anton didn't engage. Not with hostility, at least. His face, which she expected would be contorted in humour and rage, actually looked the colour of concerned.

"Well then," he said, brushing his hands on his pants. "Grew a set, did you?"

Abbey didn't answer. She felt his eyes on her as she walked away and settled in at the end of the drive so she could play in the rocks and watch the occasional vehicle pass on the lonely country road. They were fairly isolated out on Faulten Drive, the nearest neighbor being half-a-kilometer away. There were no businesses out their way, other than farming, and people pretty much kept to themselves. It was a haven for homebodies and unpleasant folk who didn't mingle well with society.

Perhaps that's why our clan of dicks moved here, Abbey thought.

She spent the better part of an hour drawing in the dirt with a stick, and building cities and worlds out of rocks. Towers would topple, upset by creatures made of leaves and odd-shaped stones, and Abbey would rebuild them, more ambitious in height every time. After a while, she felt the little hairs on the back of her neck whispering to her, a set of eyes heavy on her. She looked towards the house and saw that Anton was sitting on the boot of his car, watching her every move.

Creep, she thought, her play becoming angrier. She smashed a tower with her fist, and swiped a village away with her foot. *CREEP!* she screamed in her head. He sat there, not a care in the world, uninhibited and encouraged and entitled.

"Hey, mutt!" Anton called. "You okay?"

"No!" Abbey shouted, scooping up a fistful of rocks as she charged towards Anton.

"What the—"

He didn't have time to respond before she was within reach, arm cocked and aimed to shower her brother and his precious wheels with rocks.

"Girl!" Father bellowed, standing from his chair.

Shit. Father hates when he has to get up before his time.

"Choose wisely, girl," Father said, pointing a fat finger in her direction.

They all stood frozen in anticipation of her next move.

She made the wisest choice for her health. And her ass.

Her arm fell slack and the rocks dribbled down onto the drive, her rage deflating into sour tears.

"Good," Father said, not yet settling back into his chair. "Mind yourself. Willful doesn't become you."

No one said another word. Abbey turned and slowly walked back down the drive as Father watched on, Anton snickering some sort of smart-ass taunt. Abbey returned to her rock village, intending on taking out her frustrations on her unsuspecting villagers, but the village had changed. Moved. The rocks had been arranged into a circle, with a stone structure in the center; it was a crude representation of the cottage from the night before. Around the cottage, tiny purple lilies had been stuffed down between the rocks. If she stared just right, and squinted her eyes just so, the tiny purple flowers looked like the faeries.

Abbey raised her head, looking up and down the country road, trying to spy any evidence of movement or travel. It hadn't rained, so any passerby would have disturbed cloud of dusts, but the air was still and clean. No one had come by road, at least. And the brush was too thick to traverse by foot. Her eyes flowed up the edge of the drive towards the house.

Surely Anton or Father would have noticed…

A lily, larger than the tiny ones on the stone model of the cottage, had been set on the edge of the drive, it's starburst, purple petals looking quite out of place on the bed of gravel and mulch. Her eyes kept going, and found another lily. Then another. Abbey stood and followed the flowers, one placed every five meters or so; not enough for anyone else to notice, unless they were looking. Abbey followed the trail all the way back to her tree, where a half-dozen lilies were arranged into the shape of a heart. Abbey looked into the woods.

A hand, grey and crippled, held a lily out from behind a tree. Abbey walked into the woods and took the flower. The hand pulled back behind the tree, and Abbey stepped around the wide trunk.

It was her, all right. Her witch was there, old and broken and terrifying, but different now. She stepped away from the tree so Abbey could see her, and spun around. She was wearing the yellow sari, wrapped into an outfit like Abbey had shown her the night before. She still looked a right mess, but at least her more private parts were covered.

"Thank you," Abbey said, her cheeks flushing a rosy red.

The witch reached out her pointed finger, and Abbey jumped back.

"Sorry," Abbey said. The witch looked like she had been wounded by Abbey's fright.

The witch moved slower this time, extending the finger again and touching Abbey's chest.

"Ahhhbayyy," she said, straining her mouth into the correct shapes to form the word.

"Yes!" Abbey said, surprised and thrilled and flattered. "Yes, Abbey! That's my name!"

The witch smiled and nodded, pleased with the success. She patted her own chest. Abbey waited patiently as the witch contorted her mouth and throat, preparing for the next word.

"Faelithh," the witch said, a heavy lisp wetting the *th* at the end.

"Faelith?" Abbey said.

"Faelithhh," the witch said, nodding her head in approval.

Abbey curtsied. "It's a pleasure to properly meet you, Faelith."

Faelith bowed, her spine curling and head nearly touching the ground. Her carefully secured garment loosened, falling into a pile around her ankles. She straightened her back and looked down at her exposed body, then looked at Abbey questioningly.

"It's okay," Abbey said, reaching down and grabbing the sari. "You'll get used to it."

Abbey stepped towards Faelith and stood on her tippy-toes so she could wrap the sari around her neck. She walked around Faelith, cloaking her in the garment, and secured it at the front in a slip knot. Abbey patted the outfit, pleased with her work, and stepped back.

"Good to go," she said, smiling at Faelith.

Faelith smiled, a warm smile, and placed her hand on Abbey's cheek. Abbey nestled her whole head in Faelith's massive palm.

"You're welcome," Abbey said.

"Abbey! Come do your chores, if you're bored!"

Abbey looked through the trees at the house. Mother was on the front porch, towel on her shoulder and spoon in hand.

Obviously she talked to Father about my near-miss outburst.

"I gotta go—"

When Abbey turned back, Faelith was gone, the glimmer of the gold sari disappearing into the trees. With a spring of newfound spunk, Abbey skipped towards the house.

SUNDAY WAS BETTER THAN ITS PRECEDING SATURDAY.

It never typically was, but this week was an exception.

Usually, the family would get together around ten in the morning —would be sooner if it wasn't for Aunt Petal's incessant need to be properly preened before going out in public. Once her face was applied and hair adequately coiffed, she and Uncle Herman would come over, and the family read scripture and discussed sin while engaging in gluttonous feasting on bacon, butter-marinated eggs, and sweet breads. Abbey sat as she always did, demure, nodding along with Uncle Herman's hypocritical preaching and smiling sweetly at Aunt Petal and Mother who drew heavily on menthol cigarettes between swigs of stale coffee.

They were a supposedly God-fearing family, saying their prayers at night to absolve the sins of the waking hours, but going to an actual church was an inconvenient commute. So they gathered at the acreage, spending the morning being falsely pious and pseudo-social. Although strictly bound to the good book for outward appearances, they loved to curse and smoke and drink. They twisted and used the word of the Lord as justification for their rampant misogyny and abuse, and just about any other discriminatory and hateful behaviours and thoughts that needed rationalization.

Abbey really didn't like the "church" service, but it wasn't terrible; at worst, it was boring. At least on Sunday—God's day—the lashes would be lighter and the anger diluted. Abbey actually hoped she'd be bored—that the service would linger on, and discussion would swell into the afternoon hours. But it still wasn't enjoyable, as such. More devoid of overt pain, than anything.

This day, though. This day was different.

On this Sunday, intrigue and magic waited in the shadows of the woods. Faelith was there. Abbey could feel her, listening to the family as they conversed, watching Uncle Herman's arms reaching for the heavens as he delivered his bullshit message from God. Every so often Abbey would steal a glance at the forest and spy the tail of that gold sari wisping through the trees.

"What do you think of it, girl?"

Uncle Herman's voice drew Abbey back into the service. She was unaware that a huge smile was plastered on her face.

"Something funny?" Father asked.

"Sorry," Abbey said, directing her attention to Uncle Herman. "I'm sorry… think of what, Uncle Herman?"

"Of our verse, One Corinthians 11:9. 'Neither was man created for woman, but woman for man'."

All eyes were on Abbey, even Mother's and Aunt Petal's.

Really? Abbey thought, saddened by the weak women at the helm of the family ship.

"Well," Abbey started, struggling to voice words that didn't coincide with her thoughts. "I… I think we were created for ourselves."

Mother looked at her feet in worry and shame. Perhaps she didn't disagree with rebellion, but rather the consequences.

"How so?" Father asked, looking over the top of his readers.

"Well, Adam was created… and he needed companionship—"

"A helper," Aunt Petal interjected.

"A servant," Uncle Herman added.

The words came—from where, Abbey didn't know—but they felt good and strong as they passed her lips. "But why would someone whose sole purpose of being a helper have free will of their own?" Abbey said. "Eve had needs, and the fortitude to choose to take the bite. Seems to me she was created for herself, as well. And Adam was not created with Eve in mind, therefore he was created for himself—"

"Enough," Father said. "They were both created for God. Let's move on."

Abbey was satisfied. Uncle Herman's grin had turned to a pout, and he continued his self-righteous teachings without the same enthusiasm as he had before Abbey's challenge. She realized she hadn't actually made him question his belief in women's purpose, but rather he was ticked because Abbey had dared speak above his authority. Meant to be seen and not heard, and all of that. Father wasn't quite as rattled, dismissing her passive challenge as mere stupidity.

That's what Father thinks of me. A stupid girl, no matter how smart I am. Silent, no matter how loud I scream.

This didn't bother Abbey, not much anyways. Father meant nothing by it. It was how he was raised—all he had known. Men were entitled, women were lesser, subservient. He was thrilled to have Anton, but annoyed by her existence. Angered, even.

No mind, she thought, halting the downward spiral of her thoughts. *There are more beautiful things to think about on this day.*

The sermon dragged on, morphing into a discussion about neighbors and coworkers, sharp blades of gossip slicing everyone within mind's reach. When Anton excused himself to go polish yet another ten centimeters of his iron beast, Abbey felt she was safe to open her journal and sketch to pass the time. While the conversation lingered, she drew a picture of the cottage in the woods, the tentacled faeries canoeing lily pads across the sparkling waters, and Faelith lighting candles on the porch. Abbey was so lost in her art that she failed to notice Mother appear at her shoulder.

"Abigail?" Mother said, touching her arm. "What's all this, then?"

"Uh, just some drawings," Abbey said, closing the journal. She was too slow, though. Mother's hand jammed a wedge in before the cover was fully closed. Mother opened the journal wide again, and leaned over to look at the drawings. Abbey inhaled Mother's perfume, some cheap, gas station splash-on Father had bought for their anniversary. It reeked of sadness and desperation. The perfume, mixed with undertones of muscle balm—used on strain caused by Mother and Father's row earlier in the week — made Abbey's eyes water.

"Quite lovely," Mother said, running her finger over the faeries, stopping short of Faelith. "But what is this terrible creature?"

"Nonsense," Uncle Herman said as he passed behind them. "The girl's imaginary creations are causing her to become willful in real life. Mind that."

Mother nodded, not taking her eyes off Faelith. "Horrible beast, that. Abigail, don't draw such nonsense."

"She's not nonsense, Mother."

Mother looked down at Abbey, words caught on her surprise, but simply straightened up and turned to the house.

"You do need to mind yourself, Abigail. Mind your attitude."

Mind yours, you helpless whelp, Abbey thought. Mother didn't look back, but shook her head as she walked into the house alongside Aunt Petal. They would no doubt complain about the sassy girl Abbey had become, and brainstorm what they could do to dampen her wild spirit. *They don't know wild*, Abbey thought.

Once everyone was safely engaged in their regular Sunday business, Abbey went to the woods, skipping and dodging trees at a doe's pace. It occurred to her after running until her chest was heaving and sweat beaded on her upper lip that she could indeed be chasing a mirage; perhaps the cottage wasn't really there, and neither was Faelith. It had all been a dream. But just as doubt slowed her pace, the trees parted, revealing the deep-woods oasis.

The garden was gorgeous, rainbow sprays of flora sparkling in the midday sun, but the faeries were nowhere to be seen. Abbey pouted. She had hoped to see the twisted little things, their horrible beauty as enticing as it was terrifying. And they seemed like lots of fun.

"Hello," Abbey called out, standing on her toes and peering into the cottage windows from a safe distance. She still wasn't entirely sure about Faelith, and had no desire to see how she reacted to trespassing. She approached the pond and looked into the water, a mirror of stillness, and spotted the faeries, motionless, tentacles fanned out, lining the floor of the pond.

"Oh," Abbey gasped, searching their tiny chests for breath and their eyes for movement. The contents of Abbey's stomach curdled as she considered she might be looking at beautiful little corpses. In a panic, she plunged her hand into the water and grabbed a faerie. The little creature was a limp and heavy rag, dripping, tentacles hanging through Abbey's fingers. Tears welled in Abbey's eyes as she stroked the tiny, silver cheek with her pinky finger.

"Ohkaaay."

Abbey jumped at the sound of Faelith's voice, and dropped the faerie in the water with a tiny plip. The faerie floated to the bottom, finally settling into the sand, tentacles splayed out like a star. Faelith came up behind Abbey and patted her back.

"Ohkaaay."

Faelith took Abbey's hands and held them together, patting the top one and pointing to the water.

"Ohkaaay."

Faelith dropped Abbey's hands and pointed into the air. She made a circle with her long, massive arms, and held the circle to the sky. She slowly knelt until she, and the circle, were touching the ground. From the ground, she pointed to the sun.

Abbey thought.

Then she understood.

"Nocturnal!"

Faelith cocked her head.

"Night. Dark. They only come alive at night."

Abbey crossed her fingers, making an X towards the sun, then covered her eyes, mimicking the dark.

"Yassss!" Faelith said. "Naight!"

Abbey nodded, satisfied.

Faelith crouched over and took Abbey's hand, and they walked into the cottage. Faelith disappeared into the kitchen again, no doubt preparing some sort of delicious snack. Abbey hummed a song, her heart light as she browsed the livingoom's knicks and knacks, settling in as a wanted guest of the mythical cottage in the woods.

They were beautiful, all the treasures of the witch. Jewels and baubles, candles and dried flowers, powders and potions in glass vials. Abbey didn't know what much of it was, but marveled at the mystique of it all. All surfaces were overflowing with squirrel piles of goodies Faelith had collected, each special in its own way, Abbey decided. To others, leaves and tattered strip of fabric would be rubbish, but to Faelith, they must be treasures. Abbey touched tiny pelts of fur draped on the hearth, and smelled opened jars of berries and dried insects. She ran her fingers though tangles of yarn and cascading vines of ivy hanging from the wall. *One could get lost in the textures and smells,* Abbey thought.

Abbey walked along, lightly grazing everything with the tips of her fingers, taking in the magic. A beautiful purple lily hung upside down from the ceiling, dried and decorated with copper wire. Abbey looked closer, the wire bent into cursive design, and saw that it was braided with beautiful red twine. No, not twine.

Hair.

Abbey pinched the strands of hair between her fingers and tugged, untangling it from the copper wire. She held the hair in front of her face, watching it wind and coil back to it's original shape.

A ringlet, thick and shiny, a chunk of stained bone attached to the roots.

Gloria.

Abbey dropped the hair on the floor and walked to the kitchen. She didn't know what she was going to do, what she was going to say. How would she confront this creature that didn't really speak her language? And what was this witch? How did she have Gloria's hair? How did she travel to and from basements and kilometers away to the school? How was any of this possible?

Faelith was hunched over a rustic, wooden island, her back to the door, shoulders heaving as she prepared the food. Abbey took a step into the kitchen and cleared her throat, announcing her presence.

Faelith turned, happy to see her, smiling big and wide. Her mouth was dripping with flesh, blood staining the grey skin on her chin and throat, dribbles of gristle hanging from her lip. Abbey swallowed hard, willing both scream and vomit to stay subdued as she eyed the fare on the cutting board. A medley of rats, birds, and large rodents filleted and skinned, raw and gooey, cut into shapes and placed on a serving tray garnished with cheese and sprigs of mint and rosemary. Abbey gagged, the smell of warm copper finally reaching her nostrils. Faelith lifted the tray and held it in Abbey's direction, proud of her culinary delights.

"Uh, no thanks," Abbey said. "I gotta go."

Abbey waved and pointed at the door. Faelith's proud smile faded to suspicion, but she shrugged and turned back to the cuisine, popping a thick chunk of meat directly into her throat and working it down to her belly like a snake.

Who are you, and what did you do to Gloria? How did you…

Abbey jogged past the faerie garden and into the woods, the smell of blood lingering in her nose and on her tongue the whole way home.

What are you?

8

<hr>

The bell rang, and everyone was in their seats. With the exception of Gloria. Abbey stared at the void at Gloria's desk, an empty seat in an otherwise full-to-capacity classroom. It wasn't unusual for one or two students to be absent — this time of year the snots and sniffles were out in full force — but Gloria's absence glared at Abbey like a neon sign. The teacher began her spiel about assignments and upcoming exams, but it was muffled background noise to the worry in Abbey's head. Thoughts of red curls and chunks of skull, hair-clogged drains and bits of bloody rodent meat threatened to drive Abbey mad.

"Thank you for joining us," the teacher said, waking Abbey from her torment. "Feeling better?"

Gloria strode in the classroom, red curls bouncing on one shoulder, the other side of her head wrapped in gauze and bandages. She nodded sheepishly at the teacher then slid into her desk, never once looking in Abbey's direction. Abbey stared at her, willing her to turn and look, but Gloria's eyes sought everything but: her books, her clothes, the teacher. *She's avoiding me*, Abbey thought.

With a quick flick of her wrist, Abbey pushed her textbook on the floor and it landed with a resounding thud, drawing the attention of the entire class, including the teacher. Well, not the entire class. Gloria flinched, but didn't look. Not even for a second.

"Problem, Abbey?"

A few snickers came out of her classmates, but no reaction from Gloria.

"No, ma'am," Abbey said as she picked the book off the floor.

The lesson went on, talk of Russian famine that claimed more victims than Hitler's war, but Abbey heard none of it. The only thing rattling around her brain was the sound of Gloria's wails that past Friday, and Faelith's cackle, before they had become friends.

Faelith is still that beast from under the stairs, stupid girl.

Lunch came, and Abbey couldn't find Gloria. She didn't make an appearance in the lunch line or the cafeteria and was nowhere to be found in the halls or the locker room. Abbey abandoned the search, finally giving in and having a go at her tray of mac and cheese at a table by herself. She kept her eyes pinned on the door, hoping that Gloria might be hungry enough to sneak in for some food.

The afternoon bell rang and Abbey floated through her classes, neither hearing nor caring about anything but her distant friend sitting on the other side of the room. Gloria arrived late to each class, giving Abbey no opportunity to corner and interrogate her, and her desk was near the door, so she managed to escape at the bell before Abbey even had a chance to get out of her seat.

Gloria remained elusive the entire day, until the break before last period. Abbey decided the risk of being tardy outweighed another night agonizing over Gloria, so she skulked by the lockers as the hallways emptied. Gloria had nowhere to hide. Abbey crouched down by the water fountains across from her classroom door, hiding behind the edge of the lockers, waiting on Gloria like a predator for prey.

This is creepy, Abbey thought, suddenly regretting the trick to catch her friend. She stood to leave, but it was a moment too late. The clicking of Gloria's shoes signaled her approach from the end of the hall. Abbey froze, holding her breath and willing herself to invisibility, but she knew the confrontation was imminent. She released her breath, preparing herself for the exchange, but the footsteps stopped. Abbey waited, her pulse quickening and mind racing.

What is she doing? Does she know I'm here?

The air thickened, Abbey's breath coming out in clouds. A dense fog hovered just below the fluorescent bulbs in the ceiling, darkening the hallway to dusk. Muffled lessons from behind the closed classroom door faded into silence, and even the chatter of auxiliary staff and tardy stragglers in the distance disappeared. Abbey's fear overcame her embarrassment, and she stepped out into the hallway.

"Gloria?"

Gloria was there, head down and red curls hanging over her face, an armful of books clutched to her chest.

"Gloria, I'm so sorry about the other day. Are you mad?"

Gloria lifted her head to the sound of Abbey's voice, her head tilting, questioning and not understanding. Her red curls parted to the side, and Abbey could see her face, ashen white, hollow eyes staring from white pupils. The books pressed to her chest were grasped by bloody hands, pages soaked and curling from the blood pouring from the chasm where Gloria's lower jaw had once been but was no longer. All that remained was a tongue, swollen and coated in blood, wiggling and protruding from an open throat.

And from that open throat came a giggle, high-pitched and manic, blood sputtering into the foggy air. Gloria dropped the books on the floor, and crimson smeared across the white tile as she walked towards Abbey, dragging bare and broken feet through the blood-soaked pages. Gloria approached, giggling, tilted head twitching and neck cracking as she tried to see out of milky eyes. Gloria leaned in and said something, words marred by a heavy wheeze, and pressed her half mouth to Abbey's lips. Abbey gagged, the taste of copper and rot riding on Gloria's breath, and pulled away, tears of fear, sadness, confusion streaming down her cheeks, curdling with the blood dribbling from her lips.

"Abbey?"

Gloria sprayed blood as she spoke, a fine mist of death that coated Abbey's face.

"Abbey, what's going on?"

Abbey blinked, each time clearing a sheet of blood from her vision. She rubbed her eyes hard, worrying that she was actually pushing them back into her skull, then opened them once she was sure she had massaged away the blood.

Gloria was there, in the flesh, all the flesh. Her jaw was intact, books in her arms, feet healthy and shoed. Her green eyes were glossy with worried tears, her teeth fretting her bottom lip.

"Abbey, talk to me. What's going on?"

Gloria released her hold on the stack of books and put a hand on Abbey's shoulder, giving her a firm shake.

"I'm good," Abbey lied. "Just a little woozy. Been a bit under the weather."

Gloria didn't believe her. Abbey could see that all over her face. But she conceded, nodding and backing away a step before glancing at the door to the classroom.

"Uh, should we?" Gloria said.

"Gloria, I'm sorry."

"For what?"

"The other day. The cafeteria. Are you okay?"

Abbey's eyes evaluated the bandage on Gloria's head that masked her wound and part of her curls, missing and otherwise.

"Why are you sorry? I'm the one who should be sorry."

"Huh?"

Gloria's downturned lips tried to turn into a smile, and she dropped her books on the floor, leaping onto a startled Abbey and grasping her in a bear hug.

"Oh, I thought you hated me. I didn't mean to be too personal, Abbey. You were so mad when you walked away."

"But, your head."

"What?"

Gloria stood back, and Abbey tried to read her.

"What happened?" Abbey asked.

"I fell. Clutzo Supremo."

"Just… fell?"

"Tripped, yeah. I was in such a hurry to catch you when you ran off, I guess my foot caught on something."

No. There's more.

The lock of hair in Faelith's cottage.

Abbey could see it on Gloria's face, the way her smile faded and her eyes darkened.

"Tripped. Kinda felt like someone reached out and tripped me, or something."

Something.

"Why have you been avoiding me?" Abbey asked, carefully studying Gloria's face.

"I thought you were still mad," Gloria said. "And I was embarrassed, and a bit scared. The way you freaked out when you saw me."

Running out of the bathroom, screaming like a banshee, covered in your hair.

"Yeah, I acted a damn fool," Abbey said, forcing a smile.

"Guess it was a fool-ass day all around," Gloria said, a fat smile appearing on her lips again. "C'mon. Let's get to class. No more foolishness."

Abbey let Gloria put her arm around her and lead her to the class, trying to hide her suspicion.

~

"No, you are not."

"Please?"

Abbey looked up at Mother, willing her eyes to be as large and pleading as they needed to be to sway the matriarch into submission.

"Why do you need to go out there this time of night?" Mother asked.

"It's just out back, by my tree."

"It's pitch dark. Bedtime's in an hour."

"It's for an assignment."

Mother looked down her nose, eyebrow raised. "An assignment. Written outside in the dark."

"Well, no, it's a story assignment. But I need to be out there. You know, for mood."

"Let her go," Father gruffed from his armchair. "Be quick, girl, and mind you listen for us when we call."

Mother sighed and rolled her eyes. "All right. I hate you out there after dark, with the coyotes and the badgers and such. But if you insist on being ridiculous—"

"Thanks Mom," Abbey said, kissing Mother on the cheek.

"Take the torch," Mother said, thrusting the flashlight into Abbey's hand. " And no more than an hour, you hear?"

"One hour," Abbey said, not sure if she could keep that promise.

She bounded out the door and towards the tree, journal tucked under one arm, no intention of writing a single word. She needed to see Faelith, to confront her about the lock of hair.

The woods were darker than usual, the moon obscured by the rising fog of the humid autumn night. Abbey shivered as she walked through the trees, their branches contorted claws reaching for her and blocking her path. Abbey wondered if she could find the cottage this night.

How did I find it before? she wondered, realizing she had no idea how she had happened upon it in the first place, and, more unbelievably, a second time.

Abbey had her doubts she would make it back before Mother's

deadline, or if she would even make it to the cottage by then. She wasn't even sure that she would make it there at all. The woods around her seemed foreign, and her sense of direction skewed, muddled by the heaviness of night and her thoughts.

A cracking twig from a mass of branches ahead lifted Abbey's spirits, and her step quickened in the direction of the sound.

"Faelith!" she called out, her voice echoing through the trees.

She was answered not by Faelith's cackle or distorted speech, but by panting and a guttural growl.

"Faelith?"

Another twig cracked, and a set of lights appeared from behind a wall of brush, two moons moving in the dark. The small celestial pair was upon her before she realized what they were. A wolf, mangy and tall, jowls dripping with the salivation of starvation, padded towards her at an alarming pace.

"No," she said, as if addressing a dog. "Bad boy. Stop."

It did not stop. It leapt through the air with desperate grace, impacting Abbey with its full body weight and sending her crashing to the forest floor. Abbey screamed, the wolf's jaws thrashing and searching for the blood of her throat, but Abbey tucked her chin to her chest, denying it access. The wolf grabbed her shoulder and shook her like a rag doll, trying to expose its target. Abbey fought back, but, even in its depleted state, the wolf had the drive of a ravenous predator. It rolled Abbey around, tiring her with the struggle, tearing into the flesh on her arm and wearing her down. Abbey was about to give in, knowing that even if she got loose and ran the wolf would surely outrun her, no matter how weakened it was by starvation.

Suddenly, a grey hand wrapped around the wolf's lower jaw and snapped down, tearing the jaw off in a single movement, ripping meat and bone away and throwing it into the trees. The wolf froze for a moment before mewling from an open throat, and the hand returned, pulling out the tongue like an oral intestine. The wolf dropped to the ground, writhing in pain, until a massive, contorted bare foot came down on its skull, smashing it like an egg, blood and brains compacted into the loam beneath.

"Faelith," Abbey breathed, looking at the witch instead of the murdered canine under her foot.

"Sahhyyyfe," Faelith said, reaching out to help Abbey off the ground. Abbey accepted, watching the tongue in Faelith's other hand as she stood from the ground. That tongue stayed there, swinging to and fro as they walked hand in hand to the cottage in the woods.

FAELITH WAS IN THE KITCHEN, SEEMINGLY ENAMORED WITH THE new piece of meat she was preparing. Abbey cringed as the witch licked the wolf's blood from her fingers after setting the appendage on the counter and retrieving a Bowie knife from a drawer.

What am I doing? Abbey thought, wincing at the blood, at the witch, at the thought of those glowing eyes beneath the stairs. *She's a monster…*

But at least she's someone.

Abbey left the witch to her culinary preparations and went to the living room, to the copper wire entwined with Gloria's hair.

And that's what this is. Gloria's hair. I know it, for sure.

Before losing her nerve, Abbey went straight for the kitchen and sidled up to Faelith as she was tenderizing the tongue with her fists. Abbey's stomach was a tight knot, fear of pain—death, even—clenching her throat in a vice. She didn't know what this creature was capable of, and what she wanted.

She's still a feral beast.

"Gloria," Abbey said, slamming the ringlet down on the counter beside a pool of blood.

Faelith stopped pounding the meat. She looked at the hair, giving it a scratch with the end of her red talon, and shrugged.

"Yes."

She started pounding again, adding a pinch of seasoning from a jar beside the stove.

"Yes?" Abbey said, trying to tame the anger in her voice, knowing a fight with this creature would be short-lived and easily-lost. "She is my friend!"

Faelith stopped again, this time looking irritated by the interruption. She sighed, and wiped the blood off on the yellow sari across her body. After her hands were slightly less offensive, she grabbed Abbey by the forearm.

Abbey's world went white. Her head exploded with heat, and the peripherals of the white curtain across her vision started to glitter and dissolve, revealing the scene in the cafeteria. The emotion of her exchange with Gloria, her hidden secret—the abuse—exposed, her embarrassment, Gloria grabbing her by the arm…

Faelith released Abbey's arm and returned to preparing the meat. Tears streamed down Abbey's face as she got her bearings, the world and her head spinning back into focus. She looked at the spot on her arm where Faelith had grabbed, and saw a smaller handprint, fading.

"Gloria."

"Mayke sahd," Faelith said. "Mayke mahd."

Abbey nodded, understanding.

"You thought she hurt me," Abbey said to herself more than Faelith.

"Yas. You hurt. Aye no like. No."

A world of possibilities filled Abbey's head, a sense of security wrapping around her like a cloak.

A feral beast, but my *feral beast.*

"You were, you thought… you were protecting me."

Faelith stopped what she was doing, taking a moment to look at Abbey as if she had just fallen from the turnip truck. "Auv course. Me pratact yoo. Me lauve you."

Abbey wrapped her arms around the witch, her fingertips unable to touch on account of the creature's girth, and squeezed with all her might.

"Oh Faelith. I love you, too."

Faelith smiled, her toothless grin still terrifying and disgusting. Abbey smiled back, no longer repelled.

"Faelith, Gloria is good. She is my friend. Sometimes friends do things that hurt you because they want to help. Sometimes help hurts."

Faelith looked at Abbey, her head cocked and eyes scouring for some sense in that statement, then gave up and returned to the tongue.

"Wahnt?" Faelith said, poking a talon into the softened meat.

"No thanks."

"Hrmph." Faelith shook her head at the refusal of the delicacy. She opened her mouth wide, and Abbey watched as several rows of sharp teeth sprouted from her black gums. Faelith shoved the meat in her mouth, tearing away chunks and gobbling them down until the tongue had been consumed and she was licking the gristle, blood, and rosemary from her fingers.

"Faelith?"

Faelith stopped chewing and looked at Abbey.

"Why now?" Abbey asked. "Why have we not met before?"

Faelith smiled, then continued chewing. With her free, slightly-cleaner hand she reached down and patted Abbey's pelvis.

"Have blood. Woman, now. Like me."

Abbey pondered that, her growth into womanhood, her budding maturity.

"Well, I better be going," Abbey said, still a tad uncomfortable about the witch's touch. "See you this weekend."

Faelith gave Abbey another hug, then went about her business, licking the counter clean and wiping her face with her sari. Abbey left through the front door and walked only a few moments before appearing out of the woods behind her tree.

A newfound confidence filled Abbey's chest.

She picked up her journal from the base of the tree and walked towards the house, twirling the red ringlet through her fingers.

9

———————

onths passed. The days became brighter, and the possibilities plentiful. Faelith had breathed new life into Abbey, instilling a confidence that made the world a bearable and — dare she think it? — pleasant place. Sure, her family was the same, and sure, she still had to walk the line. But she treaded forth without fear. She knew, ultimately, if she were in any real danger, Faelith would be there, watching, waiting, ready to come to her aid. She didn't know how it worked and chose to give it very little thought. Having discovered the impossible, and a true magic, Abbey set aside assumptions and logic and just went about her business, a weight lifted from her shoulders.

Abbey and Gloria became closer, Abbey emerging from her shell, encouraged by Gloria's infectious positivity and extroversion. Much to the chagrin of her family, Abbey got involved in school activities, taking a position on the school newspaper as a student journalist, and joining the cross-country running team. She couldn't run very fast, or very far yet, but being outdoors was fresh and freeing, and it made her feel strong.

And then there was Faelith. Abbey visited her regularly, mostly on the weekends but sometimes at night, always at the cottage. Even though Abbey knew that Faelith moved beyond the confines of her clearing, Abbey only saw her there. *I'll see her when I'm in trouble, sure. She'll know when I need her.* Faelith had changed, too. Abbey had shown her how to sew, so she could take all her fabrics and make herself new garments as she pleased; the old, yellow sari had quickly deteriorated into shrouds of stench, a bouquet of meat and blood and dirt. Faelith's wardrobe quickly rivaled that of woodland royalty, an entire room full of robes and dresses and scarves to suit a prosperous gypsy queen. On her own, Faelith had begun to fashion leather garments—boots and gloves, mostly—from the hides of her kills.

Mother and Father occasionally questioned Abbey's absence into the woods, but they had raised her a country girl, and she always came home on time or there about. As long as she remained on their property, and under their heavy thumb, they were content. Winter hadn't reduced her visits, the cottage becoming a cozy haven warmed by the immense fireplace and blazing wood stove. Faelith chopped wood every day, the elements having little to no effect on her leathery skin. Even so, she donned her thigh-high leather boots and billowing duster when she trudged out into the snow.

One late Saturday night, Abbey came skipping out of the woods as the sun sank heavy in the sky. Activity in the kitchen suggested it was dinner time—dark came early in the winter—and the frigid, snowy night had driven Father and Anton in from the garage. Anton had been so pleased with the addition of the huge heater Father had installed so they could work year round in relative comfort, doing the things that men did to avoid boredom. Even so, the heater was small, and the night was cold.

Abbey spun in circles, drawing hieroglyphics in the snow with the toe of her Sorel, admiring the glitter of frost in the pink night sky. She thought of the cottage, even more hidden under blankets of snow, the greenery dormant and faeries hibernating in places she could only imagine. The only hint of the building was a glimmer of candlelight in the window, twinkling through crystals of frost. She wished that her home was that cottage, rather than the sterile, frigid structure in front of her.

She came through the back door, pausing in the boot room to kick off her boots and wipe the chunks of iced-snow off the legs of her pants. After peeling off several layers of clothing, Abbey ruffled her toque-hair and went into the kitchen, where she found Mother at the counter, arms folded across her chest.

"Oh, Abigail."

What now?

"Such nonsense, Abigail."

Mother tossed Abbey's journal on the counter in front of her. Abbey looked at the cover, red leather, imprinted with roses, edges of the pages foiled like a rainbow.

"What?" Abbey asked, reaching for her most prized possession. Mother slapped her hand.

"We need to watch you closer, young lady," Mother said, grabbing the journal and opening it on the counter. Abbey felt her face flush as Mother flipped through the pages, images of the cottage, the faeries, the woods at night.

"And this? Where do you come up with it all?"

The wolf. Abbey had drawn the crumpled carcass of the predator, its jaw tossed to the side, a smear of red in an otherwise black and grey charcoal drawing.

"It's just my imagination, Mom."

"It's just you spending too much time in those woods."

"Mom, no—"

"No, that's it. I won't hear of it. You're head's lost in the clouds, Abigail. If your father knew…"

"He hasn't seen this?"

Mother hesitated, her fingers stroking the rainbow edges of the paper. "No. He hasn't. And he won't."

She flipped another page, her hand trembling ever so slightly, her face softening to sad pity. She held out the page for Abbey to see.

It was the best drawing Abbey had ever seen. It was the acreage in the throes of winter, thick snow coating the ground, bare shells of trees skulking in the background like alien invaders. And the riding mower, an odd splotch of green and yellow on the grey and white landscape, parked in the middle of the snow. Behind it, deep tracks leading from the barn, rolled through deep crimson…

"Abigail, what is this?"

I don't know.

"I…"

I didn't do this.

"Um…"

Is that blood?

Abbey took a step forward and grasped the journal, holding the page up to her face and squinting her eyes.

Is that…

"…a hand?"

Mother grabbed the journal and tucked it into her skirt, covering it with her apron. "Abigail, there's something wrong with you. Something terribly wrong."

"But I didn't—"

"Didn't what? Draw this? Abigail, don't be ridiculous—"

"What are you going on about?" Father said, stomping into the kitchen, slush from his boots dripping onto the floor.

"Oh nothing," Mother said, giving Abbey a hard look before looking back at her husband. "And what are you at, there? I just cleaned this floor!"

Mother shuffled Father towards the boot room, and took the journal out of her skirt, thrusting it in Abbey's direction.

"Take this," she whispered. "Better you be caught with it than me. Keep it in your room. He won't bother with it there."

Abbey nodded and went straight to her room, eager to see if there were any other drawings her hand and mind had mysteriously concocted without her knowledge.

~

THEY WERE BEAUTIFUL, THE DRAWINGS. MYRIAD COLOURS, textures; it was the heart and soul of the woods, the cottage, the many knick-knacks of Faelith the witch.

Abbey had seen all that before. She had drawn them, those depictions of her time in the woods at the cottage in the clearing.

What she hadn't seen were the black and white sketches, crude drawings scratched on paper, charcoal depictions of pain and death splattered and accented with brilliant shades of red. The one Mother had shown her, the backyard of the acreage with the mower dragging through blood and body parts. Another was of Abbey's tree, crimson noose hanging from a cockeyed branch. Anton's car, painted a garish scarlet, tools floating in puddles of oil and blood on the floor of the barn. There were no people in the drawings, only death.

Who drew these?

Did I draw these?

Sometimes she fell asleep, pencil in hand and paper pressed to her face. Often she daydreamed, eyes unfocused, other senses engaged as the pencil scratched the page. She didn't need to look to create, to see while she translated her thoughts to the page. Her mind saw well enough. But had she been so distracted, so careless that she had forgotten such dark and horrible drawings?

She had anguish and pain. She knew that. The drawings were the manifestation of that pain, she told herself. An outlet, when violence was not the correct answer. And there had been many times where violence had seemed a palatable possibility; the prongs of a fork to Uncle Herman's testicles, an axe to Anton's head. The thoughts were fleeting, but they were there, usually rearing their terrifying, sharp-toothed heads while Abbey was in a state of extreme distress.

These pictures are me. I drew my anger to murder my fear.

Did I create Faelith, too?

Panic clenched Abbey's heart, and she swiped the thought away.

No. It's real. It's all real.

Unsettled but satisfied with her conclusion, Abbey went to work, coloring a picture of her and Gloria running through the trails in town. Colours and musical notes bounded off those ruby ringlets, dancing through the air before landing in Abbey's ears and eyes.

It had been a beautiful day.

"Abigail!"

Had been.

"Yes, Mother. Coming."

Abbey slid the journal between her mattress and boxspring and went to the door, readying herself to be around her family for dinner. When she reached the top of the stairs, she looked down and saw Mother draping her coat over her shoulders.

"Where are you going?" Abbey asked.

"Out for dinner, Abigail. Remember?"

She hadn't remembered. They probably didn't tell her in the first place. Abbey was always the last thing on their minds, unless they were angry and needed an outlet.

Perhaps I shall get them a journal for Christmas, Abbey snickered to herself, taking care to keep her smile in her head.

"Be good, and mind your Uncle," Mother said, taking her handbag from Father.

"Uncle?"

No.

"Aunt Petal has her meeting tonight, so Uncle Herman agreed to come keep an eye on you," Father said. "Anton has a date later on, and we didn't want you thinkin' you could take off into the woods on yer own, brazen as you've been."

"Yes, Father. Mother."

Uncle Herman dare not touch me, now he's in Faelith's reach.

"Have a good time," Abbey said. She peered over the bannister at Anton, who was in his regular groove on the sofa.

"He's going out after nine," Mother said, seemingly reading Abbey's mind. "And he damn well better be home before midnight."

"He's soon an adult," Father said, taking Mother by the arm.

"But the weather…"

Abbey didn't hear any more of the debate. The door shut behind her parents mid-discussion, and they were off into the night. A small part of Abbey wished their car wouldn't make it home; she hoped that perhaps their belts would be too tight and blood thick with cheap wine, and they wouldn't spy that patch of black ice hidden beneath the blowing snow. And that Uncle Herman would share the same fate, striking the headlights of an ongoing tractor-trailer on the nearly abandoned highway leading from town.

Put that in your journal and sketch it, Abbey smirked, retreating to her room and pulling the little red journal from beneath her mattress. She flipped through, half expecting wheeled tragedy and skid marks to be drawn on the once blank pages, but it was exactly how she had left it. She flipped to a page and started writing prose, a poem about the cottage on a bright summer day.

After filling three pages with the words in her head, Abbey heard the front door open.

Great. Here we go.

She looked at the clock.

8:30. Anton's still here. He can entertain Uncle Herman for a while.

Pencil scratched across the paper, Abbey paying little attention to the thumping and banging going on below. After a while, footsteps thudded up the stairs. Abbey turned and looked at her doorknob, heart caught in her throat, waiting to see the knob turn. But it didn't. Anton's door opened and shut, and the spring on his bed squealed and compressed. Abbey sighed and rolled over, content that Anton would be leaving soon. The sound of the television below blared out, signaling that Uncle Herman had settled in for the night, drink in hand.

"Abbey."

Abbey yelped, and the journal fell to the floor as she spun around on her bed.

Relaxed too soon, you idiot.

She had failed to consider that Uncle Herman's footsteps may have accompanied Anton's up the stairs.

Uncle Herman's not an idiot. Anton's right there in the next room.

"Hi Uncle Herman," Abbey said.

Besides, Faelith…

Abbey leaned over and grabbed her journal. She could feel the intensity of Uncle Herman's stare into the gape of her neckline as she reached to the floor.

"Parents out on a date, eh?"

"Guess so, yeah."

"And what's this here?"

Uncle Herman shut the door behind him and sat on the bed, lifting Abbey a good ten centimeters with the weight of his fat figure. He reached over to touch the journal, but Abbey yanked it away.

"My journal," she said, willing calmness into her tone.

"Ah, a teenaged girl's journal." As he spoke, a grin cracked across his face, exposing yellowed, uneven teeth. "All yer secrets 'bout your boyfriend."

"Haven't got one," Abbey said, looking away. She could taste the cigarettes on his breath.

"Now why is that, dear? Little beauty like you."

He reached out and put a hand on her knee. She resisted the urge to pull away.

Abbey felt a surge of clarity and bravery.

"I don't like that Uncle Herman."

She grabbed his hand, lifted it, and placed it on his own leg.

"Excuse me?" he said.

"I prefer you not have your hand on my leg. It makes me uncomfortable."

Uncle Herman's mouth opened but he struggled for words, his fingers drumming his knee. Finally, he concocted a clever response. His fingers stopped, and the grin was back.

"Uncomfortable," he said, tongue brushing his upper lip. "Why's that, sweetheart?"

"I don't like you touching me," Abbey said, matter-of-factly. She didn't break eye contact with him.

"Make you feel funny?" he said, sweat glistening under his nose. "Down there?"

"Go," Abbey said, standing from the bed and pointing at the door. "I want you to leave."

For a moment Abbey thought he might go. For just a moment, with the air between them thick with hesitation from both sides, Abbey thought she might get through this with her comfort and dignity intact.

Uncle Herman stood, but he did not go.

After realizing he had no intention of leaving, Abbey still had no fear. She imagined him attempting to approach her, but grey hands grasping his shoulders, ripping him in two and tossing his halves to opposite sides of the room.

Uncle Herman walked up to her and placed his hand on her face.

His skin was damp and warm, almost sticky.

She could feel the heat radiating from his body.

He backed her against the wall. Faelith did not come.

Abbey looked at her door, at her window, at the space beneath her bed. She listened for sounds from the vent in the floor.

Nothing. Nothing but Uncle Herman's moist breath sputtering over his panting tongue.

Abbey thought of one more out. A backup in case her saviour waited too long to come to her rescue.

"Anton!" Abbey called, panic finding its way to her voice, her journal dropping to the floor.

She could hear Anton shuffling about in his room.

"Anton!" she called again, sobs in her screams.

The noise from his room stopped, only briefly, then he turned on his stereo, the base thumping through the wall and into Abbey's bones.

Anton didn't answer her pleas.

Uncle Herman did not go.

And, worst of all, Faelith did not come.

10

─────────

The night was frigid, and Abbey's gooseflesh felt raw against the fleece of her parka. Her feet throbbed, tucked into Sorels one size too small, sock-less toes jammed into the front. Her whole body ached as she charged through the trees, hot tears stinging against cheeks prickling from the cold. She shoved her way through the thick brush, barely noticing branches tearing through her down jacket and nicking the bare skin on her calves.

She burst into the clearing, tears frozen to her eyelashes and frosted snot soaking the scarf around her face. She stole a look at the frozen pond as she went by. The faeries were out of hibernation, for the moment at least, tiny blades strapped to their feet. They were wrapped in tinsel parkas, with knit sleeves covering their tentacles. They twirled and whirled, leaping through the air in triple, quadruple, quintuple jumps, leaving spirals of shaved, glittered ice in the air behind them as they spun. Abbey was distracted from her mission. For a brief and glorious moment, all she saw was the faeries, all she felt was their playful jubilation as they performed on that pond, the light of the moon gleaming off their violet hair.

"Bootiful."

Faelith wiped Abbey's cheeks with the sleeve of a newly created fur coat, then wrapped it around her shoulders.

Abbey cuddled into the warmth of the pelt for a moment, closing her eyes and breathing in the smells of the hide and the woods.

Then she pulled the luxurious fur from her shoulders and threw it on the ground at Faelith's feet.

"Why?!" Abbey screamed, spitting the words at Faelith as loud as they would go. "Where were you?"

Faelith did not answer. She hummed a little tune, tapping her toe along with the dance of the faeries.

"You hurt Gloria when you thought she had hurt me. You thought she was gonna hurt me more, so you stopped her."

Faelith looked at Abbey, then walked away, humming her tune deep in her belly. Abbey dropped to her knees and balled up a wad of snow, firing it at the back of Faelith's bald head. Faelith's head snapped forward, and her grey hand wrapped around, rubbing the spot where the snowball had struck. She turned and looked at Abbey.

Abbey found a rock and hurled it at Faelith, striking her in the cheek, opening a gash and releasing a dam of blood over the witch's leathery face.

Faelith didn't flinch, allowing the blood to run down her face and soak her clothes.

"You weren't there!" Abbey shouted, at Faelith, at her family, at the world. "I needed you, and you weren't there!"

Abbey collapsed into the snow, her tears evolving into violent sobs. She closed her eyes, pressing her face into the snow, focusing on the piercing stabs of cold over the sting of every other pain. She felt the tingling of sleeping limbs, and warmth flooded her body. She opened her eyes and sat up. The faeries were all over her, tentacles licking her skin like feelers, the silver glow of their skin warming her. Faelith was there, too, sitting cross-legged, naked in the snow beside her, stroking her matted, tear-drenched hair.

"Yoo wah?"

"What?" Abbey asked, swiping her nose with the forearm of her coat.

"Yoo wah me?"

"What?" Abbey snapped, her frustration growing. "I don't understand you, stupid witch!"

The air around them silenced, and the faerie's glow extinguished. The red light glowing from Faelith's eyes burned on Abbey's face. Abbey gasped as Faelith drew in a deep, seemingly endless breath, her chest expanding and ribcage creaking.

Faelith closed her eyes, lips moving and flexing, preparing words more carefully than before. Abbey felt a wave of shame, of guilt for chastising the old witch, who was making every effort to learn how to communicate. Abbey was about to apologize, when Faelith's eyes snapped open and smile widened, tearing her face open from ear to ear. Abbey shivered as Faelith moved close to her face, hot breath preceding sharp, precise words.

"You. Want. Me?"

Abbey didn't respond. Couldn't.

"You. Want. Me. There? Help. You?"

Abbey trembled, afraid of the witch, terrified of her home, but absolutely paralyzed by her solitude.

"Yes," Abbey breathed. "Yes, I want you."

Abbey collapsed into Faelith's arms and the sobs returned full force, shaking her body like a seizure. Faelith held her tight, warming her, caressing her hair. She rocked Abbey back and forth like a babe, humming a tune deep in her chest. The glow from the faeries warmed them as they sat in the snow, rocking, singing. Abbey's muscles melted, her tension draining like a bathtub, and soon she was lulled to sleep.

～

THE GLOW WAS NO LONGER WARM, AND FAELITH'S EMBRACE NO longer soft.

Abbey woke, teeth chattering in the cold, body aching. She sat up, and something grabbed her hair. She pulled away; her scream rang into the night, but whatever had a hold of her did not relinquish its grip. Abbey flailed, trying to fend off whatever meant to drag her into the night, but found only rough, sharp nature.

Abbey steeled herself, taking gulping breaths to try to catch her runaway panic. Her hair had become matted in branches when she sat up. With trembling hands, she unknotted her hair from the bush and crawled out from beneath its thorny grasp.

She was in the woods, neither the clearing nor her home in sight. It was late, she knew that, but it was light enough to see. The sky was a pretty pink reserved for snowy nights, the rose glow covering the glittery snow as if in a fairytale. Though pretty, Abbey's skin was hurting from the freezing temperatures. Her breath frosted her eyelashes as she started walking, intent on arriving at any destination that might provide some warmth.

It didn't take her long to find familiarity. Within a few moments of shuffling her feet through the snow, she was at the edge of the woods, looking at the silhouette of her tree against the backdrop of her house. That house. The place where her Uncle was, where her parents didn't care, and her brother hated her. The only thing that drove her forward was the chill in her bones and the pain in her limbs, frozen digits growing number by the second. She passed the tree, eyes focused on the light ahead, trying to spy Uncle Herman through the patio door. The house was dark, a faint glow flickering from the television.

She didn't hide her arrival. Abbey flew through the door, choking a sigh of relief as a warm wave of air welcomed her into the house. She walked into the kitchen, ignoring the blaring television in the other room, and heated herself a cup of milk in the microwave. Once the warm mug was clasped in her hands, she made the dash for the stairs, focused on getting to her room and closing the door on the day behind her.

"What are you doing, dumbass?"

Anton was on the couch, hand orange with Cheeto dust, eyes glued to the screen. The sight of him made Abbey sick—his indifference, the knowledge that he was there, one room away, while Uncle Herman…

"Going to bed," Abbey said.

"'Bout time," Anton said, tossing another Cheeto into his mouth. "Mom and Dad gonna kill you, they find out you were in those woods again. And late, at that."

"And I'm sure you'll tell 'em."

"Or Uncle Herman will. He's probably mighty poisoned by now."

Abbey stopped and actually looked at her brother, grin slathered on his face, amused by the lashing she was going to get.

"Where is he?" Abbey asked, her stomach churning, eyes glancing up the stairs towards the door of her bedroom. She realized that she had expected Uncle Herman to be in plain sight, watching television. Not Anton. "And when did you get home?" Abbey looked at the clock. Anton did too.

Oh shit. It's three in the morning?

Anton furrowed his brow, rubbing his eyes and looking at the clock again.

"I… I honestly… I got home just after midnight, and…"

"Where's Uncle Herman?"

"I've been here that long? Man, I had plenty to drink, didn't I—"

"Anton, where's Uncle Herman?"

Anton paused, finally looking at his sister. "What happened to you?"

Abbey looked down at herself, her torn clothes, her scratched and bloodied skin.

"Like you'd care," she said, a blade in her voice. Anton winced. She smiled.

"I assumed Uncle Herman was out looking for you," Anton said. "I checked your room when I got home, and he wasn't on the couch, and when I saw that you weren't there, I figured he went hunting your ass."

Did he?

Is he out there? Still looking for me?

Anton placed the bowl of Cheetos on the coffee table and shut off the television. He looked sick.

"What is it?" Abbey asked.

"Mom and Dad."

"Yeah?"

"It's 3am, Abbey. Where are they?"

Abbey looked out the window at the gently falling snow.

"And where the hell were you? Did you just come home? Jesus, Abbey, it's three in the fucking morning! You weren't here when I got home at midnight…"

And neither was Uncle Herman.

Abbey went to the front window at the same time as Anton leapt from the couch, both reaching for the switch to the floodlights pointed down the drive. Uncle Herman's car was there, covered in a thick skiff of snow. There were no tire tracks in the fresh snow to indicate that Mother and Father had returned and snuck off to bed.

Anton ran his hands through his hair, a nervous gesture Abbey had never witnessed from him before. Her eyes fell to the floor, searching the boot rack.

Uncle Herman's boots were there, dry as a bone.

"Anton?"

She looked over at Anton, who had faded to a pale shade of white.

"Uncle Herman?" he called, running up the stairs. "You here, Uncle Herman?"

Abbey went to the backdoor, looking out the window to the porch and yard beyond. She could see her footsteps coming from behind her tree, but the snow was otherwise untouched. She went back into the kitchen and looked at the door to the basement.

The house was not silent. Anton was crashing around upstairs, moving from room to room and calling out names. The furnace was running, and the foundation creaking under the cold of the deep freeze, but a heavy quiet came from below. The deep and dark silence of the void under the stairs. Abbey went down, fear of the witch returning, lighting bulbs as she passed. The laundry room was dank and musty, as it always was, with the pile of blankets heaped in such a way to mask any squatters. Abbey pulled the blankets off, one by one, expecting a grey hand, a foot, anything. There was nothing. Abbey replaced the blankets and left the laundry room, and gave the rest of the basement a once over before heading back up the stairs.

She intended on going to Anton, joining him in the front room and possibly heading out on the roads to find Mother and Father, but she didn't make it. Her eyes were drawn to the window, the pink winter wonderland that was their back yard, and the previously untouched snow. Her footprints were still there, visible but fading in the falling snow, but now there was something else. The snow was soft and powdery, light and gleaming. In that field of untouched, crystalline white was a red slash severing the serenity. A trail of crimson down the middle of the yard.

Abbey opened the door and stepped outside, bare feet dipping into a gritty, warm pool of blood on the patio. She followed the crimson trail, blood and flesh and snow squelching up between her toes as she walked out into the yard. The sky was still a sheet of pink glowing light, providing enough illumination to see the carnage in the center of their land.

Uncle Herman. He was there, spread out on his back like a star, shivering from the cold and inching away from the house like a hobbled animal. His arms and legs had been severed, each limb strewn to opposite ends of the yard like post markers to the four corners of hell. Uncle Herman's body was bruised and torn, his naked flesh tortured by both the pain and the cold, yet he donned a high, firm erection that pointed to the starless skies.

"Abbey," he hissed through bloodied air. "Help…"

Abbey watched as he floundered there, limbless, naked, humiliated and overpowered, and she felt nothing. Not fear, not shock, not pity. Nothing. She didn't want to run away, she didn't want to help, she didn't want to know what had happened or why. She just wanted to stay there. And watch.

It came as no surprise when the sound of the mower engine reached her ears. It moved across the yard at a fair clip, pushing powdery snow aside with it's blade as it came. Herman's shrieks grew quiet in her ears as it approached him. Sound ceased in her head. All she heard was the blade as it dropped, passing over Herman's exposed body, slicing off the tip of his nose, the pudge of his belly, and the shaft of his manhood.

He didn't scream any more. He laid there in the snow, twitching, blood dribbling from his circumcised nose, joining in a river with his tears and the melting the snow beneath his head. A similar puddle formed between his legs, crimson spurting out in a spreading slick atop the ivory-white snow. Soon Uncle Herman was no more than a shell of meat in the center of a ruby pool, bright and colorful in contrast to the white and grey world that framed it.

The world froze for a heartbeat, then thrust forward at full speed, an explosion of terror. But Abbey remained still, calm, silent.

Anton screamed.

"Abbey? Abbey!"

She looked towards the barn, rolling door opened to the drive. Anton's car was in there, red and shining in a world of grey, its driver and passenger protruding from a smashed windshield. Mother and Aunt Petal lay half on the hood, half on the dash, glass and metal skewering their chests, throats, and abdomens.

What will people think, the stains on those darling skirts, Abbey thought.

Anton ran only as far as Abbey, stopping and viewing the wet mess that was his former uncle. He babbled like a toddler, incoherent thoughts garbled with gags and sobs, and he ran towards the rogue mower that was heading towards the back of the garage. As the engine of the mower died, Abbey looked into the woods, expecting to see remnants of Faelith passing in the night.

Abbey did not see the witch.

She did not see the woods.

She saw Father, hanging from a branch on her tree, swinging back and forth, flesh rubbed raw and noose soaked in the blood from a chaffed-raw neck. His tongue was blue and hanging from swollen lips, eyes purple and dark in the night.

He was gone.

And it wasn't suicide, as the noose might suggest.

His hands and feet were bound by his belts, belts that had broken her own flesh many times through the years. Her flesh now shared a spot on that leather with the chaffed skin from Father's wrists and ankles.

Abbey stood. Silent. Unmoving. Looking at nothing, and feeling less than that.

She stood in that spot, in the bitter cold, toes freezing to black as chaos ensued around her. Anton's screams. Slamming doors and cries for help. Blue and red lights flashing on the snow like an early Christmas show. The songs of sirens and a chorus of strangers moving in the night, scrambling to assess the hell unleashed upon this tiny nook of the earth.

PART II

"There is something at work in my soul, which I do not understand."

— Mary Wollstonecraft Shelley, Frankenstein

11

―――――――

*C*link.

The sound of the spoon on the inner wall of the coffee mug was piercing, almost nauseating.

The smell of old books was usually intoxicating, but the manuals and journals stacked ceiling high on generic pressboard bookshelves carried the odor of chemical and stale smoke.

Abbey wouldn't look up at her. She knew she'd be looking into probing eyes staring over glasses balanced on the tip of a hooked nose. And those eyes would be reading her, her every movement, every twitch in her body.

"Abbey, are you taking your medication?"

That's all I am now. A beast held at bay by pharmaceuticals.

"Abbey?"

And that's why I'm here. Why she's here. To supervise wildlife.

"Yes, I am."

"Regularly?"

"Daily, as prescribed."

"You seem angry, Abbey."

"I'm fine."

"Then why are you here?"

Because I have to be.

I am afraid.

"I'm quite fine," Abbey said, straining a smile. "I'm just checking in."

"Checking in?"

"Yes."

Take the hint, bitch. I don't want to talk to you.

"You are here because you need to see me, so I can keep refilling your prescription."

Of course. You think I like sitting here, having you judge me? Using me as entertainment?

"No, our talks help."

"You don't talk, Abbey."

C'mon lady. I've served my time. Let's just do this and go about our business for another three months.

"What should I say? Life is pretty boring. And boring is good, yes?"

"Is it?"

"It is. I've had enough excitement for one lifetime."

The doctor stared at her, watching the curve of her brow, the twitch at the side of her left eye. Abbey finally looked back, staring, willing her to stand down. The doctor's pencil moved but her eyes did not, remaining firmly planted on Abbey.

"How's work?"

"Work is work."

The doctor set the pencil down on the steno pad on her lap.

"Abbey."

"Yes?"

"You need to think about what you want to get out of these visits."

Drugs.

"My anxiety—"

"You want to just triage that, Abbey? Keep the edge off with medication? You're better than that. If you were more receptive to treatment—"

"I am receptive to treatment. I go out of my way to come here, take time I don't have out of an already impossibly tight schedule—"

The steno pad closed and the prescription pad opened.

"Look, Abbey, I'm not the enemy here." The doctor started scratching words on the prescription pad. She finished by dotting the pad with a firm stab of her pen.

She's frustrated, too.

"If this is what you want, Abbey, then so be it. I'll keep writing these, and you'll keep not giving a shit. You can hide behind the medication, Abbey, but it'll never make you happy. Not truly happy."

Abbey snatched the paper from her hand and stood.

"I'm perfectly fine with just being comfortable. Happiness is a stretch."

The doctor shook her head and closed Abbey's file. Abbey walked out of the office, feeling the doctor's eyes on her back as she left.

IT WAS WARMER THAN IT HAD BEEN IN A WHILE. THE ONLY SNOW that remained was on the shaded street corners, in alleyways that saw only dirt and grime. Abbey walked at a fair clip, pissed off that she had sacrificed most of her lunch break for her mandatory appointment. She was not required to go, but if she didn't, she would run out of medication. She'd been down that road before, and the anxiety had been debilitating. Locked away in her apartment for a month, screaming and crying into pillows, using alcohol to numb herself enough to go fetch groceries. It had been horrible, and had almost killed her.

But the appointments were aggravating. Abbey preferred to go through her life like a side-scrolling video game, one task to the next until the end of her days. She only hoped to make it another step, another minute, another second. And some days, it was second to second.

The street meat vendor on the corner by her office building was peddling some fusion fare. Abbey selected the chicken option on the menu, and a gingerale to settle her roiling guts. As she waiting for her food, she watched the city move around her. People dressed to the eights, strutting about on heels and shiny loafers, noses buried in apps and emails, nary a smile in the crowd. Here and there people were interacting, friends sharing a story, couples exchanging a touch. Those people. Those were the people who were smiling.

Abbey had no people. She had her coworkers, her therapist, the clerk at the market. And Netflix. Netflix was pretty easy to get along with. Abbey didn't mind the solitude though. People were generally garbage, and Abbey didn't want to sift through the bad to find the occasional good. She knew what to expect from herself, and that was enough.

The vendor handed her a foil wrapped meal, and Abbey headed towards her office building. As she walked, cars whizzed by, mufflers growling, exhaust spewing into the air. People passed her on the sidewalk, a few looking, most so involved in their own scurrying that they barely noticed another cookie-cutter version of themselves passing by.

All we are. Ants on the same pile.

A bistro table outside the office building was awfully tempting, and equally awful. The courtyard was crowded, and the traffic on the adjacent street was thick. Abbey wanted to be somewhere outside where it was quiet, but one doesn't find such things in the downtown core. Regardless, the sun was warm and the sky blue, even if she could only see a sliver between the screaming sky scrapers, billboards, and traffic lights.

The meal was good, a mix of Korean spicy chicken and Spanish paella. Abbey savoured every bite, watching the lone birch tree trembling in the feeble breeze. The tree was alone there in that courtyard, planted by the company for aesthetic appeal, but it looked sickly and contrived, stuck there all by itself. Abbey watched the tree and swayed back and forth with the branches, admiring it's pitiful beauty, when her shoulder lurched forward. Her meal, heavy red sauce and all, poured into her lap.

"Hey!" Abbey said, turning.

The man looked down at her and shrugged, a sheepish grin on his face. He had been walking with two other men, all phones in hands, and had bumped right into her. She wasn't even overlapping the sidewalk, tucked away at her table. And he didn't say sorry. He didn't say anything at all. His feet never even slowed, nor did his lips or fingers. He kept talking to his buddies, his fingers still dancing over his screen.

"Fuck you," Abbey said.

She watched as the man disappeared into the crowd. His hair shining, the shoulder pad of his blazer glowing a faint silver as he swatted at the empty air beside him…

"No," Abbey said, louder and harsher than she intended.

Patrons at the other tables looked at her, one shaking his head, the other clucking her tongue. The sound was like a nail up Abbey's spine.

Clucking. Mother used to do that. All the time.

Abbey glared at the woman. The woman saw, and shook her head, quietly scolding Abbey under her breath.

"Fuck. You," Abbey said, articulating every letter.

Lunch was over. Abbey wiped the remainder of her lunch off her lap with her scarf, and threw the whole lot of it into a nearby rubbish bin. She didn't have a change of clothes, but what she did have was a bright red stain on the front of her taupe pantsuit, and a meeting starting in fifteen minutes. When she entered the building, she went straight to the bathroom to try and do what she could to clean up the mess.

"Bad one, that," Brenda said, looking down at Abbey's trousers when she stepped in front of the mirror. "The fusion guy on the corner?"

"Yup," Abbey said, wetting some paper towel and rubbing the front of her trousers.

"That's not going to work," Brenda said, looking at her watch. "Henderson meeting in ten? I got you covered. Stay here."

Abbey stayed. She went into a stall and shut the door, leaning her head against the cold steel. She hated this place, the fluorescent lights, the carpet that itched even through properly-pointed high heels, the paper-pushers doing busy work which never really amounted to anything. She had worked her way from the mail room into a role in human resources, investigating employee claims against each other and upper management. Meetings were never productive, and people never happy. Defensive and hostile were the moods of most days. But the money was decent, allowing her to live in a down-town apartment and squirrel away extra in case of the rainiest of days. Since she rarely went out, and had little in the way of hobbies other than reading and streaming movies, that money had grown to be enough to cover a full-on monsoon season. Or four.

"Abbey?"

"Yeah."

"Here."

Brenda hung a pair of black trousers over the stall. "You're a tiny bit of a thing compared to me, but these'll be better than those boys staring at red on your crotch. Men get so squeamish about the rag."

Abbey blushed. She hadn't considered that people might think that. She never really cared what people thought at all. She would have gone to the meeting, blood-a-blazing, and never given it a second thought. Thank goodness for Brenda, an ally in a swarm of hostiles.

The trousers were too big, but sat nicely on Abbey's hips if she folded over the waistband. They weren't perfect, but they would do. Sagging pants were less noticeable than bloody ones. She gave her hands a wash and splashed a bit of cold water in her face. The woman in the mirror was aged well beyond her thirty-odd years. Grey bags framed hollow, haunted eyes, dark hair dull and plain, skin wan and sallow. And now, with the baggy pants and oversized white shirt, she looked like a corpse in the clothes of the living.

"Better," Brenda said, coming out of a stall and giving Abbey the once over.

Abbey smiled as best she good, looking into Brenda's warm, dark eyes. The older woman was handsome and kind, and soothed Abbey when work was especially caustic. Abbey reached out and brushed a clump of hair off the shoulder of Brenda's blazer.

"Ready for this?" Brenda asked, scratching at her head.

"As I'll ever be," Abbey said, looking away from her reflection in the mirror.

"OH, COME ON."

He was a stallion in a suit, looking as sharp as the glare he gave the woman across the table.

"Mr. Knight—" Abbey started, but he held up his hand, stopping her with the flash of his palm.

"Abbey," he said, grin at the corner of his mouth. "She's overreacting, can't you see?"

"I'm not, you vile rodent!" The raven-haired woman spewing anger at Callen Knight was Lydia Barnes, an engineer who had been with the company for a few years. He was a silver fox, a gorgeous man who had been with the company over twenty years. Abbey stared at them, then down at her notes, pretending to read wisdom that wasn't there.

He was innocent, Abbey knew that. He had violated no company policy and hadn't even been indecent. Lydia and he just suffered a workplace relationship gone sour, and every tick and tock of the day there was some sort of indiscretion or misunderstanding that led to a meeting with HR. Abbey struggled, day after day, looking at black and white policies but feeling the grey of social hierarchy and interactions suffocate her like a gag. Whether the offending party was guilty or not, Abbey felt the pull, an overwhelming orbit, leaning her to favour the accuser. When she went the route of common sense, of policy and evidence, she re-lived the situation in her mind, wondering if she had just stifled another victim. Even squabbles over stolen lunches and abuse of the photocopier left her mind rambling at night.

The proceedings went on, ending in a fuck-you/fuck-you deadlock between the parties, each claiming they would seek their own legal counsel. But Abbey's job was done, neither being involved in any violation of company policy.

Abbey returned to her desk, an empty wasteland of papers and stationary supplies, and flopped into her chair. She caught her reflection in her computer monitor, an ugly frown slashed across her face. She stared at the miserable woman, then her eyes swept her desk, her walls. Nothing. Her degree hung crooked on the wall, an imperfection she had noticed five years previous but hadn't bothered to fix. Other than that, there was no other art in her office, framed or otherwise. No pictures, no photographs…

Pictures of what?

Abbey reached into her purse, finding the bottle of pills she had picked up from the pharmacy. They looked so inviting, so delicious. But then she looked up at the walls, empty, taupe, lonely.

She stuffed the pills back in her purse.

Abbey didn't hesitate this time. She stood from her desk, purse in hand, like she had imagined doing at least a hundred times before. She left her office, door open, lights on. She walked into Robert's office and didn't shut that door either.

"Hi Robert."

"Abbey," he said, looking startled. "What can I—"

Abbey pulled his notepad from in front of him, reached over and grabbed the pen from his hand, and scrawled a message on the yellow paper. When she was done, she pulled out her phone and took a picture or her words.

"Abbey, what is this?"

"My resignation," she said, pushing the paper across the table. "You've been good to me, Bob, but it's time."

He opened his mouth to argue, but didn't. She could feel him looking her over, her baggy clothes, the sickness in her eyes, on her skin and in her hair. He stood and took her hands, giving them a firm squeeze.

"I know, Abbey," he said, his eyes growing wet. "Where will you go?"

"Out of the city," she said, looking out the window at the blue sky. "Away from this. I need a change. A complete change."

"You'll always have a place here, if you need."

"Thanks Bob."

She didn't linger. She didn't want an awkward goodbye—any more so than it already was—and didn't want to have to articulate details she didn't have. She had been with the company since she had graduated, and in the city several years longer than that. And she didn't care. She hadn't cared about anything in a very long time. That was her world now, sterile and empty, concrete and congested. She needed to cough it out of her lungs.

ABBEY'S APARTMENT WAS A SHORT JAUNT FROM HER OFFICE building, a single LRT stop and a one block dash before she greeted the doorman, rode her elevator, and disappeared behind her apartment door. She scurried through her place, a criminal on the run, sorting through what was important and what wasn't. Save a few of the essentials—clothes, toiletries, her laptop—most of what she owned was the latter.

She had been out of the foster system for ten years, on her own in the shadow of a metal and glass city, clawing her way up from the trenches to support herself and her solitary lifestyle. One online degree and three ladder rungs later, she was HR at a big company, paying her way and then some. Her apartment was simple but chic, and filled with the bare minimum—food, clothes, toiletries, a television, a couch, and a bed. Simplicity made packing easy.

Abbey's frantic gathering slowed to a steady pace as the night wore on, the decision resting easier with each passing hour. She had been moving fast for fear she might change her mind, but as time passed, she realized there was no going back. She didn't want to. She wanted out. Needed out.

Wanting a break from the final few boxes and trips to the dumpster, Abbey poured herself a Merlot and perched on a barstool at the window. She stared at the lights of the city, wondering if she would miss them.

"You will," she said to the reflection in the window. "But there are other lights in other places, far more pretty than this."

Abbey resisted, but her mind pushed, bringing her to the woods, the stars, the lights from the fires and the faeries at the cottage…

"No," Abbey said. She drank her wine in two generous gulps, then returned to the counter, filling her glass with the rest of the bottle. She would not be looking out the window again. No more night sky, no more lights.

TWO BOTTLES OF WINE AND HALF A NETFLIX SERIES LATER, THE couch became Abbey's final resting place for the night. The apartment was empty, Abbey's clothes and essentials packed up into two suitcases and several boxes. The sounds of the television echoed as if in a tin can, rivaled in volume only by Abbey's snarling snores, drool tainted red with the leavings of the bottles of wine sitting high on her belly. Traffic revved up below, the sounds of bars leaking out into the street after closing time crawling up the windows.

The hoots and hollers of a herd of particularly rambunctious white collar millennials managed to find their way to Abbey's ears, waking her from the peace of unconsciousness. She spat profanities and saliva at the window in a futile attempt to stifle the noise and resume her slumber, but the noise continued, and sleep did not.

Abbey rolled off the couch, lingering on all fours until the room steadied enough for her to get up, and swayed her way to the bathroom. She released like a geyser as soon as she hit the toilet seat, and let her head rest on a knee well after she had voided her bladder. Not to be left out, her stomach spoke up. She dropped to her knees and spun, just in time to aim the contents of her stomach at the water in the bowl. She heaved until her guts ached and her throat burned, and kept going a minute more, screams and vomit and tears pouring from deep within her soul. She shivered, her naked body pressed against the unforgiving tile and cold porcelain. Abbey's mind and body ached. She couldn't move, paralyzed by the cold, the hurt, the emptiness. As she writhed against the toilet, feeling like she might die right there on the spot, warmth shrouded her shoulders. Abbey breathed slow, feeling heat radiating from just beyond her bare back.

"Not real," she breathed through sour breath.

Her hair, which dangled in the toilet, matted and soaked, parted and lifted from her face. Abbey didn't move as she felt hands, hot and rough, take strands of hair from her face, pulling it back and tying it in a knot behind her head. Abbey reached back and laced her fingers through the phantom hands, squeezing the contorted bones and leathery flesh.

The vomit came again, this time with more force, producing little more than screams and bile. The large hands held Abbey's head as she urged, then rubbed her back when she was done. Abbey resisted the disbelief, enjoying the sensation, unquestioning.

"Not real," she chanted, over and over again.

And then the hands were gone.

Abbey turned and saw nothing and no one behind her in the bathroom.

"Not real," she said as she stood.

"Not real," she said as she washed her face in the sink.

"Not real," she said as she went to the kitchen and cracked open her new prescription bottle, downing another pill with a swig of wine straight from the bottle.

"Not real," she said as she resumed her position on the couch, turning up the volume and drowning out the function of her own brain.

12

———

he orange wagon had a certain appeal.

  Until now, Abbey had no need for a car; her apartment was a stone's throw from her office, and she did nothing else with her life. She had her driver's license, and could drive quite comfortably. She just hadn't done it much.

"This one's an old girl," the sweaty salesman said, his eyes flickering towards the shinier, pricier models on the lot. "A girl like you should get the fun she deserves. How about the Mustang over there? Or I have this Lexus in a pearl white…"

As he droned on, Abbey looked down at her clothes, simple but name brand, the ostentatious logo shouting at people who didn't know her, but used these little trademarks to judge her.

"I prefer this one."

The sales man gave her the once over again.

I'll take it along with your eyes, asshole, if they touch me again.

"You have kids," he said, more a statement than a question.

"No thanks. Just the car."

He laughed, a forced and uncomfortable sound. Abbey did not. She looked at him, all business, impatient for the keys.

"Lighten up, ma'am."

And there it is. Aged and desexed me in an instant.

"How much?"

"Straight to business, eh?"

Abbey stared at him, unblinking. He hesitated, then the smile disappeared. He turned and walked back to the neon trailer plastered with signs touting honest and out-of-this-world deals. Abbey gave a cursory glance around the lot, briefly considering the sportier models, but was happy with her initial choice. She patted the hood of the orange, wood-paneled wagon.

"It's just you and me, old girl."

Abbey walked into the trailer, plastic blinds rattling against the door as it closed behind her. The salesman was sitting behind a desk, chortling to the other chubby peddler across the way.

"Impatient, sweetheart?" he said, initiating a fake shuffle of the papers in front of him.

Abbey walked over, placed her palms on his desk, and hovered over him. "I have better places to be than that dingy lot, or in this sweat-smelling, donut-littered shack. I have a long drive ahead, and I'd prefer to be on my way."

Abbey placed a cashier's check down on the desk. She had intended on paying more, and had the cash in her purse to do so, but changed her mind.

More than he deserves. Some other wilting flower can line his pockets today.

The salesman moved to stand, placing his own hand on the desk, mouth opened to begin an argument, but he stopped. Abbey flinched. He looked past her, over her shoulder, and his jaw snapped shut. His hands returned to his lap for a moment before he shook his head and rifled through a few papers before sliding them across to Abbey.

"Uh, I need you to fill these out, and I need a copy of your ID."

Abbey nodded and handed him her card. He hurried to the photocopier in the corner, glancing a few times over his shoulder, and Abbey's. Abbey turned, looking behind her at his perplexed looking partner in crime. The other man shrugged his shoulders and raised a brow at the nervous man at the copier. Abbey took a long look behind her, scanning the wall, the centerfold calendar, the old, dusty sales awards.

A shiver scraped her vertebrae, settling on the hairs on the back of her neck.

Not real.

The paperwork was filled out in a flash, Abbey's rushed chicken scratch barely legible in the too-small boxes asking for seemingly endless information. Soon, Abbey had her card and keys in hand, and was transferring boxes and suitcases from the taxi to her new ride.

"Have a good day, ma'am."

Her original salesman had not emerged from the trailer to bid her adieu. His partner had come out, for the sake of good business, to wish her well and send her on her way. The other one sat hunched behind the blinds, finger hooked through the slats, looking like a kicked puppy.

"I'm sorry," the other man said, looking back at the trailer. "I don't know—"

"It's quite fine," Abbey said. "He's just embarrassed about his behaviour. I hope."

"Okay," the man said, reaching out to shake Abbey's hand. She smiled and slid in the driver's seat of her new friend, and caressed the dash.

"Barnes. That name will suit you just fine."

The engine purred to life, and she pulled out of the gravel lot, GPS off and radio on.

"Well Barnes, we have miles to go. Better make yourself comfortable."

~

THE HEAT OFF THE BLACKTOP RADIATED IN WAVES OF DISTORTED air off in the distance. The old wagon's air conditioning worked up a sweat, keeping Abbey cool and fresh behind the wheel hour after hour. She drove, knowing only that she was moving forward. It was her second day on the road, and she was actually quite liking it. They had never taken road trips when she was a kid, and her teens and twenties had been dedicated to mere survival, so this was her first foray into this territory. She picked up snacks and compact discs at the first gas stop, along with a pair of aviator sunglasses to complete the feel. She had traveled almost twelve hundred kilometers, with no inkling of stopping.

The wagon's ride was comfy and its space plentiful, but it was a pig on gas. Abbey didn't mind. She liked the old side-of-the-road stations where the clerks were short on teeth and long on conversation, with always a tale to tell, tall or otherwise. She saw one of the old yarn-spinners when she pulled into a generic set of pumps on a bunny trail a kilometer off the highway.

She got out of Barnes and stretched her arms to the sky, lifting her heels off the ground. It felt good to be out in the fresh air; the smell of the country was sweet and delicious on her tongue. And hauntingly familiar.

Not far from home, now, I suppose.

She jammed the nozzle into the gas tank, then leaned up against the car, giving it a pat on the hood.

"How are you holding up, Barnes?"

Abbey heard the crunch of gravel and suspected she would spend the next minutes speaking to someone other than her car.

"Strange name for a car."

It was an old man, hair as long as the tip of his beard, rolling a sprig of wheat around on his tongue.

"Figured Barnes and I should be on a first name basis," Abbey said, "since we're together for such long stretches. And she's an old girl, motherly..."

Abbey's eyes looked off into the swaying fields, green and gold, softly rolling hills and dense forest in the distance.

"Beautiful, that," the old man said, looking too.

"Lived here long?"

"Yes, m'lady. My whole life."

"This is a beautiful area."

"Sure is." The old man looked back to Abbey and Barnes. "Out for the long haul, eh?"

"Pardon?"

"Boxes. Plenty o' them. And suitcases. They're going where you're going, and neither of you are making a return trip, methinks."

"You think correctly, sir."

He laughed, a gasping guffaw dipped in tar and nicotine, then spit out a heavy wad on the gravel at his feet.

"Sir. Ain't heard that one, no, not in a long time. Not since I was at the school."

"The school?"

"Yes, ma'am."

Abbey looked at the station, nameless and plain, diner attached, the entire property surrounded by trees.

"There's a school out here? What town is this?"

"Don't pay much mind to the signs, eh? Well, you and everyone else these days."

His eyes were distant, but not sad.

"Our quiet little corner of the world."

Quiet. Corner, Abbey parroted in her mind.

"Lamarque," the man said.

"French?" Abbey asked.

"Tavern keeper, yes. Passed through here heading east. Laid her name on this area. But there ain't much Francious about us. We're as English as they come."

"Oh not all of us, you fool-ass."

A plentiful woman emerged from the station, apron tied around her waist and hair piled on top of her head in a haphazard bun. As she approached, Abbey could smell her—bacon grease and fresh baked bread.

"Bonjour," the woman said, bowing. "Common sai Vue? Je'mapple Marie."

"I'm sorry," Abbey said, feeling her cheeks flush. "I don't speak French."

"Ah, well, there's no shame in that," the woman said, stepping over and slapping Abbey on the back.

"Pride in that, though…" the man said, grinning.

"Chuck!" Marie screeched, slapping his round gut with the back of her hand. "We don't harp on the French here, now do we. Western pride without eastern slander, yes?"

"Yes ma'am," he said, rubbing his stomach.

"Now then, from what I overheard, you are traveling about with nowhere to go," Marie said, locking arms with Abbey. "Why don't you stay a spell, have a bite to eat?"

Abbey hesitated, the woman's touch hot and prickly on her arm. Marie read the signal and stepped away.

"Okay," Marie said, folding her hands in front of her. "My manners allude. What, my lovely young thing, is your name?"

"Erm…"

"C'mon then, don't be bashful. We aren't gonna eat you."

Chuck and Marie laughed, a joke repeatedly enjoyed by secluded gas station 'billies, Abbey was sure.

"Abbey."

"Abigail. What a lovely name," Marie said, acting like she was tasting the name on her tongue.

"No," Abbey said, firmer than she intended. "Just Abbey."

"Ah," Marie said. "Abbey. Very good, then. Come along Abbey. Park this—"

"Barnes," Chuck interjected.

"Barnes?" Marie said, scrunching her face at Chuck.

"Barnes," Chuck repeated. "The car. She's named it Barnes."

"Barnes," Marie said, looking over at Abbey's partner. "Well, each to their own. Looks more like a Karla to me."

The gas tank had been full for five minutes, but Abbey had not made a move to leave. She replaced the nozzle and the gas cap, and had been leaning against Barnes listening to the banter. She felt less than moderately uncomfortable, which is the best she had felt around other people in years.

"Yes, I wouldn't mind a bite to eat."

Chuck and Marie look surprised, but beamed as soon as Abbey's words had sunk in.

"Well that's lovely, dear," Marie said. "I was quite certain you was gonna blow us off. You seem the type, you know."

"Never mind that," Chuck said, waving at his wife. "Why don't you park Barnes over there by the trailhead and come join us."

"That'd be lovely," Abbey said, eyeing the side of the building. There was a marker indicating the beginning of a trail system into the woods. Abbey's stomach fluttered, a comatose butterfly squirming to life, but the feeling was fleeting. She moved Barnes into a spot and killed the engine, being sure to lock the doors before she went to the diner.

THE BACON WAS DELICIOUS, AND THE EGGS WERE COOKED TO perfection; they weren't raw enough to be snotty, but soft enough to be soaked up by the homemade bread Marie had loaded into the basket on the table.

"This is delicious," Abbey said through a mouthful of food. "I was starving."

"You need to eat, girl, keep yourself healthy," Chuck said from behind the counter.

Girl.

Abbey's shoulders tensed.

"Pay him no mind, Abbey," Marie said, giving Chuck his

umpteenth whack on the gut. "I'm sure you don't need another nag in your life."

Abbey didn't know how to respond to that. She had no nag in her life. No bolster, no cheerleader, no lover. Nothing. And she preferred it that way, and that way was horrible. A painful dichotomy.

Marie sat next to her, taking care not to get too close.

"You know, I have an ear, if need be."

Abbey looked at the woman, the motherly rouge on her cheeks, the concern in her eyes.

"I'm fine. Just travelling."

"Mmhmmm," Marie said, crossing her arms over her chest. "Just traveling, sure. Running away from nothing, going to nothing. Sure of that."

Abbey's muscles flexed, telling her to get up and go, and she just about did just that. But a heavy weight pressed her buttocks heavier into the red vinyl stool. She swung her feet off the barstool, trying to stand, but stayed firmly stuck in place. She tried to move her arms, to get some leverage to push herself up, but her arms stayed glued to her sides.

Not real.

Marie looked at her, brow twitching in bewilderment, but she quickly looked away. *She* was able to rise from her stool, so she did, and moved to her place behind the counter.

"Tell you what," Marie said as she wiped the counter, deflecting attention from Abbey's odd behaviour. "We own all of this—the station, the diner, and the little motel out back. It's clean and safe; no one's interested in causing trouble this far out of the way. If you like, we can put you up in a room for a bit, until you find out where you're going."

Chuck turned his head to Marie, and Marie gave him a look.

"Free of charge," Chuck said.

"That's not necessary," Abbey said. "I have plenty of cash."

They looked at each other, and Marie smiled.

"And sure of yourself, in that regard. You obviously feel safe with us, making that kind of declaration. That, or you have no intention of staying."

Abbey was surprised that she had decided to stay. In her mind, she had already concluded her drive, the night in that motel room seeming more than just appealing. And she was also surprised she had no qualms about these folks, people in the middle of nowhere that she knew nothing about, who were offering a complete stranger complimentary respite. There were no other patrons in the diner, and no other vehicles in the parking lot.

Perhaps they are murderers. Cannibals.

Perhaps I don't care.

Abbey wiped her face with the napkin on her lap.

"I am very tired," she said. "It's been a long day. A good night's rest sounds wonderful. Shall I leave Barnes where she is?"

"You can move her right outside your room, if you like," Chuck said. "You ladies seem close, so I'd hate for her to be too far away from you."

Abbey smiled. "Thank you. You've both been too kind."

"Just kind enough," Marie said, reaching under the counter and pulling out a key card. "Make yourself comfortable, dear. We're here, all day every day, at least one of us. Chuck might step out for groceries or supplies, but the other is always available. We live in the trailer out back."

Abbey nodded and took the key.

"Chuck, help the lady with her luggage," Marie said, shooing him towards the door.

"That won't be necessary," Abbey said, flushing red again.

Marie made eye contact, then nodded, knowing. "Well if you decide to move it from Barnes into the room… if you should decide to stay awhile… let Chuck lift them heavy boxes for you. Makes him useful."

Abbey smiled, and it wasn't forced. She liked these two. Good people.

She pulled Barnes around the diner and gas station to the strip of motel jutting out back. It was a two-story, outer walkway style, with a basic pool in the center of a u-shaped line of rooms. Abbey parked her car next to the stairwell and retrieved her suitcases from the boot before hauling them up the stairs to her room on the second floor.

The room was clean and simple, two double beds and a surprisingly modern flatscreen television on the wall. There was an empty mini fridge in the closet and a tray of toiletries in the bathroom. Abbey flung her suitcases on the bed next to the window, opting to sleep deeper in the room, next to the closet.

Like a damsel in a horror movie, she chastised herself. *If someone or something breaks in, why do I want to be farther from the door? So I can lock myself in the bathroom with no escape, I suppose.*

Before her mind could start running laps around her anxiety, Abbey clicked on the television to a late night talkshow, and hit the shower. The hot water rinsed off Barnes' stale interior, and relaxed bunched-up muscles that had been cramped behind the wheel for hours on end. She stepped out the shower and toweled off, not caring to look in the mirror or even brush her mangled hair. After donning several layers of clothing to protect her skin from strange bedding, she retrieved several pill bottles, hiding them next to the King James in the drawer beside the bed, popping several in her mouth before her head hit the pillow.

Underneath those covers, in a world she didn't know, in a place she did not yet hate, Abbey felt mildly comfortable.

Now this. This could be real.

13

———

The morning came and went, unbeknownst to Abbey. She slept away the dawn, and the soft mid-morning light, waking to the heat of the midday sun. Exhaustion had allowed the drugs to take hold, and she slept, uninterrupted, for over twelve hours. She sat up, her muscles stiff and aching, mouth gritty and bone dry.

She checked the mini-fridge, knowing full well it was empty, then dunked her head under the tap and drank greedily, sucking back the water until it sloshed in her belly when she moved. A quick splash to the face and outfit selection and she was out the door and down to the gas station.

"Morning, love," Chuck said, rising from his wooden rocker and giving her a pat on the shoulder. He instantly pulled his hand back and shoved it in his pocket. "Oh, erm… sorry there."

Marie must have talked to him. Clever woman.

"It's okay, Chuck," Abbey said, meaning it. "Hey, which way to town?"

"That way," Chuck said, hooking a thumb over his shoulder. "You could walk, unless you plan to pick up some things."

"I do, actually. Stores there?"

"A few. The market, boutiques, hardware. The usual small town staples."

"It's alive!" Marie said, coming out the diner door, bell singing into the afternoon air. She didn't come anywhere near Abbey, though, nor extend a hand. "Did I hear you're going into town? Doing some shopping?"

"Yeah," Abbey said. "Few groceries, maybe look at the shops."

"Groceries, eh?" Marie's smile was bigger than her girth. "You're sticking around a while." A statement and a question.

I guess I am.

"Well, as I was telling you," Chuck said, looking at Marie, a wink on his eye," town's that-a-way, just a few blocks before you hit main street. Not much to look at, but there just the same. You could walk, if you didn't have an armful, but parking is plentiful and free. Just hang a left out of our parking lot and follow the road. You'll see the rest of town as soon as you're around the bend."

Simple enough. Abbey offered another thank you—one of many she would give these two, she was sure—and walked back to Barnes. She glanced at the trail just beyond the motel, marked by a map with coloured paths outlining different routes. Abbey walked past her car to the sign, marveling at the intricacy of the area that looked like little more that a field with meager clusters of birch and poplar trees.

"Not much," Marie said, coming up behind her. "Great for the athletic types. All gravel trails, well maintained, several loops, different distances. Are you a runner?"

Abbey's mouth fell open, and she felt a crimson tint touch her cheeks.

"No dear," Marie said, daring to touch her shoulder. "Not like what we discussed yesterday. A runner. Jogging."

"Oh," Abbey said, glowing redder by the minute. "No, not anymore. Used to be. In school."

Images of Gloria sprinted across Abbey's mind, her red curls bouncing off her running shirt, Abbey's breath heavy and heart pounding in her chest as she worked to keep up with her...

"These trails cover a fair distance and are safe and friendly." Marie held tight to Abbey's shoulder, giving it a few pumps with her pudgy hand. "You are safe, here Abbey. It's a friendly place."

Abbey didn't know what to say.

"You look in need of a friend, my dear," Marie finished, turning and waddling back towards the diner. "Nothing but friends here. And," she said, turning and giving Abbey a stern look, "we are well enough off the beaten path, and you look like you've travelled quite a distance. It'd be an extremely lucky shot in the dark if he found you here. 'Sides, that's what we got sledgehammers and chainsaws for."

"I don't know what you—"

"Course you don't," Marie said, winking.

Without giving Abbey a chance to argue or respond, she hustled back to the diner, laughing to herself the whole way.

Abbey sighed. *Better she thinks that I'm being chased by something other than a past full of fiction and sickness. Let them think I'm sane, if only for a while.*

LAMARQUE WAS SMALL. ASIDE FROM A STREET OR TWO OF SIMPLE little houses, the population, as far as Abbey could tell, resided mostly on outlying farms and averages, leaving a little strip of commerce isolated like a sore thumb in the middle of nothing. A market, a little restaurant and bar, boutique clothing store that had clothes Abbey could imagine no one out here affording, and a tiny Bank of Montreal branch, out of place in the country surroundings.

Money makes the world go 'round, even out here.

Abbey popped in and withdrew some cash, not certain if the little mom and pop shops even accepted cards. She walked the winding street, taking a look through the boutique and some flea markets, picking up some nifty outfits—boho tunics and leggings—to replace the cold, sterile pant suits that were standard uniform of city bitches. She even picked up a pair of running shoes to replace the shiny patent pumps that squished her toes into an actual triangle. Her last stop before hitting the market was a shop specializing in second-hand goods and creations by local artisans.

The little bell on the door tinkled as she passed through.

"'Allo, miss," the shopkeeper said, popping out from behind a mound of dusty knickknacks. "How's the day treatin' ya?"

"Just fine, thanks. Checking out the town."

"Visitor. Nice. What do you think of our little Lamarque?"

"Quaint. Quiet."

The shopkeeper laughed, a high pitched and airy sound forced through tired lungs. He stood from his pile on the floor, abandoning the display for a moment to give her his full, undivided attention.

"Quaint and quiet be an understatement," he said, brushing the dirt off his stained corduroy pants. He came over and held out his hand. "I'm Peter."

These people want to be touched too much, Abbey thought, shaking his hand anyways. She might be a lot of things, but rude was not one of them.

"Abbey. Pleased to make your acquaintance."

"Abigail," he said, giving her hand an additional shake before he released her.

Abigail.

Her mother's voice.

"Just Abbey," she said.

He was tall, thin man, teeth yellowed, skin too. His left eye looked at her, and his right stared off at something on the wall. He was balding, a greasy comb-full of hair twirled over the top of his head, a far cry from the bushy, handlebar mustache perched atop his upper lip.

"Looking for something in particular, or just perusing?"

"Just browsing," Abbey said, trying very had not to stare at the man. "I'm staying at the motel down the road, the one with the gas station."

"Is there another?" he laughed, putting his hand over his mouth. "I'm sorry, love. Of course you are. There ain't nothin' else round here. Rude of me, though."

Abbey shrugged and let her eyes move over the shelves, trying to signal the end of the conversation. She was growing uncomfortable. She'd had enough peopling for one day.

"Got some good stuff here," he said, moving back to his pile but still talking to her. "All from the locals, all hand made or hand-me-down. No junk. I don't take junk."

The majority of it looked like junk to Abbey, but everyone had different tastes. Old pottery, ceramic decorations, a clay tea set. Abbey tucked some used books under her arm. There was a beautiful park with picnic tables across the street where she could sit out in the sun and read.

I wonder if there's a big tree I could lean against, soak in the sun and the smells and sounds of the wilderness.

Abbey shook her head, quickly brushing the thought away with the swipe of her hand in front of her face. Peter looked up at her, brow raised. She looked away, falsely focusing on a red vase on the shelf beside where she stood.

After perusing the odds and sods of the shop, Abbey took the books up to the counter and pulled out her wallet to pay.

"No ma'am," Peter said, stepping behind the counter and pulling out a brown bag. "You can have these, but you shan't be paying. Not today. A gift for being new in town."

"That's not necessary," Abbey said, reaching over the counter with the cash. "I'm only passing through, and—"

Behind the counter, just over Peter's shoulder, was a small box, wooden, painted black with intricate designs of purple and pink lilies. It was enchanting. Peter noticed Abbey's attention and looked over his shoulder at the box.

"That?" he said. "Old music box. Had it for quite some time."

He plucked the box off the shelf, blew the dust off the top, and gave it a swipe with the rag tucked into his belt. The finish was shinier than she originally thought, and the details more magical. Tiny flowers, creeping vines, iridescent dragonflies.

Peter plucked a tin key taped underneath the box and poked it in the lock in the front. He opened the lid, and a dancer stood. A ballerina dressed in pink, surrounding by mirrors. Peter wound a metal dial on the side and she started dancing, twirling in a multitude of reflections. The song sputtered from the box, tinny and simple, a haunted melody pinging off old, internal workings.

"Fur Elise," Peter said, tapping his finger along with the tune. "Pretty standard for old music boxes, that and Tchaikovsky. This one plays both. Nowadays, digital boxes play whole ranges, and sound like full orchestras. But ones like these have a certain charm about them"

Peter passed Abbey the box, and she held it in her hands, admiring both the sight and sound. "I'll take it," she said, gingerly shutting the lid, watching the dancer fold down as the mirrors collapsed upon her.

Peter wrapped it in bubble wrap, ensuring all corners were protected for the journey home. He put both the box and Abbey's books in a large tote and walked her outside. She eyed the park across the way, deciding she would return tomorrow and have lunch there with her books.

"Good day to you," Peter said, waving as she walked back towards Barnes. "Hope to be seeing you."

"I imagine you will."

～

After several trips up the stairs, all of Abbey's goodies and groceries had been deposited into her room. Abbey took a few minutes to organize her dry goods neatly in a drawer and put the perishables in the refrigerator before fixing something to eat. She boiled water for her pack of ramen noodles, then settled in at the little table by the window to eat and watch some television.

As the noodles went down, and the news droned on, Abbey watched out the window. The new summer dusk was a blaze of oranges, pinks, and reds shining on the light wisps of clouds in an otherwise clear evening. Her window overlooked the courtyard, littered with a dozen pool chairs, a few tables with umbrellas, and an above-ground hot tub.

Perhaps I'll even take a dip one of these days.

The corners of Abbey's mouth curled up.

One of these days.

She had unconsciously decided this is where she would plant her roots. For the time being.

Avoidance had been Abbey's way for as long as she could remember—as long as she *chose* to remember. But there she sat, eating her noodles, contemplating the logistics of staying long term in a motel room. She didn't mind the cramped quarters—she had very few belongings, after all—and the price was right. Town was easily accessible, and the few locals she had met seemed nice.

And it was removed from the rest of the world.

Abbey went to the drawer beside her nightstand and fished out the pills. She opened the bottle and peered in at the tablets. The very feeling of the bottle in her hands aroused feelings of… nothing. A suffocating numbness, amnesia, a dullness that spread itself across her senses, her world, her memories.

She took all her bottles to the bathroom and poured their contents into the toilet. She flushed, watching her avoidance swirl down to the great beyond.

Resuming her position at the window, she watched the birds, the pool rippling in the waning light, the trees blowing in the wind.

This'll do just fine, she thought.

14

———————

"I couldn't help but notice," Marie said, beaming from ear to ear as she poured Abbey another cup of coffee, "that you moved your boxes upstairs late last night."

"You noticed, did you?" Abbey said, smirking.

Abbey took another bite of bacon, holding up a finger, telling Marie to wait as she chewed. She purposely took her time, savouring both the bite and Marie's need to know.

"I've decided to stay awhile," Abbey said as she dabbed her mouth with her napkin.

"Wonderful," Marie said. "Stay as long as you need, or as long as you like. Or both, for that matter."

Marie came out from behind the counter and wrapped her arms around Abbey before she could pull away.

"Ah, you'll survive. It's only a bit of a hug."

Abbey finished up her breakfast as Marie called out to Chuck, chirping at him about the good news. He was equally tickled that Abbey was staying, but kept his hands mostly to himself, giving only Marie a hug and a high five.

Abbey decided to break in her new shoes and walk into town. If she found anything more she'd like to buy, it was only a short jaunt back to pick up Barnes. She told Marie and Chuck where she was going—*funny, that, like they're my parents*—and got herself ready for the day. With fresh clothes and shiny new runners on her feet, Abbey walked to the trailhead.

She settled on the short loop, a half-kilometer trail through the trees that would take her straight into town. Once she felt more confident with her surroundings, she would explore the longer trails. She stuffed her hands in her pockets—wallet in one, cellphone in the other—and started down the neatly manicured gravel path. It was hardly nature as she had once known. And for that she was glad. The woods were thin, open fields visible through a sparse line of skinny trees. Nowhere for anyone, or anything, to hide. Even so, she breathed a sigh of relief when she reached the opposite mouth of the trail.

The park was quiet, only an elderly gentleman sitting on a bench, reading a paper. Abbey walked by and smiled, and got a warm hello in return. She kept on going, deciding that she would wander the streets a bit, get a feel for what else Lamarque had to offer. Abbey kept going around the bend, circling behind the row of shops to an area with a few storage units and a smaller gravel road, and followed that road to another section of the sprawled-out town. There she found a volunteer firehouse with an adjacent police station, and an old house. It was a huge home, two stories, and filled a good portion of the one-acre lot. The front of the building was old, oak slats and ornate garnish on the face, but the second story and back of the house seemed to be modern—recently updated with stucco siding in pastel colours.

The yard was not fenced in, and was on the corner of a turn, so Abbey followed the road, walking around the back of the building. The yard backed onto the edge of a thicker forest. Abbey circled the house, stopping at a fenced patch of land that cut into the trees at the back of the yard. She pushed through a small lychgate and surveyed the surroundings. Didn't take her long to figure out what it was.

A graveyard.

For sure, she thought, pressing her toe against a headstone that was flush with the overgrown turf.

There were at least two dozen headstones, most plain and flat, covered in moss and growth seeping from the forest. The headstones were mostly unreadable, age and weather wearing away shallow, crude inscriptions. She could pick out a letter here and there, but nothing more.

"Stay back here too long, you're liable to hear the ghosts."

Abbey spun around and found a man standing under the lych-gate. Unlike all the others she had met in Lamarque thus far, he was young—probably in his early thirties—and had all his teeth, and white ones at that. He was tall but slender, with warm brown eyes and hair. Several moments passed before Abbey realized she hadn't said anything. And was staring.

"I'm sorry," he said. "Creepy of me. I'm James—Jamie, if you like. It's what my friends call me."

He stepped forward, and Abbey stepped back. She immediately regretted the knee-jerk reaction.

"Abbey," she said, forcing herself to hold out her hand.

He smiled. "Lovely to meet you, Abbey." He looked back towards the road. "Walk here?"

"I did. Just exploring."

He paused, thinking. "Know someone in the area?"

"Oh," she said, realizing how strange it must be to see newcomers roaming around. "No, just passing through. Kind of."

"Kind of," he said.

"Well, maybe not passing through, exactly."

"No less puzzling," he said, smirking.

"What I mean is that I'm staying a while. In Lamarque. I have a place at the motel, the one by—"

"There is only one," he said.

"Ah. Yes, of course."

"Well, I'm a lifer," he said. "Lived here my whole life, as did my folks, my grandparents, so on. This little chunk," he drew a square in the air with his fingers, indicating the land around the house, "is ours. Mine, I suppose."

"Your folks?"

"They moved away to a retirement home near the city. Eden's Landing."

"Oh, I'm sorry."

"Don't be. They love it. All of their buddies are there, and none of the heavy work of rural life. That leaves me here, manning the business," he said, tilting his head to the mansion.

"Business? I assumed that was a house."

"And one hell of a house it would be!"

"I thought it was a tad large."

"It was a church at one time."

"Oh," Abbey said, looking at the cemetery. "Explains the lychgate."

"Yup. We converted it to a house when the population dwindled and shifted towards the city." He motioned for Abbey to follow him. "I live on the upper floor. The main floor is our town hall and community information center. People come here for local tax business and other permits, and tourists come for information on sight seeing, recommendations on accommodations and restaurants in the area, all that."

He and Abbey went into the house, heavy oak door groaning as they passed through. The inside was dark, with burgundy velvet wallpaper, heavy wood floors, and old-fashioned sconces lining the walls. To the left was the former church foyer, with shelves and displays of pamphlets of all kinds: maps, brochures, advertisements from the city. To the right was an office with a huge desk, tax and permit forms in files on the wall.

"You run this show all by yourself?" Abbey asked.

"I do," he said. "But it's not like a full three-ring-circus around here. Very little change and happenings in Lamarque. Population stays steady—not too many people start a new life out here—and tourism is light. People who come to the area tend to live closer to the city. Our only accommodation is the motel, and most travellers are looking for more than that."

"It's quite lovely, the motel," Abbey argued, feeling a touch defensive.

"It is," he said, "but not if you are looking for a vacation. It's pretty bare bones."

"Suppose so."

"Have a look around," he said. "Can I make you a coffee?"

No.

Abbey felt the pull, the gurgle of panic on the top of her stomach.

"Yes, that'd be lovely," she said.

"Great!"

Jamie disappeared deeper into the house, leaving Abbey behind in the foyer. She moved into the tourist office, plucking pamphlets off the shelves, perusing the attractions of the area. Dunvegan City was about a forty-five minute drive away. It boasted a steady stream of commerce and tourism to suit all walks of life. She had been there a couple times as a child, but she had been very young, and barely remembered. Had she and Barnes continued on down the highway instead of pulling off for gas, she would have ended up there.

Lucky. This is way better. Farther from home, but close enough for the feel of my outdoors.

"You take cream and sugar?" he said, coming in the room with two coffees balanced on a tray.

"Double double," she said. "So tell me, what's the population here? Lamarque, specifically."

"Around a thousand, including the farms and averages in the vicinity."

"What do people do?"

"Commute."

"To where?"

"Dunvegan City, and some outlying industry."

"That's a long commute," she said.

"Not bad," he said, "especially considering the astronomical cost of living the closer you get to the city."

"So is there much industry right around here? I mean, besides Peter's little shop."

He laughed, a sound open and full of joy. "Ah, you met ol' Peter. And he didn't scare you off? You're a tough cookie, for such a pretty little thing."

Abbey felt uneasy, fingers scraping the inside of her bowels.

Jamie noticed.

"You okay?"

"Yeah, fine," she said.

Her skin grew clammy, her neck tight.

"I'm sorry," he said. "I… cookie… just an expression."

She tried to relax. "I know, I'm sorry. Bit sensitive."

"Of course," he said, nervous fingers adding more sugar to his already syrupy coffee.

Great job, Abbey. You idiot.

"Anyways, other industry?" she asked, trying to get back on track.

"As in jobs?"

"Well, yeah. I guess so."

"Wow," he said, his face brightening. "You really are considering staying here for the long haul, aren't you?"

"Not sure how long…"

"No matter," he said, almost excited. "There are always positions to be filled. The firehouse and police station might have something—"

"I was thinking a little quieter, less intense."

"It's Lamarque," he said, rolling his eyes. "Not much intensity here."

"Even so," she said.

"Yeah, mostly they deal with traffic, and accidents on the highway."

"Nope. I'm out," she said.

"Righto. Well what about kids?"

"Pardon?" she said, feeling her face flush.

"I don't know for sure, but the school tends to be strapped for substitutes. Beyond that, the second and third grade classes share a room and a teacher. I'm sure they'd love the help."

"Teaching? I don't know. I've never taught before. I don't have my teaching certificate."

"Let me take you over so you can meet the principal, see what they can work out for you."

"Sure," Abbey said. "I really appreciate this, Jamie. You don't need to do this."

"I want to. Besides, it's not every day that someone under the age of eighty comes to town. Nice to socialize with someone from my century."

She laughed, and his smile warmed even further.

"C'mon," he said, grabbing a set of keys off a hook on the wall. "I'll lock up, and we'll head to the school."

"Now?" Abbey said, looking down at her outfit and feeling her hair. "I'm hardly fit for a job interview."

He rolled his eyes again. "Please. First, this is Lamarque. Second, these are children. Prepare yourself for snot, paint, and pee. You look like the Queen, compared to that lot over there."

Abbey eyed the keys in his hand. He watched her face, reading her expression.

"We can walk," he finally said. "It'd be silly not too. Everything's so close... Abbey, I'm sorry, is this too much?"

She stared at him, the sheepish look on his face, the way he started self-consciously scratching at his hair.

"I mean, I know we just met, and you just got to Lamarque, I'm just—"

"Enthusiastic," she said, trying to force a smile to put him out of his misery. He bought it.

"Great," he said, opening the door. "After you."

~

THE SCHOOL WAS A SIMPLE, ONE-STORY BUILDING WITH A MURAL of children playing painted on the side. Jamie took her inside, stopped briefly to have a cozy yarn with the receptionist, then walked straight back into the principal's office.

"Scott!"

"Jamie," the man said, stepping out from behind the desk and embracing Jamie, finishing with a loud slap on the back.

The principal was not what she had anticipated—a young man, no more than forty, with a hairstyle and clothes straight from the pages of a magazine. Although he was painstakingly put together and polite, there was something off about him. Uncomfortable, somehow.

Abbey didn't like him.

"And who is this?" Scott asked, taking Abbey's hand and giving it a gentle shake.

"This is Abbey," Jamie said, proud like a cat who dragged a bird to its owner. "She's new in town. Living at the motel. She thinks she might stick around a while, so she's inquiring about employment."

"A teacher?" Scott made no effort to hide his elation. She figured he would have put her in the classroom right then and there, had there not been a legal hiring process.

"I'm not a teacher... not formally," Abbey said.

Scott's expression dropped.

"That's not to say I'm not interested," she continued, "but I don't know how that works here, certification and all."

Scott rubbed his chin and looked at the receptionist just outside his door. Jamie watched Scott, practically oozing anticipation.

"Tell you what," Scott said, tapping his head. "There's an option, if you think you're a good fit here, and we're a good fit for you.

He rattled off all sorts of information, speaking of the school and its workings as if he birthed it himself.

"The school has been here for about thirty years. Six classrooms in all, one for each grade level."

"What about the older kids?"

"Some get bussed into the city for junior high and high school, most are home schooled. Pity."

"Pity?"

"One of the charms of small-town living is being part of a close-knit community. The children bond as a family until they are separated by this fragmented school system."

"I assume population is the reason there aren't any intermediate schools here."

"You assume correctly," Scott said, looking over at Jamie. "That's where I think you could help us."

"How's that?"

"Well, you're right about the certification thing. We can't have you teaching the grade levels without certification, and that takes a year, if you already have a degree."

"I do."

"Wonderful," he said, clapping his hands together. "We'll get the certification process started, if you're interested."

"In the meantime?" Abbey asked, thinking about a year devoid of paychecks. Marie and Chuck had been generous, and would probably have no qualms about carrying her if her money ran out, but Abbey didn't like relying on anyone.

"You can still work for us, in our Preschool/Kindergarten program. There are lots of wee ones in there, and Ashlynn could use the help. If you don't mind being a secondary teacher, that is."

"Kindergarten? Little kids?"

"Do you have children, Abbey?"

Abbey felt a twinge, a flutter in her belly.

"I don't, no."

She started to feel uneasy, the cold sweat of panic moistening her pores.

"Any experience with children?"

Scott started to look concerned.

Get yourself together. You need this.

Abbey collected herself and took a deep breath before starting to speak.

"I have a degree in sociology, and a solid reference from a job I held since straight out of University. I'm going to be completely honest with you," Abbey felt the heat of a thousand suns radiating from what she imagined was a dark crimson face, "I know less than nothing about children. But I am smart, I am hard-working, and I can learn."

Scott stared at her, poker-faced, contemplating or disgusted, she wasn't sure. He held out for a moment before bursting out into laughter.

"Abbey," he said. "No need to be so formal. I'll check your reference, and I'll need to do a background check, but I'm sure you'll be a great addition to the team."

Abbey wished she felt as thrilled as Jamie looked. Scott went to gather some paperwork for her to fill out, and Jamie shuffled close to her, placing his hands on her shoulders.

"I'm so pleased, Abbey! Glad I hooked you guys up."

His hands felt huge on her shoulders, his nails sharp.

"I think maybe I should take you out for a celebratory dinner…"

Her breath quickened as she watched grey fingers creep over his shoulders.

He frowned and turned towards the door.

"Scott?"

Scott popped his head in the door. The door that was two meters away from Jamie.

"I'll be a flash," Scott said, holding up a stack of papers. "Just getting the fingerprinting requisition together. Can you head over to the cop shop today, Abbey?"

"Sure can," she said, watching the confusion in Jamie's eyes as he took his hands off her shoulders to brush his own.

"I'd like that dinner," Abbey said, touching his arm.

He smiled, despite his obvious concern.

"Wonderful. We can head over to the police station, do your background check, and then head to the pub."

"Good food there?"

"No other choice," Jamie said, apology in his tone.

"Hey, stop," Abbey said. "I'm here because Lamarque is small and secluded. I needed life to slow down. I love quiet and simple. This is exactly what I had in mind."

He looked elated again.

It's gonna be okay, Abbey thought.

Scott returned with his stack of papers, and Abbey inked her information on all of them without hesitation. There was nothing in an employment history that looked askew, or that she was ashamed of. All of her shady business was buried long ago, in a youth long since forgotten.

15

*L*amarque was quiet, but the pub was not.

After an initial period of discomfort, Abbey adjusted to the lights, the noise, and the tightly packed clientele. The few glasses of beer she had downed when she and Jamie first sat at the bar helped soften her edge.

The pub was bigger than it looked from the outside, with booths up and down both sides, tables in the middle, and a small stage in the back. The menu was simple home cooking, not much different from the diner except for a higher proportion of deep fried everything. And the alcohol, of course. And although the population of Lamarque was small, it seemed pretty large, crammed into the sole restaurant in the area.

"We haven't another place," Jamie said. "The ambience here is more appealing than the diner —"

'Stop!" Abbey said, pulling a Marie and slapping Jamie on the arm. "Do I look like I'm not enjoying myself?"

"Kinda, yeah. Can't get a read. You're like Stonehenge."

That stung, but she knew it was true. She was showing exactly the amount of emotion she was feeling. She took another swig of her beer.

"So tell me about you," Jamie said.

She cringed, the softness in his eyes an illogical threat.

"Not much to tell," she said, shrugging. "I came from out east — office job, city life, standard rat race."

"Have you known different?" he asked.

She shifted in her seat, thinking of fields and forests, of the countryside, isolation, and her tree…

"Yes," she said, regretting the truth. It was an admission that would lead to more questions, ones she was afraid she might answer. "I used to live out this way. Other side of Dunvegan City."

"Really?" he said. "Where?"

Abbey stumbled over her words. "Out… there."

He watched her, paused, but didn't ask anymore questions about that.

"So what kinds of things do you like, Abbey of the city?"

"Like?"

"Yeah, like. You know, enjoy. How do you pass the time? Hobbies, favourite shows, that kind of stuff."

This must be like pulling teeth for him, Abbey scolded herself.

"I like reading, and yeah, I'm a Netflix junkie."

"Me too!" he said, as if he had struck gold. "I prefer the rough action, Game of Thrones and Frontier and such."

"I'm a Westeros junkie, myself. But I like the indie series, the dark, spooky ones."

"Not much spooky in the city, I imagine," he said.

"We have elevators and alleys," she said, knowing that's not where terror resided. Not the true terror, anyways.

"Ah, indeed. And mirrors."

"And night."

He smiled. "I'm sorry, I'm a softy. The few things I can't handle are spicy foods and scary films. The White Walkers are my limit, and even then, my drawers never stay completely clean."

Abbey laughed, the first audible expression of joy she had heard from herself in years.

Time passed, more a gallop than a crawl, and the alcohol flowed freely. Jamie seemed to be holding his own, but Abbey felt the room start to quaver a touch.

Nope. Time to go.

She had been intoxicated before, many times, but was always in reach of her couch or bed, and never beyond the confines of her locked door.

"Ready?" she said, standing from the stool.

"Yeah," he said, standing too.

They cleared up the tab, then went outside. Abbey's breath was stolen by the thief of nature, a blast of fresh air and the starry skies. She traipsed across the street, looking for cars when there was no need; there was zero traffic on the little road this late at night. Not like the city, where dozens of cars came close to mowing you down at any hour of the day or night.

Once she was safely across the road and into the park, she kicked off her runners and let the grass tickle between her toes. The air felt so good, and the quiet so blissful.

"You missed it," Jamie said, coming up beside her.

"What did I miss?" she asked, turning her face to his.

"This. The country. Nature and simplicity."

She looked back up at the sky, the breeze fresh and cool on her face.

"I did," she admitted.

The silence between them marinated, the tension growing thicker.

"I like it here," Abbey said, not necessarily to Jamie.

"I'm glad you're here," he said.

He placed his hand on Abbey's back. She looked around, at his shoulders, at the park, looking for limbs, hands, eyes...

He leaned in and kissed her, and she didn't pull away. His mouth was wet and warm, and his touch gentle.

But something was wrong. She didn't like it.

She shivered as he moved the tips of his fingers up and down her back. She took his face in her hands, breathing in his mouth, and ran her fingers down his face. She wasn't sure when it had happened, but their bodies were close now, pressed together. She could feel him harden, and she cringed.

This isn't right.

And just like that, there were hands everywhere. Grey hands, bloody eyes, a hollow cackle whispering off the fields...

"Coffee tomorrow?" Abbey said, pulling away.

He tried to pull her back into an embrace but she clutched his shoulders. He was strong, but she wasn't worried. He was a gentleman. Besides, there were massive, thick grey fingers threaded through hers, helping to hold him back.

He didn't persist. "Abbey, I'm sorry. I..."

He looked embarrassed.

Abbey leaned in and pressed a firm kiss on his lips, lingering for a moment to secure her performance.

"No need for sorries," she said. "I've had more than my share to drink, and I'm not sure... I'm just not sure."

"No explanation needed."

He didn't look sad anymore.

"You mean it?" he asked.

"Mean what?"

"Coffee?"

"Yes," she said, holding his hand. "Tomorrow?"

"Lovely," he said. "I look forward to it."

She moved away, giving an awkward wave and a curtsey, and he followed suit with an animated bow and stumble. They both laughed like donkeys in the quiet night. She shushed him, and he continued to laugh as he walked in the opposite direction, heading for his mansion. Face hurting from smiling, she walked on feather-light feet to the trailhead leading back to the motel.

IT TOOK ABBEY WAY TOO LONG TO REGRET HER DECISION.

She had walked into the trees, blindly following the gravel trail, unaware of anything but the feel of Jamie's lips on hers, of his erection against her hip. She was excited and ashamed, nervous but giddy.

But she was still Abbey, and she was alone.

Already deep down the trail, she realized that she was on a dark trail, at night, alone. That, and she was corked enough to have impaired mobility and sense. She gave herself a good shake and kept on walking.

Too late now to go back. Besides, where would I go? Jamie's place? No.

Not yet.

She kept on walking, focusing on one step at a time, keeping her eyes down on her feet, not in the trees.

It's not far. Should be able to see the end of the trail straight away.

She dared to raise her eyes, to look forward to the end of the tunnel of trees, but saw nothing but trail ahead. The trees loomed over her, angry fingers with splintered bones, blocking the stars and the moon.

The trees were not this thick.

And then she heard it, the crackle of fire. And that oh-so-familiar cackle.

Abbey started running, the sound of her feet hitting the gravel and her heart pounding in her ears drowning out anything and everything around her. She ran and ran, twice, three, ten times the distance she had gone coming into town. She pushed on as the brush grew thick, piercing her flesh and binding her ankles. But she had more strength than she did as a child, and she lunged forward, swinging her arms and kicking her legs, breaking free of the brittle confines of the woods.

And it let her go, suddenly, releasing her like a slingshot to the lot beside the motel.

Abbey hit the pavement with a thud, pain radiating from her palms and knees straight to the base of her skull. She threw her hand over her mouth, stifling a scream.

I don't want them to come running.

They'll know.

They'll know I'm crazy.

She scrambled to her feet, walking backwards to the stairs at the side of the motel, eyes pinned on the trailhead.

Not real not real not real.

She reached the garbage can beside the stairs and puked every bit of her meal and drinks into it in great globs that burned her eyes and nose. Eyes wild, she scanned the motel for other occupants, or for Marie and Chuck, who would worry over her more than she could tolerate. She didn't find Chuck and Marie, or other occupants. What she did see she turned away from, ignoring it, eyes squeezed tight, internal mantra denying its existence.

Not real, not real.

By the pool, splayed out in a lounge chair, naked body spread-eagle, white and bright as the moon, a creature that writhed and contorted in rhythm with its own guttural cackle. It was twice as large as the chair it occupied, anaconda-like limbs dangling in the lit water, sending off ripples like sparks of electricity.

And the smell. Like hot, rotten meat.

Abbey felt her way along the wall, finally reaching her room. Her card was already handy, cocked and aimed at the slot. She burst into her room, slamming and locking the door behind her in one fluid motion. She drew the blinds, ripping down one corner in the process, then went even deeper, locking herself in the bathroom.

The bathtub was a cold bed, hard and unforgiving. But shut in there, behind two doors and the shield of a faded, stained shower curtain, Abbey felt safe. Her adulthood Blanket Fortress of Solitude.

～

THE MANSION SPOKE TO HIM. IT ALWAYS DID, ESPECIALLY WHEN HE came home. Changes in the weather, the warming of the season, always made it speak more, the wood moaning in response to the penetration of the summer winds.

Jamie slammed the heavy wooden door shut and dropped the iron bar lock, barricading himself in for the night. Overkill, but he enjoyed the aesthetic. Made him feel medieval, badass. He gave a quick glance to the front offices, then went to the kitchen to gorge himself on whatever junk he could find. Two chocolate muffins and a bag of Cheetos later, he poured himself a tall glass of milk and wobbled his way up the stairs, splashing droplets of his drink every time he swayed and bumped the wall.

More to drink than I thought.

He wandered to the media room, intent on playing some video games, but thought better of it, feeling the spin in his head and the roll of his gut. He opted for sleep instead. He went to the master bedroom at the end of the hall and peeled off his clothes, tossing them in a pile against the wall with the rest of the week's outfits.

Too bad she wasn't a maid, he chuckled to himself.

He swayed forwards and back as he emptied his bladder, missing the bowl on all sides, then passed his hands under the tap before collapsing on the bed and turning on the television. He settled on a horrible movie, a pretentious play on the concept of God and Mother Earth, and settled back to watch the curve of his favourite actress's breasts and buttocks.

Fucking maid, he said, Abbey on his mind.

His hand slithered down his chiseled abdomen, his fingers playing at the hair on his inner thigh, tracing lines up the seam of his testicles before wrapping his fingers around his already solid shaft.

"Abbey."

He pictured her, in a maid's uniform, bending to scoop up the pile of clothes, nary a stitch of clothing covering what was under the apron and puffy white petticoat.

Harder he pumped as the woman on the screen moved around, nipples erect, and the phantom woman in the room joined in, shedding her apron and fingering herself in front of him.

The pressure built, and the stroking became frantic until he exploded over his stomach.

"Abbey!"

His voice was large, alone in that mansion, the only evidence of a living being. It surprised him, the way it echoed off the walls and down the stairs; he hadn't thought he'd said it that loud.

He stood carefully, using a pillow to contain the mess, and hopped in the shower. The hot water felt good, washing away the day, the smoke and grease and booze of the bar, and the generous amount of ejaculate on his skin. It had been a while, and he had worked up quite an appetite, flirting with Abbey the whole day.

Bitch better be worth it, making me work for it like this.

Satisfied that he was clean, Jamie got out of the shower, toweled himself off with the least offensive towel balled up on the floor, and slid under the covers. His eyes immediately grew heavy, as did his head, sinking deep into his feather pillow.

The crash from downstairs nearly stopped his heart in fright.

It was loud enough to shake the pictures on the walls, and sounded like metal.

The bar lock.

He jumped from the bed and, wrapped in his blanket, ran to the top of the stairs. The bar lock was still engaged. He took the stairs slowly, one at a time, ducking down to see if anyone was waiting in the shadows for him. Everything was exactly how he left it. He made the rounds of the entire main floor, flicking on lights, checking corners and closets, even looking through the kitchen cupboards.

The sound absolutely came from down here, he thought, giving a glance to the windows and the back door, all of which were locked and intact. He went up the stairs again, looking back at the front door and the iron bar, trying to remember the sound in his head.

"A dream," he muttered to himself.

He reached the top of the stairs and started towards the bedroom when he spotted his untouched glass of milk on the entertainment stand in the media room.

"Yes!" he said, grabbing the glass and chugging a few huge gulps of the lukewarm beverage. As it registered on his tongue and was halfway down to his belly, he spat it out, sputtering and urging. It was more than warm. It was hot, thick with sour chunks of creamy, solidified curds he could have chewed like cheese. He looked down at the glass, difficult to see in the dark of the room, and flicked on the light switch to get a better look at his contaminated beverage.

Jamie looked, and then he looked again, having difficulty processing what he was seeing. The glass was full of milk, but tainted, discoloured milk, curdled blobs of crimson swirling through the white, moving as if they were alive. He dropped the glass. It shattered, freeing the milk and its animate curds over the hardwood floor and his feet. He screeched and danced, trying to get the blood-creatures off his skin, and ran for the bedroom. As soon as he was behind the slammed and locked door, he rubbed his eyes and smacked himself across the face. Hard. Several times, until it really stung, and a warm trickle of blood dribbled from his nose.

Then he laughed.

You've had plenty to drink, mate.

Even though he thought it, he didn't believe it. He was holding his breath, trying not to make a sound for fear that whatever was beyond the door might hear him and come for him. He waited a full minute before deciding he was, indeed, being ridiculous, and opened the door to verify that he had simply dropped a glass of milk on the floor.

Jamie approached the wet, white puddles with caution, half expecting them to come alive with writhing, crimson worms. Once he was standing right above the broken glass, he could see that it was just milk, but there were spreading droplets of crimson tingeing the white. He frowned, then looked at his feet, wet with milk and blood.

"Ah shit," he said. He lifted a foot and spied a shard of glass sticking out of his arch. He braced himself and yanked out the shard, releasing a steady flow of blood over the hardwood. With little concern about containing the mess, Jamie hobbled to the master bathroom, leaving a trail of blood in his wake. He sat on the edge of the tub and ran his feet under the water, using his best contortional abilities to reach under the sink and grab some bandages. Once the wound was cleaned, he dried his foot and applied some gauze, wrapping his foot tight with some old tensor tape.

The trip out into the bedroom and the sight of the impending cleanup was exhausting. He had spread blood across the hardwood, down the hall, with smears here and there on the wall.

"Tomorrow," Jamie said, shutting off the hall light and closing the door. His nerves were rattled enough that he locked the door. He had never locked the bedroom door before.

"Doesn't matter if the door is locked if the threat is already inside."

He didn't know where the words had come from. They didn't sound like his, and the thought surprised him—not something he would have concocted on his own. He turned, the world in slow-motion, and faced the creature on the bed.

On her haunches, arms and legs long and bent like a praying mantis, skin white and distressed like mottled bone. This beast was massive, sprawled across the entire king-sized bed and then some, heavy girth balanced on spindly limbs.

And her head. Bald, skin stretched to the limit, black veins throbbing atop the too-large cranium. The face was empty—a blank canvas of skin, until the creature opened her mouth. A black, toothless cavern, hollow and dripping with charcoal gore. Her eyes became visible, slits of red splitting the solid white face, black sclera punctuated by a bloody pupil, oozing crimson tears down her ivory face.

Her voice signaled his end.

A guttural cackle, from deep within the witch's gut, carried on heavy brays of air, taunting him, laughing at him, the brunt of her joke.

"Abbey," she howled.

16

It was early morning, the sun still below the horizon, when Abbey woke, a knot in the tub. She eased herself to a sitting position, stretching her limbs and rubbing her neck in an attempt to knead and pull out the kinks. Complaints were lodged by both her stomach and her muscles, and her mouth tasted of vomit and booze. Without time to reconsider, Abbey opened the faucet full blast, letting cool water pelt her. From cool, to warm, then steamy hot, Abbey remained seated on the floor of the tub as the water washed away the sins of the previous night.

Wriggling out of her wet clothes was easier than she thought. She managed to undress without ever having to stand. She dumped the clothes outside the tub, scrubbed her body and her hair, then closed the faucet. In one quick movement, she was out of the tub and wrapped in the bathrobe that hung on the back of the door.

The room started to dance, twirl, and swirl, sloshing her stomach and hammering her head. She sat on the edge of the tub and held her head in her hands.

Never thought myself a lightweight. Hope I didn't act a fool around Jamie.

Jamie, his wide chest and gleaming smile. Kind words and child-like excitement.

Abbey felt her face flush again, her fingers finding her lips, feeling the kiss from the night before.

Time for coffee, she thought, braving the head rush to get to her feet and prepare herself for the day. She swiped the mirror with her hand and paused at her reflection. Face pale, eyes bloodshot, and lips a black smear on her face.

"What the…"

She moved in close to the mirror and examined her lips. They were caked in a black, gritty substance. She rubbed them with the back of her hand, spreading the filth across her pale face. Against all better sense, she licked her lips, and recoiled at the metallic, earthy taste.

Soil.

Another closer look confirmed that it was dirt on her face. As the hangover lifted and everything came into focus, she could see that the room was also covered in dirt. The toilet, the floors, the sink. Even the wall had a muddy handprint on it where she had braced herself getting in the tub. She was the only clean thing in the room, thanks to the shower.

A quick rinse and splash in the sink took care of the muck on her lips and hands. There was no clean towel or article of clothing in the bathroom—her clothes were stained from the night before—so she opted to drip herself dry on the bed while she watched a spot of television. She turned the bathroom knob and stepped out into the room.

There would be no laying on the bed to dry off.

From one end the room to the other, dirt was piled high, seemingly shoveled into the room and dumped in piles on the beds, the desk, every possible surface. Dirt was ground into the carpets, in some places so deep it appeared as rolling hills. The mirror was smeared with the stuff, as was the surface of the dresser and the desk. The front of the television was covered in mud, caked dry and cracking across the lit screen. Some sort of show was playing behind the curtain of soil, muffled sound speaking through dirt-encrusted speakers.

It wasn't a show. Abbey knew that; she could hear it.

She squished through the dirt on the carpet until she reached the television, then clawed at the screen, revealing a misshapen, leathery face and hollow black and red eyes.

The low cackle continued, seeping through the television speakers and clinging like tentacles to her brain.

THE CLEAN-UP EFFORT WOULD TAKE A FULL DAY, AT LEAST. THAT'S what the cleaning company told Marie and Chuck when they came to evaluate the situation. They decided that the carpet was too stained and damaged to clean, so replacement would be the best option. Same with the mattress. The furniture had already been hauled outside to the trailer behind the motel where Chuck was washing and sanding it down. A couple coats of stain and it would be good as new.

Abbey was horrified.

"'Tis all right, dear," Marie told her for the umpteenth time. "I just wish we knew you were okay. Nothing, eh?"

Nothing. Abbey couldn't remember a single thing. Just walking home, getting paranoid in the woods, and stumbling up to the bathtub. Certainly nothing resulting in the mess plastered over that room.

"I'm so, so sorry," Abbey said, feeling sick to her stomach. Part excessive drinking, part shame. "I will pay for your time, and the inconvenience."

"Naw, don't be silly," Marie said. "You've footed the bill for the cleaners. That's plenty."

"And I'm buying a new mattress and television," Abbey said, little give in her tone.

"I said that's unnecessary," Marie said, but nodded when she met Abbey's eyes. "Do what you like, then. Whatever sets it right in your mind. But it truly is no bother. We have so many rooms, and very few guests."

"How many are staying here right now?"

"Just you, darlin'. It's off season, and we are off the beaten path. We do clog up a bit closer to summer and during the winter break, but we're otherwise dead as a doornail."

"Well I'll be sure to have your new stuff straight away."

Marie huffed, then patted Abbey on the knee. "Now how's about we set you up in a new room."

"New room?"

"You expect to be staying in that mess anytime soon? Besides, there's not many places around you can just scoop up a television and a mattress. Suppose we could shift one over from one of the other rooms—"

"No, that won't be necessary. I wasn't thinking. Of course I can move rooms if you'll still have me."

The expression on Marie's face grew warmer, if that was possible. She clasped Abbey's cheek in a pudgy hand. "Dear oh dear. We have no hard feelings about this. You're going through what you're going through, and offering a respite is the least we can do."

An overwhelming feeling of deceitfulness washed over Abbey. Marie thought Abbey was being pursued by an abusive partner. But she was not. She was only running from herself.

"Abbey, look," Marie started in such a way that Abbey winced, "I gotta check, because I think you ain't got no one checkin'. You were out drinking, yeah?"

Abbey nodded.

"You got some troubles with the sauce?" Marie asked, chugging an invisible bottle of booze.

"No," Abbey answered, a little too quick.

Do I? I don't. Alcoholics stumble around, puking-sick drunk, ponched-out bellies and red, bulbous noses.

"Mmkay," Marie said, looking at Abbey down her nose. "Drugs, then."

"Marie!"

Marie held her hands up in surrender. "Like I said, honey, gotta check on ya. We all have our things, do our sins, but where there's nobody to catch you if you fall…"

"Marie." Abbey squared her shoulders and made a concentrated effort to maintain eye contact. "I had too much to drink last night. I do that from time to time. But I haven't got a drinking problem. And I certainly haven't touched drugs, nor will I."

Marie looked convinced. "That's the first thing you've said with any kind of authority!" she said, slapping Abbey on the back.

"Ladies?" Chuck said, coming up from the trailer behind the motel.

"Yes, my lovey?" Marie chimed at Chuck.

"I'd guess that, based on the leavings of last night's shenanigans, that this young lady should toss a bit o' grease on that stomach." Chuck leaned in, whispering a dirty little secret in Abbey's ear. "I've had one too many, many a-time, my love. Don't sweat it."

Marie gave Chuck his requisite arm slap, then pulled Abbey to her feet. Abbey didn't protest. After she'd discovered the mess, she had thrown on the nearest clothes and high-tailed it straight to Marie and Chuck. The morning had passed without a single bite to eat, and a hangover nagged at her temples and stomach. A feed of bacon, eggs, and a pot of coffee would help pacify the gods waging war in her guts.

ABBEY DECIDED, OVER HER SECOND HELPING OF BACON AND third cup of joe, that she would take Barnes into Lamarque today. There was no way she was going to walk that path into town. Even though she knew the trail was perfectly safe, and the sun was still high in the sky, she had no desire to tread down that trail again. Not yet.

Barnes purred her way into town, and Abbey was lulled into

relaxation by the familiar whirr of the engine. Even though they had only known each other a short time, she felt bonded to the old car.

Pitiful, Abbey thought, shaking her head. *Human friends, girl. Flesh friends.*

She drove past the shops and the pub, twisting and turning up the road until she arrived at the old mansion. There was no car in the driveway—*had there been one before?*—so she parked Barnes in one of the empty spots. When she stepped out of the car, a gust of wind blew her hair back and slammed the car door shut, the noise jarring her heart.

Nerves rattled, she walked up to the mansion and tried the door handle. Locked.

Strange, that, for a tourist information place.

Wiggling the handle a second time produced the same result. She pressed the bell once, and a melodic series of chimes sang through the interior of the house. She waited, looking down the drive at the new summer grass blowing in the breeze, dandelions losing their heads along the expansive front lawn.

When Jamie didn't answer the door, Abbey raised her fist to knock, but a sound on the wind drew her attention. A melody, close to the tune of the doorbell, rang through the air, a chime played on crystal. Abbey pressed her ear to the door, wondering if it was the doorbell or something inside, but heard nothing but her own heart-beat against the heavy wood.

The wind was strong, blowing in gales around the building and through the surrounding trees. The sound traveled around her on all sides, from the trees, the air, the cars. Abbey thought it could be in her head, but the notes were crisp and clear. She walked around the house, peering in windows, but found no signs of life.

Perhaps he's as hungover as I am.

The music was louder behind the house, but Abbey still couldn't pinpoint the source. Though now, the instrument was clear. A voice, small and young, probably female. She looked towards the school-house, then laughed at the absurdity. *It's blocks away. I'm not a bat.*

Abbey scanned the road, the surrounding properties, the trees. So much movement and so much sound, from the wind, the song—a swirling of leaves and music. It was dizzying. She covered her ears and closed her eyes, and the world stilled, sharply and suddenly. The wind ceased, as did the sound. She dropped her hands away from her ears and opened one eye a slit. The world looked the same, nothing menacing in clear view, and the regular sounds of the world persisted: a car in the distance, the twitter of a bird.

With both eyes wide open, Abbey looked around, unsettled by the dead wind. Movement in her peripheral caught her attention immediately. A small person dressed in grey and white sat cross-legged in the cemetery nestled in the woods behind the mansion.

For sure. For fuck sake.

Against her better judgement, Abbey walked towards the woods. "Hello?"

The person didn't move, not much at least. They were back on, shoulders hunched over, shaking ever so slightly. Abbey walked through the small iron lichgate and into the cemetery, stepping gingerly so she wouldn't tread on the sunken headstones.

"Are you all right? I heard someone singing," Abbey said, taking care to keep her voice soft and gentle.

The movement stopped, and the person sat up straight.

"Was it you?" Abbey asked.

The person was so still and silent that Abbey could have mistaken them for a stone statue in amongst the graves; a faceless gargoyle keeping watch over the dead. She walked towards the person, giving him or her a wide berth, putting several graves between her and the mysterious person perched on the ground. When she was head on, standing a few meters away, she saw the person clearly.

A small girl, pale, white-blonde hair and icy blue eyes, wearing a grey raccoon hoodie complete with ears and eyes on the hood. She had sidewalk chalk in her hand, and was sketching a masterpiece on the gravestone in front of where she sat.

"My name is Abbey." Abbey didn't extend a hand and didn't step forward.

I know a thing about discomfort and boundaries.

Instead, she knelt on the ground, eye level with the child. "Do you like to draw?"

The child looked away, down at the chalk she fiddled in her fingers. A silver piece, shimmering.

"I do," the child said, barely a whisper.

Abbey felt a strange delight at the voice, as if she had cracked a code.

"Are you out here on your own? Where did you come from?"

The child didn't answer, and stopped twirling the chalk through her fingers. She set it down on the gravestone in front of her.

"Okay," Abbey said. "Too many questions from a stranger. Don't stop drawing. I'll leave you be."

Abbey stood, intending to go to the firehouse next door and tell them about the wayward child in the graveyard. She walked past the girl closer than she had the first time, and stole a glance at her drawing on the gravestone.

Abbey dropped to her knees.

"What is that?"

The girl picked up the chalk and started working on her art again.

"You like it?" she asked.

"I don't know," Abbey said, reaching a trembling finger out and touching the drawing.

A body of water, black and grey, the reflection of the moon distorted on the ripples. And the faeries, silver flesh, purple hair flowing in waves and braids, tentacles coiled around their tiny bodies.

"Where did you…"

The little girl lunged at Abbey, scratching her face and biting at her neck. The child had to be no more than sixty pounds, but knocked Abbey back like she had been hit by a truck. Abbey grabbed her by the hood of her coat and pulled her off onto the ground, then straddled her, pinning her down. They lay there, Abbey and the child, staring into each other's eyes until a droplet of blood from Abbey's clawed face dripped onto the child's fluorescent white cheek. The plip of the crimson droplet rang in Abbey's ears like shattering crystal, but not half as loud as the consequential howl from the child below her.

The girl screamed and screeched, incoherent panic reverberating through the trees and off the seemingly empty mansion. Abbey shushed her, not wanting to let her up for fear of another attack. The screaming persisted. Abbey loosened her grip and drew the girl into her arms, rocking as the screams subsided to whimpers.

~

"THANK YOU, MA'AM. KIND OF YOU TO BRING HER IN."

What else was I gonna do? Run screaming from a little child?

"It's no problem," Abbey said.

"Well *those* might be," the fire chief said, pointing at Abbey's face.

He said something to one of the paramedics checking out the little girl. The paramedic grabbed a suture kit and sat down next to Abbey.

"Let's take a look at those," she said as she pulled on a fresh pair of gloves. "Mighty deep gouges for such little nails."

The woman laughed, a cough covered in nicotine and late nights, and got to work cleaning and dressing the claw marks across Abbey's face.

"She okay?" Abbey asked, looking over at the little girl who was curled up on a bed in the corner of the fire station. "I held her down pretty hard."

"Dare say you did!" the paramedic laughed. "Rabid little beast like that."

"What's her story?" Abbey asked.

"Dunno. Probably retarded. On the spectrum or somethin'"."

The hairs on the back of Abbey's neck stood at attention.

Something not quite right with that girl.

"Seems okay to me," Abbey said under her breath. "Never know what's going on in someone else's world."

"I've seen her around lots," the paramedic said.

"She's young. She probably goes to the school, yeah?" Abbey said.

"Probably. I dunno."

After Abbey's wounds had been dressed, she pulled her phone out of her pocket and dialed the school. A light, airy voice answered the phone.

"Lamarque Elementary, Maggie speaking. How may I help you?"

"Hi, Maggie. It's Abbey, from the other day. With Jamie."

"Of course! How've you been?"

"Well, that's what I'm calling about."

"Oh dear. Do tell me you can still come and take the position. The teachers and children are quite excited."

"Oh yes, that's not why I'm calling. There's been a bit of an… incident? I've come across a stray child, and I'm wondering if you might know her.

Silence on the other end of the line, followed by a sigh.

"White blonde, looks like a tiny pixie?"

"Erm… yes."

"Suzy. Please hold."

Sounds of shuffling came across the line, and a muted conversation; the hold button at the school appeared to be Miss Maggie's had over the receiver. After a hushed conversation, Maggie came back on the line.

"Where are you, Abbey? And is she with you?"

"Yes. We're at the fire station. They're checking her out."

"Scott is on his way," Maggie said. Abbey swore she heard the woman roll her eyes. "Trouble, that girl."

Abbey felt heat wash over her body. An anger, a craving to defend the girl.

"I was meaning to call you, Abbey. Can you come in tomorrow, start your training?"

"Yeah… yes, sure."

"Great! See you at, say, 8am?"

"I'll be there."

After she was off the phone, Abbey realized she hadn't been fully prepared to go back to work just yet. She wasn't quite settled into her new place—even less, with the events of the previous night—and she craved some calm and quiet. Though that meant more time for her to linger in her own head, and that was dangerous territory.

No, better to keep busy.

Scott was there in a matter of minutes, which is about how far the school was from the fire house. He got out of his car and walked up to the open bay door, smile on his face. Once he caught sight of Abbey, his smile faded.

"Oh Abbey," he said. "What did she do to you?"

"It's nothing, really," Abbey said. "I startled her, I think. Out behind Jamie's place."

"Let me guess. The cemetery."

"Yep."

"Macabre little one, Miss Suzy is. That'll be the third time this month she's hidden away there by the forest, drawing on the headstones."

One of the firefighters came over, leading Suzy by the hand.

"Suzy," Scott said, his voice firm. "You can't wander off like that. Mom would be worried sick, you know."

"I know," Suzy said, hiding her face in her coat. "But I was following…"

She trailed off, saying no more.

Scott shook his head and took Suzy by the hand. "Come on, Suzy. Go hop in the back of my car. I'll take you to the school."

Suzy shuffled away, kicking gravel and dragging her feet the whole way to the car. Once she was in the backseat with the door closed, Scott turned to Abbey. "She's odd, you know."

"How so?" Abbey said, watching the little girl fumbling with her belt in the back seat.

"In her own little world. Talking to herself, following things that aren't there."

"Oh," Abbey said, her eye twitching and stomach roiling. "Is she... is there someone she can see? Talk to?"

"Her family doesn't live here in Lamarque. And we don't have those kinds of services here, regardless. She may need help, but she's too young for the school to recommend services in Dunvegan City."

Abbey's eyes were glued to the car. "Do you think she's..."

"Autistic? Schizophrenic?" Scott asked. Abbey winced at the question. "No, Abbey. She's just extremely shy and introverted. Very smart child, just grew up pretty isolate, I think. She just started with us, so hopefully we can bring her out of her shell."

Nothing wrong with shells. Shells are safe.

"You'll get to know her well, Abbey. She's in your class. Tomorrow, then?"

"Tomorrow," Abbey said.

She watched as Scott got in the car and said a few words over his shoulder before backing out of the drive and heading towards the school.

As Abbey walked back to Barnes, who was still parked in Jamie's driveway, she thought of the girl, of the music, of the empty mansion with the locked door. The wind picked up again, swirling her hair and chilling her bones.

17

———————

After signing a handful of papers, perusing manuals thicker than phone books, and watching outdated training videos on food safety and child abuse, Abbey was thrown into the classroom just a few short weeks after starting at Lamarque Elementary. The kindergarten was more of a preschool or daycare than an actual school, with more focus on social and spatial development than academic achievement. Because many parents worked in one of the bigger centers, requiring them to commute, the children were dropped off before the start of the school day, and not picked up until suppertime. Suzy was one of those children.

"Okay, children!" Miss Ashlynn said, clapping her hands. "Two minutes until clean-up!"

Mumbles and grumbles erupted around the room, but it didn't dampen the woman's sunny disposition. She was one of those people hard-wired to be a teacher—positive, unflappable, organized and peppy. Abbey felt like the anti-Ashlynn, a cloud in the presence of a rainbow.

"Try to follow along while I'm doing circle time with the kids," Ashlynn said to Abbey. "We sing the welcome song, talk about our letter, number, shape, and colour of the week. Once you've heard it a few times, maybe you'd like to give it a try!"

"Sure," Abbey said. She wasn't sure. In fact, she was quite sure she did not feel up to the task at all.

The children finished putting away their toys and books and took their places on the colorful carpet in the center of the room. Miss Ashlynn started singing the welcome song, and everyone clapped and tapped their hands in time with the words.

Hello to everyone
And how are you today?
We come to our circle time
To laugh and sing and play...

Suzy was clapping, but she wasn't singing. An emotionless robot, going through the motions, looking pained at every line and every clap of the cheery little ditty.

...and when we're up we're up
and when we're down we're down...

Suzy's focus lifted from the rainbow carpet in front of her and met Abbey's eyes. They stared at each other, and Abbey forced the best smile she muster.

... And when we're in the middle
we are neither up nor down.

The corner of Suzy's mouth curled up ever so slightly, which seemed to startle her. She dropped her chin back down to her chest and started to fiddle with the velcro on her glittery shoes. Abbey watched in fascination as Suzy's pale white arm started to glow. Abbey cocked her head, watching the expressions on the faces of the children on either side of Suzy, but no one else seemed to notice the phenomenon.

So we roll our hands so s-l-o-w-l-y...

The entire class started rolling their hands super slow, some giggling in anticipation of the impending explosion of speed. Suzy was rolling her arms too, casting shadows with the silver light. Even she seemed unaware of her new glow. And with good reason. It wasn't coming from her.

It was coming from the silver, tentacled faerie perched upon her shoulder.

And roll 'em really fast...

The children erupted into laughter as they rolled their arms at lightning speed.

The faerie weaved its tentacles through Suzy's hair, braiding her blonde locks with its own purple tresses.

Give your hands a clap clap clap...

The faerie smiled at Abbey, baring sharp, crimson teeth as it coiled a tentacle around Suzy's throat.

And put them in your lap, tap tap.

The children finished the tune by tapping their hands against their thighs and folding them neatly in their laps. For a few seconds, anyways, before they started wiggling and poking at their neighbours.

"All right, children, we have a new teacher with us today," Ms. Ashlynn said, motioning an open hand towards Abbey. "Everyone give a big, glittering hello to Miss Abbey!"

"Good morning, Miss Abbey!" the children chanted in unison.

"Hello," Abbey said, trying to fake some enthusiasm.

"Well then," Miss Ashlynn said, raising a brow at Abbey. "Can anyone tell me what our letter of the week is?"

Abbey looked back at Suzy, at her pale skin and half-hearted smile. There was no glow, no tentacles. No faerie.

Not real.

～

THE MORNING WAS FILLED WITH SONGS AND READING, PAINT AND play dough, laughter and tears. Abbey hadn't realized how exhausting it was working with little children—bundles of high emotion and manic energy. Some were quieter than others, but all needed a great deal of care and attention.

After wiping the last bit of food off the last little face, Abbey and Ashlynn spread out the nap mats and started directing yawning children to their places of slumber.

"Some of the kiddos have a harder time falling asleep," Ashlynn explained. "They may need a little extra attention, a pat on the back or just sitting beside them so they feel comfortable."

Most of the kids already had their heads on their pillows, some were chatting with the person beside them. Ashlynn turned the light off and played some soft lullabies on the speaker on her desk.

"I'm going to take my lunch break while they're sleeping, if that's all right with you," Ashlynn said.

"Of course," Abbey said. "I'll keep them alive until you get back."

Ashlynn didn't laugh. She looked over her shoulder as she left the room, glancing over the children and nervously at Abbey.

Bitch thinks I'm psycho, Abbey thought, stifling a laugh. *Oh sister, you have no idea.*

The children settled well, only a few were stirring five minutes after Ashlynn had left the classroom. Abbey walked up and down the rows of mats, making sure everyone was tucked in and sleeping, or at least drifting. She took a close look when she reached Suzy, whose mat was tucked into the corner of the room against the wall. Suzy was awake, eyes wide, blanket up to her nose. Abbey sat against the wall next to her.

"Can't sleep?" Abbey asked.

Suzy didn't reply. She looked up at Abbey with her big blue eyes, then pulled the blanket over her head.

"I don't sleep well, either," Abbey said to the blanket. "I have… scary dreams. I used to do the same thing you're doing now. I'd hide under my blanket, pretend it was my own little world where no one could see or hear me; where I was the only one that existed, and the entire planet was limited to my Blanket Fortress of Solitude."

Suzy pulled the blanket just below her eyes. Abbey could see that the corners of her eyes were scrunched.

"Is that… a smile?" Abbey asked.

A soft chuffle came from under the blankets. Suzy pulled the blanket under her chin, revealing the most surprising smile.

"Did you really hide under your blankets?" Suzy asked.

"Yep. Sure did."

Suzy's eyes grew distant, and her smile faded.

"What were you hiding from?" Suzy asked.

Abbey tensed.

"Nothing, actually. Nothing real, anyways."

"Something pretend?"

"Possibly," Abbey said, trying not to think back to the time under her blankets. "Monsters, I suppose."

Fairy tale creatures, and real-life monsters.

"Can I tell you a secret?" Suzy asked.

"Sure," Abbey said.

Suzy sat up and inched closer to Abbey so she could whisper in her ear.

"Monsters are real. I see them too."

The room was no longer dark. In the blink of an eye, the classroom was aglow with a glistening silver light. Abbey looked up. Tentacled faeries, dozens of them, flitted and fluttered around the ceiling, casting moonrays of light over the sleeping children. Suzy kept looking at Abbey, not seeming to notice the creatures above.

"Why do you say that, Suzy? Have you seen a monster?"

The faeries floated down, gliding on glimmering wings until they were all over Suzy, clinging to her clothes and tangled in her hair. They were gnashing their teeth and drooling globs of blood over Suzy's dress. It was all Abbey could do not to swipe them away.

"Have you?" Suzy asked, still as a stone.

"Yes," Abbey said, lower lip relinquishing its strength and beginning to tremble.

"And what did you do?" Suzy asked.

"I ran away."

"Where?"

"Here."

"But why?" Suzy said, tilting her head. "There are monsters here, too. There are monsters everywhere."

The faeries were multiplying at an alarming rate, flying in through the vents and squeezing under the door, filling the classroom, settling on every surface and cloaking every child. They started making a racket, pushing books off shelves and turning on the toys. Abbey stood and started shooing them away, but they flocked in full force.

"Stop!" Abbey yelled in a whisper. "You'll wake the children!"

Not real not real not real.

Abbey looked back at Suzy, who was looking at her like she had ten heads.

"What's wrong, Miss Abbey?" Suzy asked, tears welling in her eyes. "Do you see a monster?"

The window smashed, the force of a dozen faeries striking it at once. The curtain flew in, and glass rained down on the floor. A few of the children sat up and started to cry.

"Oh!" Abbey said, torn between running to the window and tending to the sobbing children.

Suzy started crying too, a painful wail that screamed through the room.

"What happened?" Miss Ashlynn burst through the door, a bite of her lunch still in her mouth.

Abbey couldn't produce any words. She pointed at the window, mouth gaping, hand trembling. Ashlynn ran to the window, crunching through the glass in her nude pumps. Suzy's wails grew louder, and more children started to cry. Abbey closed her eyes and covered her ears, trying to gain some composure and be a responsible adult for the children.

"Well you don't see that every day, now do you?" Ashlynn said.

Abbey opened her eyes. The faeries were gone, and the room was dark again. Ashlynn pulled open the curtain, revealing the shattered glass. Sunlight poured into the room and all the children sat up on their mats.

"Okay, children, I think nap time is over," Ashlynn said. "Please stand up and go sit at your tables. Stay away from the window until we can get this cleaned up."

Ashlynn turned to Abbey as she guarded the broken glass on the floor. "Can you fetch a broom from the closet down the left hall?"

Abbey nodded and scurried out of the classroom. She was happy to be on her own again, if only for a few seconds. She looked down the empty hallway, several doors on either side. She didn't have to search to find the closet.

One of the doors creaked open and a grey, mangled hand reached out, clasping a broom and dustpan in its red talons.

Abbey went to the hand, accepted the broom and dustpan, then flung the door open with a force that nearly ripped it off its hinges.

There was no one in the closet, and nothing in there that should not have been. Just cleaning supplies, a mop bucket, and toilet paper. No witch. No monster. Abbey looked at her hand, and the broom she held firmly in her sweaty grasp.

She returned to the class, numb and sick to her stomach, and started sweeping up the glass.

"Imagine that," Ashlynn said. "We have little ones bouncing off the windows all the time, but never a big sucker like that. I'm gonna have to put decals or something on the outside to let them know it's a window, not a door!"

A crow, neck snapped, blood trickling from shiny blue feathers, lay in a pile on the floor. Abbey swept the glass around it as Miss Ashlynn handed coloring sheets out to the students. When the glass was cleaned up, Abbey donned a pair of gloves and put the crow in a plastic grocery bag before cleaning up the mess of blood.

"I'm going to run this outside," Abbey said, holding up the bag. "I need some fresh air, anyways."

"Sure thing," Miss Ashlynn said. "You okay, Abbey?"

"Yeah," Abbey lied.

Once the corpse was disposed of in the dumpster behind the school, Abbey debated bolting. She could just walk away, get in Barnes and drive back to the motel and watch television and eat and drink until she was in a coma.

But that wouldn't work.

She would find no peace there, either.

There are monsters everywhere.

"ONE FOR THE BOOKS!" SCOTT LAUGHED, AND EVERYONE HELD UP their glass to cheers. "Hell of a first day."

Abbey clinked her glass against Scott's and Ashlynn's, the only two in reach at the large table in the back of the bar. They had all come to the pub after the last student had left. Abbey had wanted to see Suzy go, to get a look at her family, but she was picked up while Abbey was in the classroom with the other children.

Talk of the dead crow created some laughter, which the staff wanted to continue over food and beverages. Plus, they wanted to check out their newest staff member.

Everyone already thinks I'm a weirdo, Abbey thought, looking around at the quiet snickers and raised brows. *They're not wrong.*

"Here's to Abbey," Scott said, lifting his glass for the second time in the same minute. His drinks had gone down smooth and quick, which gave Abbey a quiet sense of joy. She didn't feel so bad ploughing through several margaritas before the food had even arrived.

Everyone laughed and drank, drank and ate, then drank some more. The mood around the table was jovial and light, a far cry from the turmoil in Abbey's head. A dead crow was a freak accident to them, but a deeper event to Abbey. As many times as she told herself it wasn't real, that it had been the crow that broke the window, she couldn't quit imagining the faeries swarming the classroom.

I'm losing it. Again.

"Abbey?" Scott said, leaning in a tad too close for comfort. "You. You all there? All right?" He stood and wrapped his arm around her, leaning on her for support rather than offering his. Despite using her as a brace, he stumbled, his weight tipping the stool Abbey was on and sending them both to the floor.

"Holy shit!" he said, rolling over and looking at Abbey. "I'm sorry."

Ashlynn came to Abbey's aid, offering a hand to help pull her off the floor. Abbey refused, instead placing her hands in grime and liquor on the floor to push herself up.

"I'm okay," Abbey said. "You?"

Scott stayed on the floor, making no attempt to get to his feet. "You know, this is probably for the best. Someone pass my drink down here."

Everyone laughed. Abbey laughed, too, although it was fake. Forced. She wasn't amused. She wasn't thinking about their fall to the floor or Scott's drunken antics. Her mind was far away from the pub.

"It's cool, guys," she said, maintaining the false smile plastered across her face. "I'm gonna go wash up. Will someone order me another?"

No one volunteered. They stared at each other, some turning away, others playing with the utensils in front of them. Abbey walked away, hearing the gossip flare as soon as she was away from the table.

After peeing and washing her hands, arms, and face, Abbey left the bathroom, intending on relaxing and trying to have a decent time. She stopped in front of a large mirror in the hall and ruffled her hair and clothes, trying to present as someone other than a high-functioning drunk, when a creak caught her attention. The exit door just beyond the bathrooms was open a crack and moving in the night wind. She went to shut it, then thought better, considering that one of the cooks may have left it open to step out and have a smoke. She poked her head out the door and looked into the alley behind the building.

It was a ghost town, the flip side of all the little shops on the lone street of Lamarque. And there was indeed a figure leaned up against the wall, a glowing cigarette between his fingers.

"Oh, hey," Abbey said, nodding at the smoker. "The door was open. I was gonna shut it, but thought I should check if someone was out here."

Fingers walked their way up her spine, settling heavy on her shoulder. Fueled by alcohol and bad judgment, Abbey walked out into the alley. The door shut behind her with a heavy click.

"Jamie?" The light in the alley was dim, but she could make out enough to be sure that it was him. She walked towards him, peppering him with questions. "What are you doing here? I stopped at your place a few times—and there was a thing behind, in that cemetery… are you okay?"

Abbey stopped walking and talking. Jamie wasn't moving, or even acknowledging she was there.

The fingers, nails dragging up her back, pinching her neck.

"Jamie?"

Abbey backtracked to the pub door and gave the handle a tug. Locked.

"I'm… Scott and the others are inside having a drink… a few— well, a lot of drinks." Abbey laughed, a nervous whimper. "Wanna come on in and have a few?"

There was another moment of silence before Jamie awoke with a jolt, giving his head a shake and looking at Abbey.

"Abbey!" he said, taking long strides towards her and swooping her up into his arms, swinging her around like a child. "I'm sorry I missed you! How was your first day of work?"

He set her down, her head spinning and muscles clenched tight.

"It was… eventful. Would you like to come inside and hear the great tale of the crow?"

It was as if he hadn't heard her at all.

"Abbey, you look wonderful tonight."

Abbey looked down at her outfit, covered in paint and snot and old whiskey from the pub floor.

"Thanks, I guess. Should we go inside —"

Jamie moved in, planting his mouth on hers, his tongue thrusting into her. She pulled away, pushing on his chest and backing down the alley. He grasped her shoulders and pulled her closer.

"Jamie, stop," she said, trying to wriggle out of his grasp.

"Relax, Abbey. I just really like you. I don't want to blow it."

"Well you are."

"Look, I'm not gonna try anything. You're drunk."

"And what the hell are you?"

Abbey lifted her leg, jamming her knee into Jamie's thigh and kicking him back with what little strength and coordination she had. He stumbled a few steps and raised his hands in the air.

"All right, all right. Relax."

"You made that request already," she said. "Denied."

"I just… you taste so good. I really, really like you Abbey."

"I like you too, Jamie, but you're acting weird. And making me uncomfortable."

"Fair enough," he said, putting his hands in the pockets of his jeans.

Abbey breathed a sigh of relief and tried to deescalate the already ridiculous situation. "Now, shall we go inside? With other people?"

"No." His voice was sharp and harsh. Abbey decided it was time to bail. Not comfortable turning her back on this man who was practically a stranger, she started moving backwards as fast as her drunken gait would allow. Jamie stood in place, head down and hands in his pockets. Abbey had just about reached the end of the alley when Jamie raised his head.

"Hey! Bitch!"

Abbey stopped.

What in the actual fuck?

"You think it's okay, being a damn cock-tease like that?" Jamie shouted.

"I—"

The fingers penetrated her spine, cradling her heart and giving her strength.

Stand up for yourself.

"I sure do," she said. "It's more than okay."

"Get me all randy and leaving me hanging, though there's not much *hanging* here."

He unzipped his fly, exposing a raging erection, stroking his engorged shaft as he moved swiftly up the alley towards her.

Abbey knew she should run.

The front of the pub was literally around the corner where there were people—witnesses, and protectors.

But she stayed put, cemented in place, her courage massaged by the hands inside of her.

"Ah, come around, have we?" he said, quickening his strokes as he reached her. "Atta girl."

When Abbey was an older teen, fresh out of high school and maintaining her own place in the city, she might have seized the opportunity for such physicality; she might have let him have her, or, at the very least, release *on* her. She had done more and worse in her young adulthood, in the pursuit of acceptance and affection. Jamie was obviously drunker than she was, and found her attractive.

But he was also dominating and aggressive.

She drove her knee into his crotch and grabbed his dick, giving it a firm twist as she kneed his balls a second time. And a third.

"There," she said, satisfied that his forward momentum had been quashed for a good while. "Was it as good for you as it was for me?"

He crumpled into a pile on the ground, mewling like a tortured animal. Abbey walked away, confident that she was safe to turn her back on the incapacitated prick. She reached the street and looked back, verifying that Jamie was still in a heap on the ground. He was, and he wasn't moving. And he was much more damaged than he should have been.

His eyes had turned crimson with blood, and his tongue was hanging out of his mouth, half bitten off, a pool of blood growing beneath his smashed and mangled head. Cracked ribs jutted out from beneath his clothes, and his left leg was turned sideways, snapped off at the knee.

Abbey felt a scream brewing in her gut. A scream for the graphic sight in front of her, and a scream of fear. For Jamie, for herself.

Now she ran.

She didn't turn towards the pub, but went the opposite way, towards the school and Barnes. Her feet didn't slow until her body slammed into the side of her car.

She thanked fuck that she had grabbed her purse when she went to the bathroom. Keys out and in the ignition in one fell swoop, she wrenched Barnes into drive and pinned it, squealing her tires and sending gravel spraying over the lawn of the school. After a few fish-tails and swerves and curves, she was on the main road, heading back to the motel. When she passed the pub and the alley beside, she saw Jamie.

He was standing, eyes drooling blood down his face, limp cock hanging out of his fly, waving a hand with five badly broken fingers. And he was smiling, wide and wicked, a bloody slash across his face.

Abbey couldn't take her eyes off him, her neck craning and eyes trying to focus on what she couldn't possibly be seeing. Barnes did her best, but couldn't keep course on her own. The car lost control, swerving over the road peppered in country town gravel. Abbey fought the steering wheel for control, but lost.

Barnes jumped the curb and plowed through the grass, crashing through a park bench and a garbage can before reaching the head of the trail leading back to the motel. They would have kept going, too, if the forest had been more forgiving, the tree roots less deep.

Her world fell slow and silent. Abbey was a figurine sealed in a shaken snow globe, tumbling through the air with shards of glass and chunks of Barnes until she came to rest on the forest floor.

18

Everything hurt. Her head, her body, her soul.

Abbey came to and started feeling around her body, fingers squelching in mud, skin throbbing from lacerations and bruising. She opened her eyes and saw twigs and muck, the earthy flooring of the forest floor. Her mouth was tacky and tasted of copper, her tongue coated in a thick paste of blood and dirt.

It took everything she had to sit up, her body complaining through every muscles engaged and every joint maneuvered. Abbey sat upright for a moment, trying to quell the chaos in her head. The trees came into focus, as did her memory.

Barnes.

Abbey braced herself on a tree and stood, looking back along the trail of carnage. The woods were littered with metal and plastic, and a tower of steam was visible through the trees. Barnes radiator was sputtering the vapours of death.

"No," Abbey said, walking towards her fallen comrade.

Barnes had hit the large poplar head on, crumpling like an accordion, her hood wrapping around the tree in a firm and final hug. The windshield was smashed and littered over the ground, speckled here and there with Abbey's flesh and blood.

Abbey flopped down on the boot and cried. She cried and shook, and screamed at the tree, caressing the blood-smeared car as she unleashed a chorus of profanities intended for everyone and no one. She closed her eyes and let the tears flow, willing the night to take her right then and there, laying on the body of her best and only friend.

Beyond her eyelids, a flicker of light. Strobing, cool then warm then cool again, bright as headlights from deep in the woods. Abbey opened her eyes and looked into the ruby-red pupils of a faerie.

"Fuck. Off."

Abbey swiped at the little creature, knocking it off Barnes and sending it twirling and screeching through the air. Abbey closed her eyes again. And again, the light shone in her face.

"I told you—"

The faerie grabbed Abbey's arm, hauling her off Barnes with supernatural strength, and pulled her a few steps deeper into the woods.

"No!" Abbey shouted, swatting at the thing like it was a mosquito. "Not real!"

The faerie hovered in front of Abbey's face, tentacles on its curvaceous hips and black lips drooped into a plump pout. It waved a hand, beckoning Abbey to follow, but Abbey didn't budge. The faerie stomped its foot in the air then flitted off into the trees, light dimming as it disappeared out of sight.

The air cooled significantly with the loss of the faerie's light. Abbey shivered. Her body was broken, and she felt sick, like she might vomit damaged chunks of her organs if she moved even a single muscle. She looked at Barnes, then into the woods after the faerie.

What am I gonna do when they find me? A DUI? Don't need that on my record.

Abbey decided to make her way back to the motel to sleep off the alcohol, then report the accident in the morning. But then visions of Jamie appeared in her mind, his bloody, exposed body in hot pursuit.

What if he's coming after me?

She looked back towards the town and her heart hammered in her chest, every pulse a painful jolt through her body. She turned the opposite way, and saw a faint light deep in the trees, a pulsating glow from the faerie, she assumed. Every pulse brought a delicate flash of euphoria, a mental morphine that dulled the pain and fear. As the light pulsed, improving Abbey's condition with every wax and wane, the faerie appeared again, holding a tentacle out to Abbey.

Abbey followed.

Not real. It's okay to go because it's not real. But it feels good, so that's okay.

She followed the faerie that wasn't there, dodging branches and trees through the ever-thickening bush until she was surrounding by forest and darkness, and was hopelessly lost. Nothing was familiar. She couldn't see the light of the road or the town or the motel. And then, a fire flared before her eyes, raging between the trees a few meters ahead. The faerie flew to Abbey's side and lifted her hand, pulling her towards the fire. Abbey followed the heat and the light until she broke free of the trees and was standing in a clearing far bigger than was possible in the spray of forest between the motel and the town.

And there she was, in the center of the clearing, tending to a fire surrounded by stones and bricks. She looked up at Abbey, and a smile ripped across her malformed, pale face.

"Hallo, love," Faelith said.

∽

ABBEY SAT QUIETLY BY THE FIRE, WATCHING FAELITH WORK AWAY at meat skewered on a spit, her mottled skin gleaming with golden sweat. Faelith caught Abbey's eye, then looked down at her own nudity.

"Make you uncomfortable," Faelith said, her voice a guttural lisp.

"Yes," Abbey said. "All of this does."

"Ah. It is only body," Faelith said, grasping her massive breast and giving it a tug in Abbey's direction. "You old enough, be used to it now. Body beautiful. Body functional, unique. Body womanhood."

It was all so surreal. Abbey felt lost in a fog, one she thought she had cleared through years of therapy and medication.

Not real.

"Very real," Faelith said, smacking her gangly hand against her thick thigh.

"It can't be," Abbey said, watching the witch's movements—her every muscle quivering and engaging beneath a tight, thin veil of flesh.

"Can. And is," Faelith said, ending the discussion with a firm poke of the fire, sending embers dancing into the dark night sky.

A cloud of faeries who had been mingling about the tree line flew in, swooping and diving through the embers, batting them with their tentacles and whooping like children.

"Why are you here?" Abbey asked.

Faelith looked at her, puzzled. "You are here."

"But you were gone," Abbey said. "So many years, I haven't seen you."

"Chose not to," Faelith corrected. "I was there."

Abbey considered that. Her years through the foster system, psychiatrist after psychiatrist, medication upon medication. There had always been little things that niggled at her—lights in the dark, eyes in the shadows, whispers in her ear and fingers in her hair. She had dismissed those things as the mental illness she had been given, the post traumatic stress that had altered her brain.

But maybe…

No. Not real.

Faelith sighed and shook her massive head. "Yes. Real."

The witch lifted her heavy frame from the stump she was sitting on and lowered herself to the ground beside Abbey. Abbey didn't move away. She let the woman wrap her arm around her and hold her close, her hot flesh pressing into Abbey's arm and cheek. Abbey began to cry and rested her head on Faelith's bosom.

"Are you real?" Abbey asked.

"Yes," Faelith said. She took Abbey by the chin, lifting her face so she could look into her eyes. "You are, too."

Faelith stood and fetched a thick blanket from a pile by the woods, and laid it by the fire, patting it with her massive hand. "Here. Rest. Questions later."

Abbey surrendered. She curled up on the blanket, and Faelith covered her in a second, heavy blanket that smelled of lavender and honey. The faeries dampened their light and softened their song, lulling Abbey into a deep and dreamless sleep.

THE CRACKLE OF THE FIRE WAS SOOTHING, AND THE HEAT comforting. Abbey woke to the sounds of the faeries frolicking, throwing stones at the trees and cooing like babies. She felt like she had been asleep for a lifetime, the heaviness of slumber sitting on her lungs and weighing her eyes closed. She blinked a few times, then opened her eyes to the sight of the night sky, stars twinkling like jewels.

"How long have I been out?" she asked, sitting up.

Faelith was out of earshot, gathering wood from the edge of the clearing. Abbey looked around at the new home Faelith had made for herself. The large fire pit, bricks and stones arranged in a large circle, mounds of wood in the center. Faelith had her collection of talismans and knickknacks hung from the trees around the clearing, filling every centimeter of bark and space with something colorful and beautiful, in a multitude of textures and sheens. There was no furniture or appliances like she had at the cottage, but she had fashioned seating and a table from stumps and logs that looked whittled and sanded to a smooth finish. And a pile of heavy blankets at the edge of the trees.

Faelith returned to the fire, a tree's worth of wood balanced in her arms. She smiled when she found Abbey was awake.

"Do you miss it?" Abbey asked. "The cottage?"

"No," Faelith said, without hesitation. "You are home."

Abbey felt warmth tingle in her body. She thought of her life, her routine.

"The city?"

"Ugly. Cold," Faelith said, screwing her face into a grimace. "You no like, either."

Abbey nodded. "No, I didn't."

Quite certain it was the booze thinking for her, Abbey began warming to the idea of the reality of Faelith. At least for the moment.

Faelith handed her a cup of liquid she pulled from the fire, heavy moss wrapped around the handle of the mug so Abbey didn't burn her hand.

"Drink," Faelith said. "Heal."

Abbey drank. It was sweet like nectar and spicy like peppers.

"Why now?" Abbey asked.

"Because you hurt. Broken. Car threw you."

Abbey looked down at her body, clothes soaked in blood and caked in mud.

"No, not the tea, Faelith. You. Why are you here now? Er… or why do I see you now?"

Faelith stopped moving around and focused on Abbey. "My love, you are ready now."

"For what?"

"To believe. To be."

"Be what?"

Sirens in the distance pierced through the night. The faeries squealed and extinguished their light, hiding behind trees and rocks as the sound grew near.

"How long was I asleep for?" Abbey asked again, looking in the direction of the noise of the emergency vehicles.

"Long enough," Faelith said. She embraced Abbey once again, then crumpled down on top of the fire, covering herself with Abbey's blanket.

"Faelith! The fire!"

"Ma'am!"

A police officer came around the trees, flashlight in hand, saying something into his walkie talkie.

"Ma'am, are you all right? Is that your car back there?"

The campsite had died, decomposed, and given itself back to the forest. The talismans and knickknacks were gone, replaced by moss and cobwebs and notches of sap on the trees. The clearing was gone, grown over by a peppering of birch trees and bushes. And Abbey was sitting there, on the ground, leaning against a huge, dark boulder.

She smiled and patted the boulder as the officer helped her to her feet.

19

The nearest hospital was in Dunvegan City—a slight inconvenience, if there was a true medical emergency, Abbey thought. It did, however, give her time to collect herself and return to reality. The paramedics drove fast with the sirens on, despite the fact that Abbey was lucid, and her bleeding had calmed to a dribble.

The emergency room nurses fawned and fussed over her, marveling that there was no glass in any of her lacerations and that her bones remained intact. Abbey went through a plethora of testing—scans to check for internal bleeding and broken bones—but came out clean. Just a mild concussion, some deep and colourful bruising, and cuts requiring some stitches.

"You are one lucky lady," the nurse—Patty, her tag said—said as she stitched up a particularly nasty gash on Abbey's arm.

"I guess so," Abbey said.

Lucky, or cursed?

"Once we're done here," Patty said, "the police are gonna want to talk to you. You feel up to it? Or do you want me to use the old head injury excuse, buy you some more time to collect your thoughts."

Patty winked.

"My blood alcohol level?"

Patty paused, needle in the air.

"Just fine," Patty said, looking puzzled. "Were you drinking?"

Sober?

Ah. Slept it off.

"Had one with dinner," Abbey said, omitting the four drinks before and after her meal. "Guess that's nothing, though."

"Nope, you're good," Patty said, as she poked the final stitch through Abbey's skin. "Lemme get you cleaned up, then I'll tell the officers to come on in?"

"Yes, that's fine," Abbey said, not sure what story she could weave.

Patty rinsed Abbey's arm and got her a glass of water, then escorted two burly officers into the room, both in uniform, both looking fairly relaxed and apathetic.

Beat cops. Not detectives. Quick and easy.

"How are you feeling, Ms… Abigail?"

"Abbey."

"Sorry. Abbey."

"Surprisingly okay. A bit sore, and my head's a bit fuzzy—*I can use that, if need be*—but otherwise myself."

"Had yourself quite the wreck tonight."

"Would appear so."

"Want to tell me what happened?"

A man sexually assaulted me, I kicked him in the balls, and his lack of release killed him, decaying his body before my eyes. He chased me, and I lost control and smashed into the trees trying to escape. My witch friend healed me and cleared the booze out of my blood just in time for you guys to pick me up.

"Your guess is as good as mine," Abbey said, shrugging her shoulders. "I went out for dinner with some colleagues, started to feel a little under the weather, and left to go home and rest. Next thing I know, you were there, helping me out of the trees."

"Did you have a few drinks with dinner?"

"One. Maybe two. I wasn't even tipsy. Just a stomach bug, I think.

The officer flipped open his file and ran his finger down the page. "Yep, you're good. Blood alcohol level's in the norm."

Thank fuck.

"My partner here stopped at the pub to chat with the patrons as the ambulance was bringing you in."

Oh shit.

The officer laughed.

Thank another fuck.

"They were all a little worse for wear," the officer said, no doubt referring to Scott, who could have only gotten worse after Abbey left. "They didn't even realize you had gone."

"I slipped out the back. Wasn't feeling well, and they were having fun. Didn't want to worry them."

"Yeah, well they're worried now. Once your boss stops puking, he'll be worried too, I'm sure."

Now the other officer spoke.

"Abbey, I spoke with the hostess."

He paused, then looked at Abbey.

What did she see?

Abbey waited him out. He was baiting her for an admission she wasn't going to give.

"Abbey, tell me a bit about where you come from?"

Bloody hell.

"I grew up not far from here, but I was living half way across the country. I ended up growing tired of the city life and decided to come back this way. Stopped for gas at the motel, then figured I'd hang around for a while. Lamarque is a beautiful little spot."

He expression glowed with pride. "It really is. And you must like it, deciding to work here, and all."

Another pause. Another stare down.

"Abbey, I contacted Marie and Chuck at the motel."

Abbey said nothing.

"Marie indicated you were the nervous type, like you might be running from something."

A witch. But she was running beside me the whole time.

Abbey waited for the officer to reveal his hypothesis.

"Abbey, *are* you running from someone? Abusive partner, family member?"

"No. I'm not. I'm single and have been for quite some time. I lived alone in the city."

"Abusive boss? Coworker?"

"Why are you asking me this?"

The officer sighed and rubbed his brow. The other stepped in, trying to divvy up the discomfort.

"Abbey, the hostess said she saw you running away from the pub. That you came from the alley, and a man was pursuing you."

Abbey was surprised. Surprised that she had been seen, but more surprised that Jamie had been seen.

Let's mix some truth with the lie.

"A new friend of mine was getting a bit handsy, had too much to drink, I think. I wouldn't say I was running, but I definitely left promptly, so things didn't get out of hand."

Like murdering him with his cock hanging out.

"Who is your friend?"

"I don't want to cause him any trouble."

"There won't be. We just want the story from all angles."

"Am I in any sort of trouble here?" Abbey said, ready to put an end to the conversation. "I'll pay for any damages, of course. Not sure what happened, but—"

"That won't be necessary," the officer said, closing his notebook. "We'll have a quick look when the sun comes up, but from what we can tell, you lost control of your vehicle coming around a turn. Bit too fast, maybe, but very little in the way of damage. City will slap down a bit of sod and remove the tree you hit, replace the table and garbage can, but nothing major. Nothing our insurance won't cover."

"Thank goodness," Abbey said, holding her chest for effect. "I'm so, so sorry."

"Look Abbey," the officer said, stepping closer and putting a hand on her shoulder. "If you need help, we're here for you. There's a crisis center here at the hospital, and a counsellor you can speak to. Confidentially. There are options, you know."

"Thank you sir, but there's no problem. I assure you."

The officer nodded, not an ounce of belief on his face. As he and his partner were leaving the room, he turned back.

"Abbey?"

"Yeah?"

"Who was that friend again? The one in the alley?"

Abbey smiled sweetly and took a sip of her water.

The officer nodded, and they left.

Abbey finally took a breath.

Not in trouble, so that's good.

The room was dim, night hanging around outside the window, and the lights inside were dim—just bright enough for nurses to see the vitals they collected on the hour. Abbey searched the corners of the room, looking for things she had spent years choosing not to see. They were there, loitering about her room, iridescent wings, purple hair, red eyes. And Faelith, a two-dimensional image cloaked in the design of the floral wallpaper. Abbey reached out and touched the faint outline of a hand on the wall. And the hand touched back.

THE DOCTOR KEPT ABBEY UNTIL THE NEXT DAY TO MONITOR HER vitals, keeping an eye out for any adverse effects. Abbey didn't mind. The hospital, though uncomfortable and reeking of sanitizer and fresh death, was safe.

And Faelith was with her, a pattern in the wallpaper, staying perfectly still whenever nurses and doctors passed through on their rounds.

In the morning, after Abbey took a round of painkillers with some cardboard-flavoured oatmeal, they started talking discharge. Abbey realized she had no way back to Lamarque.

"Any chance I can catch a taxi out this way? Uber?"

"We typically don't discharge unless there's someone arranged to pick you up," the day nurse said, scowling.

"Tough game for single folks," Abbey said, giving her a hard look.

"Relatives?"

"Nope."

"Friends?"

Abbey's eyes flickered to Faelith.

"Not ones that drive."

"Well, what's your plan, then?"

Abbey didn't have a chance to answer. Marie burst into the room and right over to Abbey, hugging her so hard she just about picked her straight off the bed.

"Oh honey," Marie said into her hair. "We were worried sick!"

Chuck stood in the door, unsure of where to put himself and what to say.

"Hope it's okay we're here," Marie said.

"It's actually more than okay," Abbey said. "I was a bit stuck. I hate to ask, but…"

Marie looked at the nurse, and down at the discharge papers.

"Oh, my word," Marie said. "Don't be so foolish! I would hope you would have called us for a ride."

Abbey shrugged, and Marie clucked her tongue.

"I'm such a burden," Abbey said.

"You are no such thing," Marie said as she gathered Abbey's things. She motioned to Chuck, who handed a plastic bag to Abbey. "And I hope *you* don't mind," Marie said, "but I took the liberty of bringing you some clothes. I looked at nothing in your room, I promise."

"Marie," Abbey said. Marie winced, looking like a puppy about to be scolded. "Thank you, Marie. For everything. You are too sweet to me."

"Just sweet enough, I'd say. We'll be out in the hall, let you get dressed. You need any help?"

"I'm actually quite fine, surprisingly."

"I want to hear about it on the drive back."

Marie gave Abbey's arm a squeeze and turned to walk away. As she passed by the wall, Abbey watched Faelith materialize from the wallpaper pattern and give Marie's hair a tender stroke. Marie stopped dead in her tracks and turned around.

"Marie?" Abbey said, watching Faelith disappear back into the pattern. "Everything okay?"

"Hmmm," Marie said, looking at the faces around the room. "I think so, 'cept maybe I need to cut back on the coffee, jittery stuff it is."

Marie continued her monologue on caffeinated, sugary beverages as she and Chuck disappeared into the hall. The discharge nurse finished up, getting Abbey's signature at the bottom of papers Abbey didn't bother to read.

Pay and be gone and don't sue, Abbey thought. *That's the sum of it.*

The nurse left the room and Abbey got dressed, watching Faelith and feeling safe.

"See you at back at home," Abbey said, brushing the wall with light fingertips.

MARIE TALKED FOR MOST OF THE DRIVE, TELLING ABBEY ABOUT the people who had called the motel to snoop about the disaster-plagued newcomer. She showed pictures on her phone of Barnes and the wreck. A lump formed in Abbey's throat when she saw the pictures of her gas-powered friend, a crumpled corpse of metal and plastic. Marie noticed that Abbey was upset by the sight of Barnes, so she started into stories about the picnic tables Chuck was building and the flowers she was planting outside the diner. Abbey was grateful for the company and the conversation. It distracted her from her thoughts.

After a long drive complete with narcotic-fueled motion sickness, the old motel was a welcome sight. The parking lot was empty, both in front by the diner and to the side by the motel entrance. Abbey was relieved. She wanted to see neither stranger nor acquaintance offering well wishes.

Chuck meant well when he pulled up in front of the diner, but Abbey just wanted to go to her room to hole up for a few days and lick her wounds. She needed to gather herself before making an appearance in town again. The sight of her coworkers and Lamarque proper would only serve as reminders of the previous night—of Jamie, of the woods…

Not that she minded the woods.

"Come in for a bite," Marie said. Both she and Chuck were out of the old truck before Abbey could protest.

Well, I do need something to sink the shitty oatmeal resting on top of my stomach.

Chuck and Marie, although in her face and her business a touch more than she was comfortable with, were also attuned to Abbey's needs. They left her alone to eat, for the most part, only making appearances to refill coffee and offer condiments when the food was ready. Abbey appreciated that. Had it not been for them, she probably wouldn't have eaten anything at all. Going to bed on a stomach that was empty except for a cocktail of antibiotics and painkillers was a terrible idea. Actually, had it not been for them, she may have been going to bed another night in that hospital with oatmeal and popsicles and nurses rousing her from a sound sleep every hour on the hour.

After her stomach was full of bacon, eggs, and hashbrowns, and sloshing with two too many cups of coffee, Abbey attempted to pay, and, as always, was firmly denied. She hugged both Marie and Chuck, and it seemed they might melt from her rare display of physical affection.

"Thanks guys," Abbey said, smiling. A genuine smile.

"No big thing," Marie said, pinching Abbey's cheek. "And you know where your new room is?"

"First floor, yes?"

"Yes ma'am," Chuck said, handing her the key. "Middle of the row. First floor has easy access to the pool, if the urge arises."

"Maybe after a while," Abbey said, motioning to her injuries.

"Of course," Chuck said. "I'm an idiot."

"Absolutely not," Abbey said. "You are wonderful. You both are."

Marie and Chuck exchanged a look Abbey couldn't quite make sense of, but she disregarded it in a heartbeat, too tired to care.

Abbey hobbled towards her room, holding her bruised ribs and favouring her battered leg. She wanted to have a long shower and watch some television, but knew she wouldn't make it as far as the bathroom before crashing. She walked into her new room, a cookie-cutter image of her old one, and flopped down on the bed. Before her head bounced and landed on the mattress a second time, she was asleep.

∼

"Poor little thing, all rattled like that."

Marie set the kettle on the wood stove and threw another piece of wood on the fire.

"She's a tough cookie," Chuck said, through a mouthful of pound cake. "She'll be jus' fine."

"I know, I know," Marie said, waving her hand at her nonchalant husband. "Doesn't stop me worrying for her now."

After grabbing her knitting needles, Marie lowered herself into her armchair with a grunt. She rubbed her shoulders, aching from tension and the long drive. Though she knew Abbey would be all right in the end, the journey had been long and grueling, and might be far from over.

"Whatcha thinking about, dear?" Chuck said.

"Whaddya mean?" Marie said, her needles ticking and tapping at a frantic pace.

"Bee in your bonnet, 'twould seem."

Marie lowered the needles to her lap and sighed.

"You fretting over money? I see you turned away another few guests this morning."

Marie looked at Chuck and rolled her eyes.

"You know money ain't no big thing," she scoffed. "We be keeping the motel empty 'til Abbey has herself sorted. Can't have people around all this odd business…"

Marie looked towards the sofa.

Chuck knew it was time to retrieve the tea.

"It's just… the danger is there, and it makes me nervous," Marie said, reaching for the tray of snack on the coffee table.

The dulcet tones of Robert Stack emanated from the old tube television, stories of aliens appearing at children's bedsides and ghostly encounters involving creatures in the woods. Marie scratched at her head, and a clump of hair fell to her lap.

"I mean, the poor girl's been hurt plenty," Marie said as she filled her plate. "Damn the stress she's under, and the foulness of the world."

"Growth hurts. Life hurts."

Marie bit into the food, her sharp teeth piercing the tender, warm flesh. Blood dribbled down and hid between her chins, which she dabbed with the crocheted doily in her lap.

Chuck put the cups on a tray and carried it over, setting Marie's tea down on the table beside her chair.

"Sugar, dear?"

"Yes, m'love."

Chuck plucked a sugar cube from the tray and dropped it in Marie's cup.

"I know we'll take care of her, but nothing's for certain," Marie said.

Marie took another bite, rolling the sinew and tendon around her tongue before gulping the flesh down like a snake.

Chuck carried the tray over and placed it on the coffee table. He plucked two sugar cubes for his coffee and put the cup next to his rocking chair.

Marie picked up her tea, gave it a stir, and took a sip. "Me worries will pass, I know. But they be worries, jus' the same."

Marie looked up, her eyes black as the night.

Chuck plucked one more sugar cube, dropping it in the third and final cup on the tray.

Marie and Chuck looked at their visitor on the sofa as she leaned forward and grabbed her tea.

"No wrong with the worries. Worries mean you love," Faelith said, picking up her cup with crooked fingers and sipping the tea through black, cracked lips. "You young, Mahree. You shall see."

20

———

*T*hump.

Abbey sat up, woken from a dead sleep. She had no idea how long she'd been out, but it was dark outside. A quick look at the clock told her it was three in the morning.

Holy shit. I've been asleep for almost fifteen hours? Damn.

Staggering off the bed, she stood on her toes and stretched towards the ceilings, trying to iron out the kinks of a long and heavy sleep. Her mouth full of cotton, she grabbed a bottle of water from the mini fridge and drank the entire thing in three gulps.

Thump.

Abbey swallowed hard then held her breath.

Thump.

The light on the ceiling flickered ever so slightly, and the cheap motel picture on the wall twitched.

Thump.

She looked up at the ceiling.

Oh, the joys of first-floor living.

No stranger to apartment living, or living in a full house, Abbey relaxed when she realized the banging was coming from above.

Some heavy-footed guest tramping around, or a kid jumping on the bed. Abbey was actually kind of pleased that there was another guest in the motel. Marie and Clark deserved the business, even though they didn't seem concerned about the off-season slump.

After using the washroom and changing into some comfortable pajamas, Abbey sat on the bed and turned on the television. The selection of middle-of-the-night shows was slim and shitty—infomercials, cooking shows, and grade D sci-fi flicks. Abbey settled on a creature horror with plenty of screams and breasts.

Thump.

Marie had stocked the room with a selection of sweet and savoury goodies while Abbey was in the hospital, everything from chips and nuts to candies and chocolates. Abbey grabbed a box of chocolate covered raisins and tried to jump into the story racing across the screen.

Thump. Thump.

Like a mosquito in a tent, the noise from above bothered Abbey to the point of anger. If she'd had a broom, she would have banged on the ceiling like an irate grandmother scolding the folks above.

Thump.

Regardless of the witching hour, Abbey decided to go for a bit of a stroll. She'd had plenty of sleep, but that noise threatened to fray her final nerve. She debated about stopping upstairs and asking them to keep it down, but she didn't feel up to the confrontation. She slid into her shoes, shoved her key card in her bra, and headed out to the walkway.

The pool was beautiful, LED lights cycling through a rainbow of colours and shimmering in the black of the night. Marie and Chuck kept the pool area immaculate with daily cleaning and regular maintenance; not at all what you'd expect from a hole-in-the-wall motel. Abbey walked out to the side of the pool and sat on the tile, rolling her pajamas up so she could dangle her feet in the water. Below the surface, the faeries swam and twirled about like torpedos, playing in the warm, clean water. Every so often, one would come up and nibble Abbey's feet, coiling tentacles through her toes and making her laugh.

THUMP.

The water in the pool rippled like a T-Rex had just stomped nearby. The faeries scattered, hiding themselves in the filters and recessed lighting. Abbey looked up to the walkway, and the room above hers. There were only two lights on either row of the motel: hers, and the room above her. In the room on the second floor, a person was moving around, the light flickering under the large and repetitive movement.

Thump.

A turn.

Thump.

An arm out to the side.

Thump.

A leg.

What the fuck is going on up there?

Then Abbey heard the music. Swan Lake. And the spinning and thumping intensified.

THUMPTHUMPTHUMPTHUMP

She rose from the pool. The air felt chilly against the bare skin on her legs. Abbey walked but felt she was floating, gliding towards the stairs leading to the upper walkway. The music got louder as she approached the door on the second floor, the thumping quaking.

THUMPTHUMPTHUMPTHUMPTHUMP.

When her hand touched the brass handle, the music stopped. The thumping stopped. The lights in the motel room went out. Abbey knocked on the door.

"Hello?" she said.

A single note played behind the door. Then silence again.

"Are you okay in there?"

Another note, a progressive step in the song.

"I'm your downstairs neighbour. I heard some banging…"

The song started playing again, slowly, notes distorted, sour and tainted. Abbey pushed down on the door handle, somehow knowing it would open. The door swung open and Abbey stepped inside, allowing the door to shut behind her.

The room was the same as hers, and the same as her first one. Same layout, same bedding, same everything. The lights were off, but the glow from the walkway shone through the red curtain, bathing the room in a crimson glow. The music played, choking out from the counter outside the bathroom. Abbey walked to the source, knowing before she got there.

Her music box. The one she had picked up from the little shop in town. It was closed, but music still spoke through the wood. She raised the lid, releasing the music, its scratching, screeching, distorted cries like fingernails on a chalkboard. The mirrored platform turned, but the dancer was gone. Abbey examined it closer, bending down to see the damage. There was a little plastic foot wrapped in a ballet slipper, still glued to the spinning platform, broken off at the ankle.

THUMP.

Abbey's teeth rattled in her head from the force of the sound. It was right behind her. In the room with her. She stood up straight, drew a breath, and turned around.

The room exploded with light and movement, the bulbs in the lights increasing to a blinding intensity until they burst, raining glass and ash over the carpet. The light outside intensified as well, but did not die, lighting the room in a powerful red spotlight. And the thumping continued.

On the bed, twirling on a satin-clad toe, was the ballerina, hands out in proper form, one leg extended, bloody stump thumping on the wall with each pirouette, smearing black gore across the floral wallpaper. The ballerina was not tiny, though, like she had just stepped out the box and resumed her dance on the bed. She had grown, but not to full size. She was a young girl, a child, white-blonde hair and pale skin stained and crusted with blood. As she spun, her eyes tracked the same spot, piercing-blue, boring straight into Abbey.

"Suzy," Abbey breathed.

Suzy screamed. The noise escaped her with a projectile stream of blood, black and shiny in the red light of the room. The blood hit the floor, soaking the carpet and flooding the room in great waves. Suzy stopped her pirouette to allow the blood to cascade out of her gawping mouth like a waterfall, foaming and warm across Abbey's feet.

"Suzy?" Abbey said, looking around the room for signs of Faelith. "Suzy, why are you here? What are you… yes. What *are* you?"

The window smashed and a gust of air billowed the red curtains into the room. Glass sprayed across the bed and the carpet, floating in the accumulating blood. A flock of faeries flew inside the room, swarming Suzy as she flailed and screamed, choking on the blood pouring from her mouth and nose. The lake of blood had reached the windowsill and started pouring out onto the walkway outside. Abbey gagged, frozen in place as the faeries began clawing and tearing at Suzy, taking huge mouthfuls of hair and flesh, ripping her apart and spitting her leavings into the lake of blood below until nothing remained except the smear of her stump on the wall and impossible gallons of blood on the floor.

"Oh no, Marie," Abbey said, looking around the room, the damage, the blood. All she could think of was the destruction she'd rained down upon these poor folks. Abbey sloshed through the blood, heading for the door, when something grabbed her ankle. She tried to kick it away, but it held tight. After a brief struggle, the hand swiped Abbey's feet from under her, and she plunged face-first into the blood.

Submerged in thick warmth, the taste of copper infiltrating her nose and mouth, Abbey struggled for purchase, clawing and kicking for something to hold on to. A hand reached down into the liquid and grabbed her, lifting her above the blood so she could breathe.

It was Faelith, grey skin black with blood, eyes glowing in the dark.

"Faelith," Abbey sputtered.

"You," Faelith said, tapping Abbey on the chest.

"What?" Abbey cried. "What? Faelith, help me!"

"You are stronger than this," Faelith said, dunking Abbey below the surface of the blood. Abbey struggled against the old witch's force, thrashing about but finding only furniture and bits of Suzy to grab ahold of. Faelith allowed her up for a breath.

"What the fuck, bitch?" Abbey screamed, spewing blood over Faelith's face.

"Make you strong."

And like a vacuum had attached itself to the broken window, the room was sucked dry, and Abbey was on the carpet, bone dry. The only red in the room was the outside light filtering through the crimson curtains. Frantic and out of breath, Abbey looked around. No stump swipe on the wall, no blood, no Suzy.

The music box played sweetly from the counter by the bathroom. The lid was closed, but the music was pretty once again, sweet tones, properly tuned. Abbey crawled over on hands and knees and grabbed the box, pulling it to the floor and opening the lid.

The tiny plastic ballerina was inside, all limbs whole, pirouetting to the music, her white blonde hair tied tight into a bun. Abbey looked closer, watching the dancer's reflection in the mirror, her razor sharp teeth covered in blood and pale blue eyes surrounded by a deep red. Abbey caught her own reflection and gasped. The Abbey looking back at her had the same sharp teeth as the dancer, and dark red, glowing eyes.

She dropped the music box and kicked it away, smashing it into pieces as she scrambled for the door. She wrenched on the handle the door flew open, and she ran smack into Faelith, whose massive form blocked the whole doorway.

"What... the fuck?" Abbey stuttered, angry, terrified tears starting to flow. Faelith was a shadow, a silhouette blocking out the walkway lights. She was all black with the bright light behind her, but Abbey could see that the witch was handing her something. Something large and gleaming.

Abbey reached out and took the gift, wrapping her slender hands around the rough wood and bearing its incredible weight. She turned it, the blade gleaming in the dull light.

"Hatchet," Abbey said.

She wanted to ask Faelith another question, to give the strange gift back to her, but Faelith was gone. In her place stood Suzy, standing in the doorway. She was smiling, her face split in two by the silver blade wedged from the top of her skull to her bottom jaw.

"Oh God," Abbey said, looking down at her empty, bloodstained hands.

Abbey swooned and collapsed to the ground, Suzy's maniacal laughter ringing in her ears as the world went black.

"Good thing I gots me some common sense," Marie said, handing Chuck another cold cloth to put on Abbey's head, "or we'd be drivin' back out to that hospital."

"I appreciate that, Marie."

"I know you do, dear," Marie said.

"Suppose we needed us some excitement 'round here." Chuck nodded, wiping back Abbey's hair and switching the old cloth out for the fresh one. "And we've got that, don't we, hon?"

The uneasiness in their voices the made Abbey feel guilty and uncomfortable.

"Again, and you must be sick of hearing this from me, but I'm sorry," Abbey said.

"No sorries needed," Marie said, waving a hand. "Your original sorry will suffice. This is all part of the same ordeal. Medication has you messed up, is all. My niece took the drugs after her gallbladder was removed, messed her up for a week. Night terrors, sleepwalking, all of that."

Sure, Abbey thought. *Sleep walking.*

"What a fright you gave us, though, sure," Marie, said. "Finding you all sprawled out on that walkway up there."

"And sorry about the window," Abbey said. "Again, I'll pay."

"No ma'am," Chuck said, shaking a finger. "Ain't your damage."

"But... I was in that room, and the window's smashed..."

"Not you," Chuck said, brow furrowed.

"Mind him not, my dear," Marie laughed. "Old fart and his nemesis."

"Huh?" Abbey said.

"Why, you may think you busted out that window, but that's happened before. Not for a long while, and not on the interior of the building, but it's happened."

Abbey stared, looking back and forth between the two for an answer.

"A crow," Chuck growled. "Bloody pests. Flew right through that glass. Found him and his broken little neck on the carpet. Right mess he made of it."

Crow.

Abbey said nothing, just looked down at her feet, bare and cut from the car accident, and fresh lacerations from her traipse through the window glass.

"C'mon Chuck," Marie said, pulling him off the bed and pushing him towards the door. "Let's give her some space, and some rest."

Marie stepped in front of Abbey and bent down to meet her eye. "I will be back in two hours to give you food and medication. Are you hurting?"

"A little. Not bad."

"Then I think you should have half the Vicodin. Get rid of that poison as soon as we can, yes?"

"Agreed," Abbey said, not wanting any more clouds in her head.

Marie gave her a little pat, then the couple disappeared out the door.

"I'm the guest from hell," Abbey said, shaking her head.

The hairs on Abbey's arms stood at attention as she looked at the dresser, and saw the music box, not smashed to bits, lid closed, sitting exactly where she had placed it when she moved into the room. She went over and opened it, and the dancer started to spin and the music play. Her face, both the dancer's and Abbey's, were plain and normal in the triad of mirrors on the inner lid of the box.

Abbey slammed it shut, killing both song and dance. She opened the top drawer of the dresser to shove the box inside, and saw it. The dark wooden handle. She grasped it, pulling it out slowly, exposing the intricately marked, carefully sharpened blade.

She sat on the bed, holding the hatchet in her hands, and cried.

21

 everal weeks had passed since the death of Barnes. Abbey finished all her antibiotics and was down to only the occasional Advil for pain. Marie and Chuck had been keeping close tabs on her, making sure she ate three square meals a day and snacks in between. She'd had plenty of rest, binge watched several new series on Netflix, and even spent some time out by the pool, getting some sun.

But she didn't go out at night.

She was uneasy—terrified, more accurately—and the dark is where fear lingered. When nighttime fell, she kept the lights on, the curtains drawn, and the television loud. Even so, during daylight hours when she could see Chuck and Marie moving about, when she knew they would be popping in on a regular basis, Abbey got into her own head. And in there she wallowed and worried, images of Suzy ripe in her mind and the taste of blood still fresh on her tongue.

It was time to go back to work.

"You sure about this?" Marie asked, handing Abbey a neatly packed lunch.

"Quite," Abbey said. She meant it. The work part, at least. What she wasn't ready for was seeing Suzy.

At least she won't have a hatchet in her skull. Hopefully.

"Here ya go," Chuck said, sliding a set of keys across the counter. They hit Abbey's glass with a sharp clank.

"What's this?" Abbey asked, picking up the keys.

"This is my fool-ass husband trying to break the dishes," Marie said, glaring at Chuck. "Also, it's the keys to the truck."

"Oh," Abbey said, setting the keys back down. "I couldn't."

"It's no trouble, dear," Marie said. "Just don't head out after work. We do need to run into the city from time to time, supplies and all."

"Running for ketchup at eight in the evening, of all things," Chuck murmured into his mustache.

"Oh hush, you," Marie said.

They didn't need ketchup, or anything for that matter. Marie was worried about Abbey and didn't want her out partying.

"Marie. Chuck. I'm fine. I promise. I'm walking there," Abbey started. Marie opened her mouth to protest, but Abbey raised a hand to stop her, "and I've already texted Scott. He's going to give me a ride home."

"Scott," Marie said, raising a brow.

Marie and Chuck exchanged a look.

"What was that?" Abbey asked.

"What was what?" Marie said, as Chuck ducked into the backroom.

"That look. You know you did it, you and Chuck. What's up with Scott?"

"Quite sure I have no idea," Marie said, wiping the already gleaming counter.

Abbey drummed her fingers on the menu in front of her.

"Well," Marie said, tugging at her hair, "he's a bit of a... scoundrel. Likes to court any ladies that come to town, the ones that happen to stay here. He and Jamie come out, more during the busy season, have some food here in the diner when they have a perfectly good restaurant right in Lamarque. Horny fools."

Jamie.

Abbey felt her stomach clench.

"Oh dear," Marie said, hurrying around the counter. "What is it? You've gone as grey as the undead."

"Jamie."

"You know Jamie?" Marie asked. "Oh dear, he's quite the player, too. And quite the arsehole, if you ask me."

Maybe not anymore.

"I've met him, but I don't really know him," Abbey said. "Tourist information center, yes?"

"Catch-all business, yes. He's got it made up there, living on his parent's legacy, not doing an ounce of work on his own. Ah well. He can do his business, and I'll do mine." Marie tapped Abbey's chest. "That is, unless he starts messing with my customers and friends."

Abbey stood from her seat, surprising Marie with a huge hug.

"What's that for?" Marie said, holding on tight.

"We *are* friends," Abbey said.

Marie pulled back and held Abbey's cheeks. "No dear. You're just a customer."

The two stared at each other for a moment before Marie burst out laughing. "Of course yer my friend, you silly goose! I like you. You're good people."

You don't know me. You're lucky you don't.

～

ABBEY LEFT THE MOTEL MUCH EARLIER THAN SHE NEEDED TO, leaving several hours leeway to get into town and to the school. The walk was actually only a half hour or so, but she wasn't going directly into work. She left herself lots of time, just in case, but didn't think she'd actually need it.

She didn't think time mattered, or even made sense where she was going.

She walked without thinking, following the path in the pink light of dawn, watching her feet rather than where she was going. As she expected—willed, even—the brush got thicker, almost impossible to walk through, until she stepped into the clearing. Faelith was tending to the fire, frying a fresh cut of meat in a crudely fashioned pan.

"Come," Faelith said. "Eat before work."

Abbey had anticipated that. The witch was a grandmother at heart, force-feeding delicious food even if she was already full to the gills. And the food was delicious, and the company just as sweet.

"Eat," Faelith said, handing Abbey a plate of berries and meat.

"This isn't rodent, is it?" Abbey said, sniffing the meat.

Faelith looked at her and shrugged. "Tasty meat. Won't bite you or run away."

"Touché," Abbey said, sinking her teeth into the mystery meal.

They sat together, eating quietly, sipping on a pleasantly aromatic tea that Faelith had bubbling over the fire. Abbey watched as the faeries woke, stumbling and groaning their way over to the fire to pick at morsels Faelith set on the ground.

"Not morning creatures," Faelith said, waving at the faeries before wagging a finger at Abbey. "You work too early."

Abbey laughed. "People have to work in the morning. Many much earlier than this."

"Ugh," Faelith said, snorting her disgust. "Night so beautiful. They miss it all." Her large, black eyes looked at Abbey. She pointed her crooked, boney finger in Abbey's face. "You miss the night."

"I don't like it," Abbey said.

"You do."

"Not really, no. Terrible things happen at night."

"Terrible things happen during the day. We see them clearer at night."

Abbey was quiet, contemplating as Faelith watched her.

"What was that, Faelith?"

"Maybe rodent, possible pig. I never tell," Faelith said, licking her lips.

"No, Faelith, not the food. That night, at the motel."

"Mmm," Faelith said, knowing. "You see."

"I see. What does that mean, I see?"

"You understand, when ready."

Faelith's eyes grew heavy and sad. Faelith stood from her stump and moved over beside Abbey. In her childhood, before she had met the witch, and even a few weeks ago, Abbey would have cringed at their proximity. Now, not only did she not mind it, she was calmed by it. If Faelith had been a person strolling down a city street, she would have been a horrible monstrosity, deformed and broken. Bald, gangly and large, black eyes and sharp teeth, bones contorted this way and that. But sitting by the fire in the light of dawn, Abbey saw something different. A woman, body weathered by experience, soul ripened by the same.

And she meant Abbey no harm.

She was her guardian angel.

"Abbey is strong woman," Faelith said, twirling a lock of Abbey's hair through her fingers. "Strong then, strong now. Stronger yet, once you realize."

"Realize what?" Abbey asked.

Faelith shook her head, huffing in exasperation. "Realize strength!" Faelith said, grabbing Abbey's breast. Abbey gasped and pulled away, and Faelith cocked her head.

"What," Faelith said, looking at her hand. "Just heart."

Abbey relaxed. "No, Faelith. Not just heart. Breast. Private."

Faelith stared.

"Sexual," Abbey whispered.

"Ack," Faelith said, screwing up her face and thumping her chest. "Sexual within." Faelith grabbed her own breasts and shook them at Abbey. "These just titties, like on cow."

Abbey laughed. Faelith stared a moment, then she laughed too, wobbling her breasts back and forth like she was putting on a puppet show. Abbey realized that she no longer noticed Faelith's nudity. She was no longer shamed by it.

Why should I be? It's hers.

Faelith's comfort in her own skin was absolutely beautiful.

"I have to go, Faelith. I don't want to be late for work."

Faelith was already tending to her business, touching talismans and picking herbs and flowers around the clearing.

"Time," Faelith mumbled. "Lots of time."

Abbey left the clearing, blowing a kiss in Faelith's direction. Although the witch's back was turned to her, she caught it.

IT WASN'T AS HORRIBLE AS ABBEY IMAGINED IT WOULD BE. IN THE days leading up to a stressful event, she'd inflate it with an ocean full of helium, imagining it as monumentally worse than it ever turned out to be. Abbey did just that. She imagined a barrage of questions, about that night at the bar, about her disappearance. About Jamie. She pictured the cops coming at her, arresting her for driving under the influence. She expected little Suzy to be absent without explanation.

None of that happened, of course.

"Abbey!" Maggie the receptionist jumped around the desk to greet her. "How are you feeling?"

"A little worse for wear, but much better, thanks."

"Well, glad to have you back."

"Abbey." Scott came out of his office, arms extended. Marie's disapproval echoed in Abbey's mind as Scott embraced her. "Glad to see you. Horrible thing, that accident. So happy you made it out okay."

"Me too."

"You feel up to jumping right into the class again? I'm sure Ashlynn would love a second set of hands. The kids have been right riled up this week."

"I'll be just fine," Abbey said. "It'll be great to have my mind back here."

Scott and Maggie looked at her.

"Mind? Back here?" Maggie said.

"As opposed to where?" Scott followed up.

You idiot, Abbey thought, cursing herself.

The world dulled to a tight silence, and Abbey felt wet breath on the side of her face. Faelith's voice spat in her ear.

Say your mind, woman. Not idiot. Not their business unless you want it to be.

The world reanimated, the sound of the fans again whirring in her ears.

"Uh… lots on my mind, is all."

Stop explaining, Faelith's voice breathed in her ear.

Abbey wiped at her cheek. "I'm fine," Abbey said. "Just excited to see the kids."

Liar. Faelith punctuated it with a cackle. Abbey couldn't help but crack a smile.

Ashlynn looked up from her desk when Abbey came in, looking more nervous than excited to see her.

"MISS ABBBEEEEYYYY!!!!" The children didn't care about Abbey's mysterious incidents, though. They ran to her, hugging her legs and telling her stories of new toys and gross meals and places they had visited.

Abbey gave lots of hugs and back pats before helping Ashlynn settle all the children down at their tables for snack time. Abbey made sure everyone had their fair share of goldfish crackers and that their water bottles were full. But mostly, she watched Suzy.

Suzy was fine, no cracked skull, visible blood, or missing leg. She seemed indifferent to Abbey's presence, and no worse for wear. Abbey spent a good portion of the day watching the girl out of the corner of her eye.

What is it? What am I to see?

Though quiet and sullen, she was a regular little girl. She played with toys, coloured pictures, ate, slept, and ran around outside like all the other children. The only thing that gave Abbey pause was that Suzy wasn't overly social, but not in a dysfunctional way. When it came time for group interaction, cooperative activities, and partner projects, Suzy did just fine. But left to her own devices, she preferred to play on her own. She didn't appear comfortable around anyone.

What secrets are you hiding?

Nap time came and went without incident, as did the rest of the day. Faelith didn't have any comments, the faeries didn't make an appearance, and no blood—phantom or otherwise—was spilled. At four o'clock the children started filtering out, parents coming to gather them one by one. Abbey was tired, but she was content. She knelt by the cubbies, helping kids put on backpacks filled with the artwork of the day. When Suzy came up, Abbey gave her a warm smile.

"Hey Suzy," Abbey said. "I had a great day with you. Did you have fun today?"

Suzy nodded, but didn't smile.

Abbey paused, waiting for faeries to come or blood to spill, but neither happened.

"Can I help you with your backpack?"

Suzy nodded and turned around. Abbey slipped the pack over her shoulders and opened it up to put Suzy's paintings inside.

"The puffy paint is delicate, so take it out carefully—"

Abbey stopped mid-sentence, the words caught like a punch in the throat. She had moved the contents of the backpack around, pulling out Suzy's lunchbox and some toys and books, including her journal. A red journal, leather-bound, with rainbow foil on the edges of the paper.

"Miss Abbey?" Suzy said, turning her head.

Abbey flipped open the journal. A black square was coloured on the inside of the cover, a black sharpie darkening the name of the owner. The *former* owner.

"Miss Abbey?"

Her name.

"Miss Abbey, is my painting okay?"

Abbey flipped through the pages. They were all there. The clearing, the faeries. The picture of the mower, the bloody rope…

"Abbey?"

Miss Ashlynn's voice drew Abbey's attention. She looked up from the journal—her journal—and found Ashlynn and Suzy staring at her.

"That's my journal," Suzy said proudly, trying to take it from Abbey. Abbey held tight.

"Where did you get this?" Abbey asked.

"It's mine," Suzy said, her voice and temper rising.

"Abbey, can you give Suzy her journal?" Ashlynn said.

Abbey and Suzy both held tight to the journal, until Abbey snapped out of it, releasing her childhood art into Suzy's possession.

"Okay then," Ashlynn said, eyes on Abbey. "C'mon Suzy. Let's get you out front."

Suzy looked back at Abbey, anger on her face as she stomped out of the classroom, clutching the journal to her chest. Abbey watched her go, a mixture of rage and sadness storming in her brain.

22

———

"I don't understand," Abbey said, pacing in front of the fire. "Why did she… how could she have that?"

Faelith said nothing, just sipped her tea out of a cup fashioned from a deer's skull.

"I'm close to that place, but not that close. And how did she get it? After all these years…"

"Home," Faelith said.

"What?"

"Home. Close to home."

Abbey glared.

"That was never my home," Abbey snapped.

Faelith took another sip.

"It wasn't! It isn't!"

"It's part of you."

Abbey stomped her foot, her younger self controlling her body like a marionette.

"Okay. Be that as it may, I don't understand why she has it. How she has it."

Faelith tapped her head with a red talon. "Use brain."

"What's that supposed to mean."

"Think. Logic."

"Yes, because my world is all about logic and reality," Abbey said.

Abbey looked around at the loitering faeries and the clearing and the impossible decor littering the trees.

"Real," Faelith said, winking.

Abbey moved to argue, but stopped. She didn't know how to argue it.

"Real is different from what many think," Faelith said. "Open mind."

"Back to the journal," Abbey said, sitting next to Faelith.

"Walk through it," Faelith said. She patted the stump by the fire, and Abbey sat. Faelith stood, leaving Abbey alone to watch the flame dance in the deteriorating light of the day.

"So helpful," Abbey muttered, watching as the wood glowed, flames licking the air. "Walk through it..."

Where had it been, her journal? That night, the night that Uncle Herman... Abbey had gotten scolded for the drawings, then tucked the journal under her mattress. That was the last time she had been in her room. The police hadn't even let her fetch a change of clothes when they removed her from the scene. She never went back.

Someone had to go there.

"Who went back?" Abbey said.

Faelith looked over from her garden, meeting Abbey's eyes with a great sadness in her own.

"Who?" Abbey demanded. "They sold the house, I heard. Child Protective Services asked if I wanted any of my stuff before the place was auctioned off. Surely, they would have tossed everything. And Anton..."

Abbey checked regularly. She had to. At first she felt sorry for him. He was a victim too, after all. Even worse, a victim that took the blame. Every so often, once in a blue moon, out of curiosity and fear and shame, she looked up the inmates at The Cranston Penitentiary. He was still there, simmering in his own mental breakdown.

"I need to find out what happened to the house. And our stuff."

Needed to, but didn't want to. Couldn't.

"It matter?" Faelith asked.

Abbey thought.

"Yes. It does. To me."

Faelith's mouth opened into a crooked smile. "Good girl."

Abbey bid Faelith farewell, blew kisses to the faeries, and charged off down the trail towards the motel.

DUNVEGAN CITY CITY MADE ABBEY TWITCHY.

Though small for a city, it still had double lanes of congested traffic, neon signs, apartment buildings, and a degree of hustle and bustle that made Abbey squirm in the passenger seat of Chuck's truck.

"Thanks for bringing me in," Abbey said.

"Glad you asked," Chuck said, reaching over and patting her hand. "Had to pick up some stuff, anyways. Are you sure you don't mind if I drop you off for the day?"

"Not at all. In fact, it's better for me. Gives me time to get the info I need and visit a few people."

One. One person.

"You can always catch me on my cell if you need to bail suddenly. You've had a rough go, and anxiety is a wicked monster."

"I'll be just fine," Abbey told herself as much as Chuck.

He parked the truck in the taxi lane in front of the municipal building, drawing honks and shouts from a couple cabbies sucking back cigarettes while they waited on fares. Chuck waved his arm out the window as Abbey started up the stairs.

Dunvegan City was large, but even larger was the scope of communities that it served; it was central to a swath of hamlets, towns, and villages, and the rural communities in between. It was almost dead center between Abbey's childhood residence and Lamarque. Although each town and hamlet had its own school district, emergency services, and medical center, Dunvegan City had the big guns: a massive hospital, all the commerce giants and main-branch banking, and the courthouse. That included all the legal records for the region.

The clerk at the records desk was a short, squat gentleman who wore his round glasses at the end of his nose and his pants at the southern shore of his nipples. He didn't look up when Abbey approached the window.

"Hello," she said. "Is this where I need to go to locate information about property seizure?"

"What property do you need?" he said, not looking up from his papers.

"482 Faulten Forest Drive."

Now he looked.

"And you are…?"

"Abbey Carsten."

"Carsten…" he said, firing up his computer without looking at it. "Abigail Carsten. Imagine that."

She worried her fingers together and clicked her heel against the white tile floor. The sound hammered through the cold, hard building.

"Been back there?" he asked, eyes now on the screen.

"No," Abbey said.

He stopped typing and looked at her, wanting more.

The dampness on her cheek, the hot breath in her ear.

He's snoopy, Faelith said. *Your pain is his entertainment. Don't give him anything you don't want to.*

Abbey stayed quiet and stared right back at him. He broke first, returning to his search.

"Here it is," he said. "What information are you looking for?"

"Subsequent owners, present owners, if that's there."

"Empty," he said.

"Since when?"

"Since you," he said, looking back at her. "The county took possession after the investigation, and it went to auction. Not a single bid."

"So what then? It's sitting out there, unattended?"

"In that area?" he said, looking back at the screen. "I imagine so. It's far removed from other residences and main roads. No one would notice or care if it went to seed."

"Hmmm," Abbey said. "So what about the contents?"

"The furniture and appliances and such?"

"Well, yes. And the incidentals. Clothes and books and whatnot."

"Cleared out. The big stuff would have gone to auction, and the little worthless stuff tossed by waste management."

Her childhood, discarded as useless rubbish. Everything she had, everything she was. Gone.

Were, Faelith breathed. *Everything you were.*

"Okay," Abbey said.

"Were you hoping to go back?"

"Why?"

"Oh, I don't know. Curiosity."

"Are you asking as a county employee?"

He looked up at her, his expression sour. "I guess were done here," he said, turning back to his computer.

Abbey walked out and hailed an Uber on her phone. She had told Chuck she was hanging around downtown, but he would never know. He didn't need to. He and Marie would worry. When the Uber pulled up, Abbey slipped inside, avoiding eye contact.

"Is this location correct?" the driver asked, pointing to the screen. "It's a half hour out."

"I know. That's fine."

The lump in Abbey's throat threatened to cut off her oxygen all together.

"Cranston Penitentiary, please."

~

THERE WASN'T A WHOLE LOT OF RIGAMAROLE INVOLVED IN getting into the jail. They were more interested in people getting out than people coming in. The Uber dropped Abbey at the gates, and she walked up the hill to the front entrance after signing in at the guard post. The clerk behind the glass recited the rules and policies, the words tired after rolling off her tongue for a long and tedious career. Abbey allowed the guard to search her, scanning her for metal and emptying the contents of her purse onto the sorting table. Once they deemed she wasn't smuggling in a means to death or escape, she was allowed in and escorted to the visiting area.

The visiting room was empty. There were half a dozen tables, but Abbey was the sole occupant of the room. The prison was full to capacity, and there was visitation every day. Abbey just happened to be the only one there on this particular day.

Perfect, she thought.

The heavy metal door opposite the one she had entered through clinked several times, the disengagement of several locks. Abbey wanted to get up, to run away and forget all of this. She wanted to buy another car, leave her stuff at the motel, drive away, and keep driving until there was no one or nothing.

Calm, Faelith breathed in her ear. *Hard, but not impossible.*

Anton looked horrible, but he was the man she'd imagined he'd be. Bigger, older, muscles bulging and skin prematurely aged and badly scarred. He was covered in tattoos of trees and crows. The guards led him shuffling to the table, wrists and ankles shackled. They locked the shackles to a steel ring on the floor. Abbey raised a brow.

"He's a feisty one," the guard said, giving Anton a cuff on the back of the head. "Moody and sour. Have fun. Holler if you need anything. You have fifteen minutes."

The door slammed shut, encasing the room in an uncomfortable silence.

"Hello Anton. How've you been?"

Anton shook, his legs bouncing furiously beneath the table. He was a mess, hair shaggy, thick, unkempt beard masking the majority of his face.

"How do you think I've been, cunt?"

Abbey heard a low growl in her ear.

"I'm sorry this happened to you," she said.

"Sure you are."

"I am."

Anton wrenched at the restraints and screamed.

"You did this, you vile bitch!"

Abbey didn't argue. She didn't put him in jail, but he was angry about being there. About everything.

But then again, he had always been angry.

"What happened that night, after…"

"After you murdered our family? After you destroyed my life?"

"Anton," Abbey said, unable to control her lip from trembling and the tears from rolling down her face. "You really think I could have done that? Me? A young girl?"

Anton's eyes filled with tears, his face scrunched in pain and anger. He started speaking, mere noises escaping as he formulated the thoughts. Took him a full minute to articulate what was on his mind — what had been in his head for all these years.

"They were horrible, Abbey. To you."

Abbey nodded, trying to catch her breath, stifling the sobs heaving out of her.

"I was horrible to you."

"It's okay," Abbey said.

No. No it's not. Not even close, Faelith hissed in her ear.

"But you *murdered* them, Abbey. Our family!"

Abbey took a deep breath, attempting to compose herself. "Anton. I did not kill them. Any of them."

"Oh really?" he said. "Then who did?"

Go on, the voice in her ear said. *Go ahead.*

"I-I don't know," Abbey said, looking down at her hands.

"LIAR!" Anton screamed, pounding his fists on the table.

Yes, you are, the voice said.

"Her," Abbey said, voice firm and sure.

The word silenced Anton's tirade and stilled the very air in the room. In the vents along the ceiling, Abbey saw the glow of silver lights.

"Her?" Anton said.

Abbey leaned forward, noting the guards out the window in her peripheral who were watching the entire interaction.

"The witch," Abbey whispered.

Stillness again, and silence, until Anton erupted into convulsive laughter, a terrifying, abrasive sound.

"You stupid twat," he said, swiping a tear from his eye. "You really are insane."

"I'm not."

"Yes. Yes you are."

"She's real."

"Damn it, Abbey, you fucking idiot. No she's not!"

I am as real as the blood coursing through your veins.

"Anton, did you go back to our house?"

"What? Why?"

"Just—did you? Did you take anything?"

"I called the cops, Abbey."

"And then what did you do?"

"I was freaking out," he said, looking away, his mind in a different time and place. "I remember screaming our information into the phone, then running outside, trying to talk to you… you were in a daze, Abbey. You weren't even responding. And Dad… he was hanging there… I couldn't… I climbed the tree and cut him down. I was holding him when the police arrived."

"And they took you."

"Yeah," Anton said quietly. "I went out swinging. Stupid, that. I was just a kid, traumatized, until I cold-cocked a cop. Then I was hostile. A suspect. My stupid snatch girlfriend reported abusive behaviour, and they found my prints all over the scene, the rope, the blood…"

He looked up at Abbey, childish panic in his eyes.

"Abbey… I was so drunk. They tested me, my blood alcohol level was so high."

Abbey let him continue, letting him simmer in his despair for a moment longer.

"I don't remember, Abbey. I don't remember coming home. My car was parked sideways in the garage, with Mom and Aunt Petal… I was passed out on that couch, remember? Lost hours…"

Abbey nodded, encouraging him to go on.

"Abbey," he leaned in, whispering. "I couldn't have done this, could I?"

"Anton. You're an asshole." He started to weep, and Abbey reached over, placing her hand on his arm. "But you didn't do this. She did."

He screamed again and swiped her hand off his arm.

"You fuck face," he spat at her, banging on the table again. This time the guards came in. "You really are a dumb cunt, you know? Stupid little girl believing in stupid little fairy tales."

Abbey sat back in her chair and watched the guards release the shackles from the floor. Anton stood, then lurched at one of the guards, driving a shoulder into the man's stomach. The other guard grabbed his baton in one hand and radio in the other, but Anton was fit and quick, kicking out a leg and swiping the guard off his feet. With both guards down, Anton took his few-second head start to run through the open door and back into the prison. The guards were on their feet in a flash, hot in pursuit, leaving the door to the prison open.

Abbey listened to the frantic footfalls and screams from beyond the door, a multitude of prisoners whooping and hollering for their liberated cellmate. Backup was summoned, and an alarm went off. Abbey tried to leave out the visitor's door, but it was locked, and no one was on the other side. Everyone had jumped into action to attend to the commotion.

Abbey sat down in her chair, listening as the chaos subsided, either moving farther away or the chase concluding. Soon, the alarm and voices were silent. She went back and knocked on the glass of the visitors door, hoping she could be excused from this hell. When her fist rapped the window, the lights went off. Immediately, the auxiliary lighting kicked in, bathing the prison in a red glow.

Just like the ballerina's motel room, Abbey thought.

The door to the cellblock was open. Abbey walked through it, into the dark row of cells. They were closed and silent.

"Hello," she whispered. Nothing but the tiny scurrying and squeaking of rats and mice, the occasional lump of fur running in front of her feet as she walked. As she passed by each cell, locked and dark, she saw that there were no prisoners contained within. Cell after cell was vacant except for rodents and roaches nibbling on crumbs and debris, evidence of prior human occupation.

"Abbey."

Anton's voice, calm and quiet, calling to her from the last cell on the left.

"Anton, I wouldn't do this if I were you."

"Do what, you pussy? You scared?"

Abbey kept walking, eyeing the fire extinguisher on the wall beside the open cell. She wanted to close her eyes as the cell came into view, but she didn't. She had to see.

Anton was there, bathed in red light, naked and erect.

"Like what you see, sweetheart? Just like you liked Uncle Herman?"

"No," Abbey said, angry tears spilling down her face.

Anton giggled, high and manic like a hyena, and blood seeped from the corners of his mouth. He stepped forward, his swollen shaft brushing against Abbey as he wrapped his hands around her throat and pulled her into the cell. She tried to scream but his grip was too tight, and he slammed her against the wall of the cell.

"Mom and Dad hated you, Abbey. The whole family did. That's why you killed them. A little tantrum. You were a disturbed child, and now you're a crazy woman. Witch, my ass. You're a psycho bitch!"

He squeezed harder, and Abbey's eyes started to throb. She clung to her last bit of oxygen as the red light bubbled with black spots, whirling and multiplying. Then a figure, darker than black and taller than Anton, stepped up behind him. The look on his face told Abbey that he could feel the presence, and she could see moist, hot breath land in a fog on his throat.

Faelith's mouth opened, revealing rows of pointed black teeth. She dislodged her jaw and opened her mouth wide, striking like a snake, biting Anton's neck and shoulder. He wailed, dropping Abbey and punching the air behind him. Faelith held tight, sinking her teeth in deeper until she had ripped a heavy chunk of flesh from Anton's body. He turned, looking right into Faelith's eyes, and she spat his flesh into his face. Urine dribbled from his now-flaccid cock, and he started mewling.

"Ma'am!" a guard yelled.

"Prisoner, on your feet!"

The guards burst into the room, one coming to Abbey, who was still seated in her chair, and two attended to the prisoner rolling around on the floor.

"What in the actual fuck is this?" the guard said, pulling Anton to his feet.

"She… fucking bit me!"

Anton groped at his neck, repeatedly touching his unmarked flesh and bringing his fingers to his face to inspect for blood. "She… right here! I can still feel it!"

The guards pulled his white shirt aside to examine his skin. "No sir," the guard said. "Nothing there."

"She didn't bite him," the other guard said. "We were watching the whole time. She never left her seat."

"Not her!" Anton wailed. *"Her."*

The guards looked around the room, then started smirking. "No other hers in this room, 'less there's something you're not telling us," the guard said, grabbing his crotch.

Anton looked at Abbey, eyes pleading. "Not real," he said, tears exploding down his face.

He struggled and bellowed as the guards yanked him out of the room, earning himself a few punches to the jaw. Abbey watched him go, and a certain peace washed over her.

Real.

bbey hoped for a quick pass-through on her way to the classroom. After the eventful weekend she'd had, she was tired, and wished to do as little peopling as possible.

"Hey! I thought I was giving you a ride the other day?"

Sigh.

Scott appeared as soon as Abbey came through the door. Maggie stood to greet her, but Scott pulled Abbey into his office before she had a chance.

"Yeah, I decided to walk," Abbey said. "I had a friend to see on the way, so I figured I might as well hoof it."

"If you need anything, please don't hesitate, Abbey. I know you're new in town, and—"

"Really Scott, I've got it."

Abbey pointed out his window to the parking spots out front. There was an old, white Volkswagen bug parked in one of the spots.

"Seriously?" he said.

"Yup. Chuck took me into town yesterday, and when I was looking around, I picked it up at the used lot. She's in pretty good condition."

"Yeah."

Scott examined his shoes, searching for his next words.

"Abbey, I know you and Jamie are, uh—"

"Speaking of Jamie," she said, deflecting the impending flirtation, "have you seen him around?"

"No, I haven't. I thought you might have seen him. You seemed pretty chummy when he first brought you in here."

One track mind, Abbey thought.

"We're not dating, Scott."

"Oh. Oh no, Abbey. I wasn't suggesting—"

"It's just, I've stopped by the mansion a few times, but there hasn't been an answer."

"Strange. He's usually all over town, and the doors over there are always open. I'll check up on him later."

She knew he had no intention of doing that. Jamie's absence opened a door for him, in his mind, at least.

"Thanks," Abbey said, opening the office door. "And thanks for offering to drive me, Scott. Very thoughtful."

She closed the door behind her, and as she passed Maggie's desk, Maggie winked at her.

"Way to shut him down, girl."

Abbey smiled.

The classroom erupted into a choir of hellos when Abbey came in the room. The day was filled with crafts and songs, and went generally smooth. During nap time, Abbey kept her distance from Suzy, but watched her closely, secretly scribbling in her journal. Suzy caught Abbey looking at her and shoved the little red journal under her nap mat.

During art, the children were doing free projects, painting and creating clay sculptures and the like. Suzy was sitting off on her own, head on the table, poking a lump of Playdoh with a pencil. Abbey took the seat next to her.

"Suzy? Are you okay?"

Suzy sat up, but didn't answer, and didn't look at Abbey.

"That's okay," Abbey said. "You don't have to talk to me. I just want to make sure you're having fun here. You always seem so sad."

Nothing.

Abbey leaned towards Suzy and whispered, "This art stuff is pretty boring, isn't it?" Abbey gave the Play Doh a firm stab with her pen.

Suzy didn't say anything, but her eyes flickered to Abbey, and one corner of her mouth teased a smile.

"Tell you what I think," Abbey said. "I think you are quite the artist."

Suzy looked up at her.

"Do you want to draw in your journal?" Suzy recoiled, but Abbey held up her hands. "I'm not going to take it from you. That wasn't kind of me the other day. I won't touch it, or look at it if you don't want me to."

Suzy looked at her for a moment, then spoke, her voice high and gravelly. "Yes, ma'am. I'd like that."

Abbey nodded towards the cubbies. Suzy hesitated, then went to her backpack, grabbing the journal and tucking it under her arm. Abbey got a box of pencil crayons and put it on Suzy's table, then left her alone to colour.

"Warming up to our little ice queen?" Miss Ashlynn said as Abbey watched Suzy from across the room.

"Guess so," Abbey said.

"Strange little bird," Ashlynn said.

"Everyone has a story," Abbey said.

Ashlynn looked at Abbey long and hard, then moved around the room, sharpening pencils and wiping noses. Once art time was over, Suzy slid the journal in her backpack and zipped it up before Abbey could even get across the room. Abbey debated about sneaking a peek during snack time, see what Suzy had been drawing and what else was in the journal, but decided she should earn the girl's trust. Then she could have a proper look at the secrets between those red covers.

Four o'clock rolled around, and the children started thinning out. Abbey was stuffing backpacks and tying shoes when she felt a tiny hand on her shoulder.

"Miss Abbey?"

Abbey turned.

"Yes Suzy?"

"Thank you for letting me draw in my journal," Suzy said, whispering. "Miss Ashlynn says we can't work on stuff from home."

"It's our little secret," Abbey said, holding her finger to her lips.

Abbey's heart clawed its way up into her throat as Suzy handed her the journal. "Here, Miss Abbey. I know you like it. You can borrow it tonight if you like. As long as you promise to give it back tomorrow."

Abbey struggled to find the words, but when she did, they came out a shaky squeak. "Pinky swear. Tomorrow."

"Suzy?" Ashlynn called from the door. "Your mom's here."

Suzy smiled and walked to the door where she took Ashlynn's hand.

Abbey waved at her with one hand, the other tightly clutched around the journal. *Her* journal.

IT TOOK SEVERAL ETERNITIES FOR THE FINAL CHILD TO BE PICKED up. Once the final parent was pulling out of the parking lot, Abbey went straight back to the classroom.

"Hey Ashlynn, why don't you let me clean up? I haven't been pulling my weight around here, what with the accident and all."

"Abbey, it's no trouble, and you're still recovering."

"No, I'm quite fine. And I'd feel better if you'd let me do this for you. Hell, it's my job."

"Well… okay. But don't stay too late. Maggie likes to get home to her cats." Ashlynn snickered and picked up her coat and bag. "Thanks."

"Anytime," Abbey said.

She watched as Ashlynn walked down the hall and out the front door. Maggie engaged the lock after she left, then looked down the hall at Abbey.

"Half hour, Maggie. At most."

"No worries," Maggie called, giving the thumbs up.

And a half hour was almost more than Abbey could take.

She had seen many of the pictures already, but their memory had grown fuzzy through the years. Abbey's fingers flipped through the pages, each more painful than the last. Tears stung her eyes as she reached the mower, the bloody noose in the tree…

Suzy's drawings were better, typical rainbows and four-legged creatures of some sort. A flower here, a sun there. Crude, simple, brightly coloured.

But they deteriorated quickly. The colours faded to blacks and browns and greys, and the faces flipped to frowns. The scenes turned from generic to hauntingly familiar, the trees, the clearing.

And Faelith.

A clear likeness of Faelith, but a Faelith in agony, arms torn from her body, blood seeping from a multitude of wounds over her breasts and abdomen, branches seemingly growing out of her flesh at every angle. Her legs were shattered, bone sticking every which way, and her eyes were hollow and empty, turned up to the moon. Her mouth was gaping open, a hole black and large as the sky, splintered trees poking out of her tongue and piercing her neck.

Abbey slammed the journal shut.

She needed to talk to Suzy about the journal. About Faelith.

"Hey Abbey."

Scott stood in the doorway, watching Abbey. She hadn't heard him come in nor felt his eyes on her.

"Just finishing up," she said as she slid the journal into her purse and stood from her chair.

"No rush," he said, walking into the classroom and shutting the door. "I just wanted to make sure everything was cool."

"Yep," Abbey said, noting that he was blocking the route to the only exit.

"What's that you were looking at? You seem upset by it."

"Well actually…"

Mix a lie with a truth. Makes the lie more palatable.

"I was a bit concerned about something Suzy drew in class today. I was going to pop by her place, maybe have a chat with her parents."

"Oh shit," he said. "She's a weird one, that Suzy. Let's see what she came up with."

"It's getting late. I'd like to get there before it's too late."

Scott's eyes darkened.

"Abbey, if you are going to speak to a parent, best to let the principle in on it. Now let's have a look."

There was no give in his voice, only force.

As Abbey pulled out the journal, she felt the growl in her head. Scott leaned on the desk, brushing against Abbey as he paged through the journal, humming and hawing at the pictures until he reached the sketch of Faelith.

"Jesus fucking Christ," he said. "That's an ugly bitch. Yes, for the love of God, please go talk to momma about this one."

He laughed and placed his hand on the small of Abbey's back.

Abbey felt fire through her body, a searing rage that pulsed along with her heart, growing more fierce with every chuckle and chortle out of the man's body. He was touching her and laughing at Faelith. At Faelith's pain and suffering. Her death.

"Stop," Abbey said.

Scott looked at her, smile large and eyes hungry. Her put his hand on her face.

"Oh Abbey, you gotta laugh. Life's not so glum."

"Please don't touch me," she said.

"Oh relax. I know you're Jamie's. Doesn't mean I can't be friendly with you."

His hand moved from the small of her back, and he gave her a light pat on the ass.

She didn't think. She didn't consciously engage her muscles or contemplate her movement. She thrust her hands out, striking Scott in the chest with both palms. He lifted off the ground, flying through the air, clearing Miss Ashlynn's desk and landing on the floor on the other side.

Abbey let out a gasp melded with a laugh. Aggression, release, and an unnatural showing of strength.

"Fuck me!" Scott yelped.

Maggie came bursting into the room, first looking at Abbey, then at Scott's feet up in the air on the far side of the desk.

"Um, everything okay in here?" Maggie asked. "I heard a crash."

"Fine," Scott said, jumping to his feet and rubbing his head. "Just lost my footing, is all."

He glared at Abbey, part anger, part bewilderment and fear.

He's just as surprised as I am.

"Okay then," Maggie said. "Abbey, you look ready to go. Are you leaving soon?"

"Sure am," Abbey said, closing the journal and putting it in her purse.

"Let me walk you out," Maggie said, looking back at Scott.

"Thanks," Abbey said, flashing Scott the biggest smile she had in her pocket.

When she and Maggie reached the front lobby, a smirk played on Maggie's lips. "Motherfucker," she whispered to Abbey. "Good for you."

Abbey nodded. "Hey Maggie, can you get me Suzy's address?"

"Sure can," she said, sitting behind the desk and pulling up Suzy's file. "Problem?"

"Need to have a little pow wow with her folks. Nothing major."

"She's an odd duck," Maggie said.

Aren't we all?

"She's a ways out, up the hill a bit."

Maggie scrawled the address down on a scrap of paper and Abbey punched it into her phone.

"Thanks, Maggie." Abbey looked back towards the classroom. "You gonna be okay here? On your own?"

"Oh sweetie. We've been there done that. He ran with his tail between his legs. He knows not to try it with me again. Prick."

Abbey smiled and headed out to the van, ready to take on the world with her newfound strength.

24

———

The sun was setting, casting an orange glow across the sky. The canola fields waved in the wind, bright yellow cloves of sunshine and nature in bloom. Abbey had a mind to keep driving, to live in the moment for ever and ever, but the fields would end. Nature would end, and life would not. And the unknown would nag at her until the end of time.

Suzy's house was in Picton, a little hamlet a fair jaunt out of Lamarque. If Suzy and her family had to get anything from the Dunvegan City, they would have a fair way to go. But Picton had most of the amenities needed for day-to-day life. A grocery store, coffee shop, clothing store, gas station, police station. It would do, for a simple life.

Abbey looked at her GPS as it led her on twists and turns, into a residential neighbourhood with tidy little bungalows and tight two-story houses. It was a lovely little spot. She pulled up to the address, a bungalow on the corner, and killed the engine. The house was painted dark green with a cape cod porch on the front complete with a swing. There were some riding toys strewn about the driveway, and an old Gremlin parked up alongside the house. When Abbey stepped out of her car and slammed the door, a figure moved in the window.

Here we go, Abbey thought, forcing herself to make the trek to the door.

The world passed in slow motion as Abbey walked towards the house. She looked at the people shuffling around the street, brightly lit pathways leading to the quaint homes, patio lanterns and bulbs hanging from decks and trees. It was magical. Abbey clopped up the steps to the front door and, without pausing to change her mind, gave the door a heavy rap, followed by a push of the bell. As she waited for someone to answer, she looked around, wondering who was home. Besides the car in the drive, there were a few parked on the street: a red truck, an old orange mustang with a blue door…

"Miss Abbey!"

Suzy came flying out of the house, smile on her face, and wrapped her arms around Abbey's legs. Abbey was surprised by the outpouring of emotion. Suzy looked so different with a smile on her face. She crouched down on one knee and gave Suzy a hug.

"Hey Suzy," Abbey said. "Are your parents home?"

"Hi Abbey."

Abbey looked up. Suzy's mom stood in the doorway in a flowing yellow sundress, dishtowel over her shoulder, long, red curls wrapped in a loose ponytail that flowed down her back.

"Gloria," Abbey breathed.

"Please, come in," Gloria said, stepping to the side. "We have some catching up to do."

~

THE LEMONADE WAS SWEET, A HINT OF FRESH STRAWBERRIES bleeding off into the lemon, tinting the pitcher a soft pink. Abbey sipped at the glass, playing with the ice in her mouth, watching Suzy play in the backyard.

"It's been so long," Gloria said, appearing at the patio doors with a plate of cheese and crackers in her hand. "You... it was so sudden. I didn't have a chance to say goodbye. And I didn't know how to keep in touch."

"It's okay," Abbey said.

The two women looked at each other, and Gloria fell into Abbey, giving her a heavy hug. "Oh Abbey," she said, tears wetting Abbey's shoulder. "I'm so sorry for what happened. For everything."

Abbey's started crying, too. A good, cleansing cry. They stayed in the embrace for a long time, holding each other and weeping. When Gloria let go, Abbey didn't feel uncomfortable anymore. She felt refreshed. They both laughed, wiping away tears and sniffling running noses.

"Why are you sad?" Suzy asked, running up to the patio.

"We're not sad," Gloria said, her peach smile practically glowing in the dusk. "We're just happy to see each other."

"But you just met," Suzy said, face scrunched in confusion.

"No, my love," Gloria said. "We knew each other long ago, well before you were born."

Suzy shrugged, not giving it much thought, and returned to her play, this time mounting the swing in the corner of the yard.

"So," Gloria said. "Tell me about you. What became of little Abbey?"

Abbey flustered a bit, and Gloria shook her head. "You don't need to talk about... that. Only if you want to. I meant, where have you been? Where did adult life take you?

"The east cost. Big city living," Abbey said. Gloria grimaced, and Abbey laughed. "Yeah, it was bloody terrible. Gave a decade of my life to rat-race living and corporate slavery."

"Is that why you came out here?"

"Yeah," Abbey said. "I missed simple living, nature, all that."

Gloria's voice quieted. "Did you ever consider going home?"

"Not for a single second," Abbey said with conviction. "I like the area, the nature out this way, but didn't want to be too close to that place. It was never home to me."

"I suppose," Gloria said. "Home is not really a place, but a state of mind. Not where you're living, but how you're living there. Who you're with."

Abbey's mind went back to the acreage, to the ugliness that plagued her memories. She tried to brush away her experiences, the people and the shit that transpired there, from the first day she could remember a harsh touch on her skin to the day everyone died. Without all that, it was a beautiful spot, surrounded by nature, a quiet refuge nestled in the countryside.

How beautiful it could have been...

But it wasn't. It was tainted with pain and shame, the ugliness of the dark side of the human condition.

Abbey shook her head to dust away the memories.

"And you," Abbey said. "You have a family."

"Yes," Gloria said, beaming at Suzy. Suzy smiled back, and Abbey noticed that she had the same peach smile as Gloria. "My little family."

Abbey looked at Gloria's hands, beautiful, slender, aged. Ringless.

"Are you married?" Abbey asked.

Gloria bit her lip. "No."

Abbey looked out at Suzy playing in the yard, happy in her own little world.

"You two live alone?" Abbey asked.

"I know what you're thinking," Gloria said.

"I'm thinking nothing," Abbey said, reaching across and touching Gloria's hand.

"Yeah. We live alone."

"Her Dad?"

"One night stand," Gloria said, cheeks glowing red. "Careless times."

"All times are careless," Abbey said, offering a smile. "Looks like it turned out all right."

"It was tough, raising her on my own. Children are expensive and needy. And it's just been her and me, no off time."

"Your family?"

"They don't approve," Gloria said. "I towed the line after you left, got a job in town after I was finished school, made some decent cash and moved up. Then," Gloria looked out towards Suzy.

"Shame," Abbey said. "She's a beautiful grandchild."

"I've made some stupid mistakes."

"And you've paid the price. Now enjoy the purchase."

Gloria worried a crimson ringlet through her fingers, looking lovingly at her daughter.

"This place is gorgeous," Abbey said. "Magical."

"It really is," Gloria said, perking up. "Got it for a steal. I could never afford a place like this—a damn house, for god's sake—but it was dirt cheap. Messy business here with the previous owner."

"Ugh."

"Naw," Gloria said, a flicker of excitement in her eye. "Nothing wrong with a bit of a ghost story, yes?"

Abbey laughed, and so did Gloria. "And you. So you're here now. And a teacher!"

"Assistant teacher," Abbey corrected.

"Whatever. Same deal. Good for you."

"Kids are shit," Abbey said, and both women burst into gales of laughter.

"Where are you living?" Gloria said. "Picton's a bit far from Lamarque, but there's nothing really out that way. Bought yourself an acreage with that giant, corporate nest egg of yours?"

"I wish," Abbey said. "I'm actually... I'm renting a place just outside Lamarque. Nice little spot, awesome landlords."

"That's great, Abbey. And how cool is it that you're Suzy's teacher?"

"Yeah, odd coincidence, that." Abbey steeled herself. "Gloria, I didn't know it was you here. I'm so, so glad to see you, but I came to talk about Suzy."

Gloria's smile faded. "Oh no. What has she done?"

"No, nothing. She's a wonderful girl, quiet and well-behaved. She does have this journal, though."

Abbey pulled the red journal out of her purse and placed it on the table beside the lemonade. Gloria stared at it, her eyes glossing over. Abbey thought she saw her lip quiver, just a touch, but it might have been a play of the shadows.

"This thing," Gloria said, reaching out and running a finger over the cover. "She never parts with this. Her most prized possession, I think."

"You don't approve?"

"It's not that."

Gloria didn't say more. She looked away from the journal.

"Gloria, where did she get this?"

Gloria looked up at Abbey, tears in her eyes. "It's all I had of you, Abbey. You were gone so suddenly, without a trace. Everything else in that place wasn't you. This was. A piece of you."

"You were there," Abbey said. "At the auction."

"No," Gloria said. "We went into the place before the auction came up—it took over a year, you know. Anyways, the house was empty, and there were stories, um—"

"Ghost stories."

"Yeah, I suppose. I mean a couple people… well…"

"Died there."

"Yeah." Gloria shifted in her seat. "So we went out one night, broke in, and had a look around. I saw the journal on your floor, and, I dunno, just decided it was okay to take it." Gloria erupted into full-on tears. "Oh Abbey, I'm so sorry. I'm a terrible person."

Abbey moved beside Gloria on the patio sofa, holding her friend in her arms while they both cried.

"What's so terrible about that?" Abbey asked. "I'm touched, actually. You wanted to remember me."

Gloria looked at Abbey, her eyes glowing like emeralds in the patio lighting. "Of course I did, Abbey. You were my friend. My best friend. I loved you."

Abbey felt a flutter in her stomach, swelling and tingling through her whole body. It was more emotion than she had felt in years. Ever. She brought her hand up and swiped a tendril of Gloria's hair out of her face, tucking it behind her ear. Gloria took Abbey's face in her hands, pulling her in and pressing her lips on Abbey's. Abbey cried as she felt that plump peach smile on her mouth, the tips of their tongues tasting each other. Abbey pressed her lips harder against Gloria, breathing her in.

"Mommy loves you, Miss Abbey."

Abbey pulled away, startled and embarrassed.

Suzy was standing at the edge of the deck, giggling. Gloria smiled. "Mommy does love her," she said, looking at Abbey, eyes warm and loving. "Stay for dinner?"

"I'd love too."

~

IT WAS LIKE THEY WERE YOUNG GIRLS AGAIN, GIGGLING AND drunk on sugary root beer. Though Suzy knew little of what they were saying, she laughed along anyways, the mood contagious. Dinner was delicious, take away from a local Chinese restaurant, and it paired well with the bottle of red Gloria had been saving for a special occasion.

"If this isn't special, I don't know what is," she said.

They laughed and chatted about everything from movies to television, and, once Suzy had gone to bed, obnoxious bosses, humorous drunks, and terrible sex. Time melted away, and soon it was midnight. Abbey finished her wine with a yawn.

"I need to go," she said, letting the last drops of the merlot slide onto her tongue.

"You sure?" Gloria said, running her finger around her glass.

"Yeah," Abbey said. "I work tomorrow. And your child has school."

"Yeah, I suppose," Gloria said. "Parenting is beautiful, but it's hard."

"Adulting is hard," Abbey said, setting off another giggle fit.

Gloria walked Abbey to the door, holding her hand. They exchanged another kiss, long and lingering.

"I'm so happy you're back."

"Me too," Abbey said.

"Want to get together this weekend?"

"Sure do."

Abbey turned and walked down the steps, like treading across clouds.

25

———————

The next month was beautiful. Perfect. Abbey and Gloria spent lots of time together, picnics in the park and mid-afternoon swims at the motel, Suzy squealing with delight with every cannonball and flip into the sparkling waters. Marie and Chuck loved Gloria and Suzy, but more than that they loved the fire that had been ignited in Abbey.

"A different person," Marie said as she set the tray of lemonade and chips down on the table by the pool.

"What did you say?" Abbey said, giving Marie a coy smile.

"You are a new person, Miss Abbey. Finally, some life in ya."

Abbey smiled. She felt it, the beginnings of happiness. An awakening.

"Life feels good," Abbey said. "Hasn't felt so good before."

"Move in with us," Gloria said.

Abbey swallowed her lemonade with a heavy gulp. "Say what?"

"Move in with us. We have two spare rooms, and you own nothing," Gloria said, shaking her finger at the motel room. "Come live with Suzy and I."

"I couldn't."

"You say that like you'd be a burden." Gloria leaned over and touched Abbey's hand. "It's for me, not you. I want you there, Abbey."

"Oh, girl. Don't make me kick ya outta your room," Marie said. "Busy season is upon us, and I'm gonna need the space."

Abbey looked back and forth between Marie and Gloria, both bursting at the seams for her answer.

"That'd be lovely. I'm in."

Gloria squealed, jumped into the pool, and hugged Suzy. "Suzy, Abbey's moving in with us!"

"Really?!" Suzy shrieked, and both Mom and daughter splashed like seals, cheering and screeching their excitement.

"So happy for you," Marie said, wiping away a tear. "How far you've come in such a short time."

"Not so short," Abbey said. "Took too long to get to this peace."

"But you are here now."

Abbey never imagined she'd reach this point, where she could feel content, happy, and excited about what the future held.

After an afternoon of swimming and snacks, and discussion about shopping trips for furniture and decor, everyone was deliciously tired. Suzy and Gloria changed into dry clothes for the ride home, and Marie packed some food for the road.

"Always the mother," Abbey said, kissing Marie on the cheek.

"Someone's gotta take care of you girls."

Faelith.

For the first time in a long time, Abbey's mind wandered to Faelith. She hadn't thought of the witch, or seen neither her nor the faeries since she had rediscovered Gloria. A twang of guilt strummed her heart, but disappeared as quickly as it had appeared. Abbey felt fingers on her hair, stroking her head, and a comforting pat on her arm. She spun around, but Gloria was still in the motel room getting changed.

"Everything all right dear?" Marie asked, looking over Abbey's shoulder.

"Everything's just fine," Abbey said. "Wonderful."

ABBEY LATHERED HERSELF WITH COCONUT-SCENTED SOAP, washing the chlorine out of her hair and off her body, then wrapped herself in the bathrobe and stretched out on the bed. Her skin was pink from the sun, and she was exhausted from all the fresh air and laughter. As tired as she was, she was also giddy, filled to the brim with excitement.

I'm moving in with Gloria.

Other than Faelith, Abbey had been alone her entire life, even as a small child. She had never lived with anyone she loved, anyone that made her feel happy and safe.

Abbey laid on her back and looked at the dark ceiling, imagining scenes in the stucco. A house of her own on a sprawling piece of land. Gloria and Suzy playing in the yard and fresh steaks on the barbecue. Faelith was there, too, part of the trees, faeries lighting the night sky.

The pool light came on outside, sending a silver glow through Abbey's open curtains. Abbey closed her eyes and let the light dance through her eyelids, aquatic ripples, peaceful and quiet. She heard splashing in the pool, a soft lapping, growing closer.

Abbey sat up in bed. As far as she knew, no other guests were staying at the motel, and Marie and Chuck weren't much for swimming. Besides, they had gone to their trailer an hour ago to catch the beginning of their evening of Unsolved Mysteries and The Twilight Zone. Abbey went to the window and saw someone swimming in the pool. The walkway and overhead pool lights weren't on, so she couldn't make out who it was, only a silhouette moving through the water. Abbey tied up her robe, shoved the key card in her pocket, and stepped out of the room. She walked through the gate into the pool area and peered into the water.

The swimmer was coming towards her, bobbing up and down

with each stroke, taking slow, calculated breaths when they were above the water. As the person got closer, Abbey realized who it was.

"Gloria?"

Gloria reached the steps, her red curls loose over her shoulders as she came up for air.

"What are you doing here? Not that I mind, at all, but you just left. And where's Suzy?"

Gloria came up one step, her hair hanging heavy over her bare shoulders. She took another step and her hair cascaded over her milky-white chest, covering her bare breasts.

"Holy shit," Abbey whispered. She looked around at all the windows, knowing full well that she was the only occupant of the motel.

Gloria took another step, exposing her stomach, and the soft ginger line of her pubic hair.

"Gloria." It was all Abbey could say. They had been close, sharing brushes of skin and tender kisses, but had yet to be intimate. It was overwhelming.

Gloria stepped out of the pool, skin wet and glowing in the silver light. She walked to Abbey and kissed her, her breath hot and quick.

"Abbey," she said as she breathed into Abbey's mouth.

Gloria's hands found the tie on Abbey's robe, loosening it and sliding her hands inside. The air was warm on Abbey's skin as the robe fell to her feet, but the water on Gloria's skin was cool, enticing gooseflesh to rise over her body. Gloria took Abbey's hands and walked backwards, leading her down the steps into the water.

They stood there in the silver light, submerged to the throat, staring into each other's eyes. Abbey's hands floated up in the water, finding the moon of Gloria's breasts, sliding her fingers over her erect nipples. Gloria put her hands on Abbey's waist and pulled her in until their breasts pressed together and lips were touching once again. They moved, bodies sliding, grinding against each other, hands groping, legs wrapping, twisting through each other, pushing and rubbing. Gloria moaned into Abbey's mouth and thrust her against the side of the pool. Abbey grabbed the side of the pool and let her head fall back while Gloria's hands pushed her, moving inside her.

Abbey saw stars. Her body tensed, her mind flashed white, and all the toxicity rushed out of her. All the pain, the loneliness, the humiliation, replaced by harmony, pleasure, ecstasy.

Abbey relaxed, her body spent. She brought her head up, thrusting her hips forward, hungry for Glora's touch. She reached into the water, running her fingers through Gloria's hair and pulling her close.

But Gloria didn't come close.

Gloria wasn't there.

Abbey let her feet sink to the pool floor and lifted her hands out of the water, along with clumps of crimson hair.

"Gloria?" Abbey said, her voice high and frantic. "Gloria!"

Abbey looked through the pool, frantically groping through the water, tangled in webs of hair. The hair was so thick, it covered the surface of the pool, dimming the light to burgundy. When Abbey reached the center of the pool, she found Gloria, floating face down. She grabbed her by the arms and swam with her to the step, dragging her out onto the deck. Abbey started ripping hair away, exposing patches of white skin, piling the hair on either side of Gloria's body. She rolled Gloria on to her back and pulled the hair away from her face.

Abbey screamed.

Gloria's face had decayed, blue flesh eaten away in chunks, exposing her teeth, cheekbones, and the tendons in her neck. Her eyes were milky white, blood trickling from the corners, forming in droplets on the end of her lashes.

Notrealnotrealnotrealnotreal.

Abbey closed her eyes, rubbing them so hard they hurt, then opened them again.

Her robe was laying ten steps from the pool, crumpled in a pile on the deck outside her motel room. The deck was clear. No hair, no blood, no body. Abbey turned and looked at the pool. Clear, no hair.

No Gloria.

Abbey became acutely aware of her nudity, her groin still throbbing and nipples erect. She scampered out of the pool and scooped up her robe, wrapping it tightly around herself and fumbling for her key. She slammed her door, crawled under the covers, and cried, screamed into her pillows, punching them and cursing the world. She sobbed until her pillows were soaked, her body spent, and she fell fast asleep.

26

Abbey walked in with coffee, a peace offering for being late. Ashlynn grabbed her cup, sucking it back like a much-needed drug, and gave Abbey a thumbs up.

"Perfect," she said. "Caffeinated diabetes. My favourite."

"Sorry," Abbey said, taking off her coat and tossing it behind the desk. "Late night."

"It's fine, really. Lots of kids are out with that cold going around. And I'm okay with that. I have my sister's bridal shower this weekend, and I *cannot* get sick."

The children were playing at their centers in the classroom, so it took Abbey a minute to get a full count, but she figured out there were six missing so far, not including the four due to arrive before circle time.

"Yikes," Abbey said. "That is a lot."

"And we won't be getting any more," Ashlynn said, giving a thumbs up and pumping her fist.

"What?" Abbey said.

"The last four are out, too. No more coming today. I told you, nuclear snots."

Ashlynn started doing a goofy happy dance, and Abbey felt panic rise like bile in her throat.

"Suzy?"

"Out," Ashlyn said. "Kid's never been sick here before. She was due. Mom phoned in this morning."

"Really."

Circle time started, and Abbey clapped and sang like a trained monkey, not hearing a single word she was saying. She went through the motions of the day, but all she could think about was Suzy. And Gloria, those milky white eyes…

By the time the last child left, Abbey felt like a caged animal pacing for release. She went to the front and stopped to talk to Maggie.

"Hey, Maggie, what did Suzy's mom say when she called in this morning? Suzy had a cold?"

"Strange family," Maggie said, rolling her eyes. "Mom sounded right rattled. Said 'things' weren't well. Hung up before I could wish her a speedy recovery."

Abbey didn't say goodbye to Maggie. She charged out the door and into her car, spraying gravel as she sped out of the parking lot.

GLORIA'S CAR WAS IN THE DRIVEWAY AND HER LIGHTS WERE ON. Abbey threw the car in park and sprinted to the door, banging it and ringing the bell at the same time. After barely ten seconds, Abbey banged again, poking the doorbell with each smash of her fist.

"Gloria! Suzy!"

No one answered. Not after one minute, not after two. A few of the neighbours poked their heads out curtains and peered through blinds, trying to see who the crazy lady was that was making all the racket. Abbey reached in her pocket and grabbed her phone, trying Gloria's number for the umpteenth time as she passed through the gate and walked around the back of the house. She rattled the knob and pounded on the glass, but there was no movement or sound from inside.

Abbey dropped to her knees and slid the doormat to the side, searching for a key, but Gloria was too clever for that. She looked around, trying to see where else a key might hide, and found a rock that was out of place. Not out of place if you weren't looking for something out of place, but a beacon if you were. Sure enough, she flipped it over, and there was a key duct taped to the belly. She unlocked the door and burst inside, calling out names and running from room to room.

"Gloria! Suzy!

The kitchen.

The living room.

The bathrooms and the master bedroom.

Suzy's room, all painted pink and covered in glitter.

By the time she reached the office at the end of the hall, she had lost hope of finding them there tonight. She went in and sat at the desk, head in her hands, foot tapping an aggressive staccato.

"Relax Abbey," she said to herself. "They're just out. Doctor, probably."

Faelith's voice cut through the silence of the house.

She would have called you.

"Maybe," Abbey said. "Unless it was urgent."

You know that's not it. You feel it.

Abbey couldn't argue. She did feel it, deep in her bones. Something was wrong. Very, very wrong.

A fluttering sound rattled in the hall, the rapid beating of wings. Abbey poked her head out and saw a faerie bouncing off the door of the master bedroom, repeatedly bashing its head against the wood.

"Hey, stop!" Abbey said, walking over to the little creature. The faerie landed on her shoulder, one tentacle winding through her hair, one pointing into the room.

"What?" Abbey said, following the line of the limb.

The faerie sputtered and purred, wrapping a tentacle around Abbey's arm and trying to pull her into the room.

"I already checked in here," Abbey said, giving the room another once over.

The faerie floated off her shoulder and settled on the carpet next to the bed, clicking and chattering as it paced back and forth like a chicken, bobbing its head. Abbey knelt down on the carpet, and her knees found a wet spot. She sat back on her haunches and her hair floated up around her face.

The room was suddenly an aquarium filled with water, furniture and books and clothes floating around, faeries swimming to and fro, their silver light bouncing off Gloria's belongings. The bed stayed put, grounded by its weight. Gloria was there, kneeling on the bed, hands bound behind her and a blood-soaked gag in her mouth.

Abbey swam to the bed and clawed at the gag, screaming bubbles through the water while Gloria's bloodshot eyes rolled up into her head. Then, like a plug had been pulled from a drain, water rushed out the door, draining down the hall, pulling Abbey away with the current. Abbey banged off the walls, struggling against the rapids until she was carried out the front door on a wave and landing on the front lawn.

A man walking by stopped and rushed over to Abbey.

"Oh my goodness," he said, helping her to her feet. "You all right, ma'am? Quite the tumble off the porch."

She was dry. Her clothes, her hair. And the front door was closed.

"I'm fine," she said. "Just not paying attention, I guess."

He looked at her for a long moment as she sucked in deep breaths, shivering in the warm air.

"Okay," he said. "You here for Gloria?"

"Yeah," Abbey said, looking up at the house. "You know her?"

"Kind of," he said. "I see her every day. I'm Joe," he said, shaking Abbey's hand. The name tag on his apron confirmed he was telling the truth. "Barista at the coffee shop on Main Street. She buys a latte from me every day. Not today, though. Hasn't missed a weekday since I've been around, which is longer than she has."

"Never missed a day, huh?"

"Nope." He looked up at the house. "She okay?"

"No," Abbey said. She gave him a shrug and got in her car, leaving him on the lawn, bewildered.

~

FAELITH WASN'T THERE.

Abbey walked the trail from one opening to the other and back again, but the clearing never appeared. Abbey was frantic, needing her witch to help her make sense of what was going on.

"Gloria's gone," Abbey said out loud. "She's disappeared. She needs me, and so does Suzy."

Faelith didn't answer. She wasn't there.

She left me, too. Again.

Abbey tried again and again, walking off the path, zig-zagging through the trees, but Faelith never appeared. No camp, no silver glow from the faeries. Nothing.

Abbey screamed into the trees, fists clenched and tears streaming down her face.

"Where are you?"

~

AFTER BEGRUDGINGLY RETURNING TO THE MOTEL, ABBEY took enough medication to down a moose, and slept off the hours until morning when she could start her hunt

"I wouldn't worry," Marie said, after pelting Abbey with a lengthy inquisition.

Marie slapped a plate of bacon and eggs down on the counter.

"No thanks," Abbey said, pushing the plate away. "Don't feel much like eating."

"You may not feel like it, but you must eat," Marie said, stern direction in her voice. "You need to fuel the system, if you're going to be charging around on this wild goose chase, searching for this dame who's not likely missing. It's been a day, Abbey. She could be doing anything."

"No, something is wrong."

"Maybe so," Marie said, "but you need energy to find your answers. And more energy to help if there actually *is* something wrong. So eat, then knock yourself out sleuthing around."

Abbey agreed. She was brutally hungry, having skipped dinner the night before. She downed the bacon and eggs in hefty gulps, and Marie packed her some pastries and coffee for the road. Abbey raced out the door, and Marie called after her.

"Let me know when you find her, so I can dole out a hefty serving of I told you so!"

"Will do," Abbey called back as she jumped in her car.

MARIE WATCHED AS ABBEY SPED AWAY, TERRIFIED AND EXCITED, hopeful and concerned.

"She be all right," Faelith said, locking fingers with Marie.

"I know, and I hope so."

"She strong," Faelith said.

"Enough?"

Faelith turned to Marie and stroked her cheek. "You been good helper, Mahree."

"It's what I do," Marie said, pecking Faelith on the cheek. "It's what we all do."

The two women smiled, eyes wet with tears. Faelith tucked a sprig of hair behind Marie's ear, then walked towards the woods.

"Faelith?" Marie said, a tear rolling down her cheek.

Faelith turned. Marie could see, in the light of the moon, that Faelith's cheeks were wet, too.

"Goodbye, old friend."

"Farewell," Faelith said.

bbey pressed the pedal to the floor, ripping to town as fast as the old car would take her. Like a reel from an 8mm, images flickered in Abbey's head: Gloria floating in the pool, bound in her room in Picton, Faelith tortured and seeping blood from branches speared through her body. Abbey was so engrossed in worry and torment that she hadn't realized she'd been driving for too long.

The road kept going, twisting and turning, forest at both her right and left thick and unbroken—no turns, no signs, no lights. Abbey stepped on the gas, screeching around turns, but the road kept going and going, the forest in the ditches thicker and thicker.

You need to go.

Faelith's voice came from everyone and nowhere, in the cab of the car and radiating through the trees.

"Go where?"

You know.

"No, I don't!" Abbey screamed.

She drove, anticipating that at any moment, after the next turn, then the next, she would see the lights of town ahead.

To her.

"I'm trying to go to her. I don't know where she is."

You do.

"Fuck!"

Abbey cried, blinking hard to clear the tears so she could navigate the winding road. The town never came, just more road, more solitude.

Find yourself.

"I don't know what that means."

You will.

Abbey was quiet, watching the road ahead, thinking about Faelith's words.

Save them. Find your power.

"Faelith, I don't have time for games."

Go where you want to be. Where you always wanted to be. What you always wanted to be.

"This isn't about me, Faelith. This is about Gloria. I will not go anywhere until I find her! She's here somewhere, and I'm gonna—"

Faelith cut her off with a scream and a growl, a gnashing of teeth in her ears.

Fine. Have it your way.

Be driven out.

Lamarque suddenly came in to view after the last of a hundred turns. Abbey slowed, passing the businesses that were just waking for the day. She shuddered, Faelith's attack fresh in her mind.

After turning the corner heading to the school, Abbey pulled over to the side of the road and drifted to a stop. Red and blue danced off the trees, a stunning light show in the pink of the dawn. Police cars were scattered about, parked at the fire station and in the driveway of Jamie's mansion, angled across the street to block traffic from passing through. Officers were out in bright yellow coats, cordoning off the area in tape that matched their outfits.

A barrier of police cruisers lined the road, and there was a flurry of activity inside the mansion. Police officers hustled about, CSI's went in and out with baggies and boxes, detectives stood on the porch talking to firefighters who had wandered over from next door. Through the noise and activity, Abbey could hear crying from behind the mansion, a voice full of grief and panic.

Abbey floated around the building—as if riding a cloud in a dream—until she reached the back yard and the perimeter of the trees. A concentrated mass of officers had gathered at the cemetery, solemn expressions on tired faces, one vomiting in the bushes. Scott was there, crying and yelling, officers holding him as he struggled to pass through the lychgate.

"Scott?" Abbey said, approaching the crowd. A few officers looked towards her, but made no move to speak to her.

"Abbey?" Scott said, wiping his nose. "Oh Abbey, you said, but I didn't listen."

"Scott, what are you going on about?"

She already knew. Her stomach lurched, and she resisted the urge to run.

"Jamie, Abbey. You told me you couldn't find him—that he wasn't answering. A month, Abbey. A fucking month... *over* a month and I never checked. I assumed he had fucked off with some tramp like he always did, stayed away a spell to get a good piece of ass, maybe even run away with her. But not this."

He lunged at the cemetery again. This time the officers properly restrained him and pulled him away from the scene. As he was dragged towards the street, arms wrenched behind his back, he screamed back at Abbey.

"What did you do? You knew! You knew about this! It was right after you got here. After Jamie met you! What did you do, you bitch!?"

Abbey didn't look back at him as his screams faded off in the distance. She watched the cluster of officers at the edge of the cemetery who were looking but not really looking at something in the trees. She walked to the lychgate and leaned in to have a look.

"You can't be here ma'am," an officer said, holding up a hand.

"What happened?" Abbey asked, standing on her toes, trying to sneak a peek through the crowd.

"Did you know the victim?"

"Victim?" Abbey said. "Jamie?"

The officer nodded. "That Scott gentleman seems to think you knew him."

Abbey pushed her way through the gate, skirting the officer who didn't seem too interested in stopping her. He seemed interested in observing her reaction. She passed through the people, some in uniform and some not, until she was standing deep in the cemetery, gravestone at her toes, trees lurking overhead.

Jamie was there, in the center of the cemetery, bound to a massive wooden stake with hay and braided sweetgrass piled high at the base. His skin had melted off his bones, leaving his body inside out, a glistening mess of blood and bodily fluids. His eyes were lumps of charcoal, and his hair and pubic hair singed to a crisp.

Abbey gagged, suppressing the urge to scream and vomit.

"Horrible," the detective said. "And strange."

The coroner was up on the heap of hay and grass, scraping and bottling samples while CSI's were snapping pictures from all angles.

"Hypovolemia and first degree burns, as if he was burned alive," the detective continued. "Odd, though. No signs of fire on the surrounding materials."

The CSI's were bagging the grass at Jamie's feet, green and yellow, not a mark of black or ash. And the wood he was bound to, a heavy stake, not so much as an ember scar.

"Now tell me, sweetheart. What's your name?"

Abbey looked at the detective. He had his notebook open, pen pressed to the paper, expectant eyes focused on her.

"A teacher," Abbey said, breathless. "At the school. On my way to work, I... I saw the commotion."

"You have any relationship with the deceased?"

Abbey looked up at the body on the stake, blood and fluid still seeping from the blisters.

Be driven out.

"I had nothing to do with this," Abbey whispered.

"Didn't say you did," the officer said, clearly suspicious. "Maybe you could come back to the station with us, in Dunvegan City, answer some questions."

"Do I have to?" Abbey said. "I'm feeling a little woozy... bit upset over this... and I need to get to work."

"The school, you say?" the detective said, jotting something down on his notepad. "You'll be there all day?"

"Yes sir," she lied.

"We'll be talking to you," he said, tipping his hat. "Now you best stay out of the way."

"Yes sir," she repeated.

She looked at Jamie once more. His eyes were screaming, filled with fire and terror.

Abbey got back in her car and did a U-turn, heading full speed towards Picton.

GLORIA'S PLACE WAS NO LESS MENACING IN THE MORNING THAN it was in the evening or at night. Abbey entered through the back door, using the key on the rock, and immediately went to the master bedroom to ensure that Gloria was not tied up on the bed. After making the rounds—double, triple checking that Gloria and Suzy still weren't in the house and hadn't been there since her last visit—Abbey settled in the office once again. She rifled through the desk, sifting through mail, receipts, anything that might help her figure out where Gloria had gone.

Her car's in the driveway.

"Shut up, Faelith."

Abbey kept looking even though she knew Faelith was right. Gloria didn't leave under her own steam. Abbey had already thought of that. The car was there, as were their suitcases, toiletries, clothes. Suzy's favorite dolly, Rosa, still sat on her bed.

Suzy.

Abbey and Gloria had never talked about Suzy's father. Perhaps he came back in the picture, decided he wanted his family back.

Did Gloria go with him? Leave me here, decide on a better life?

But again, the car. The clothes and toothbrushes. Rosa.

Abbey pulled open the filing cabinets, searching for papers mentioning Suzy's father, but found nothing more than bills and mortgage statements. She looked up and down the bookshelves, the collections and first editions, the ornaments.

The photo albums.

Abbey sat on the floor, picking off albums and flipping through photos. Lots of Suzy, riding a bike, Gloria holding her as an infant, them looking lovingly into each others eyes. Abbey started crying, tears dripping onto the pages, discoloring the photos. There were photos of Gloria in the hospital, propped up in bed, holding a freshly-born Suzy in her arms, umbilical cord still attached.

But no dad. No one but hospital staff.

"Where are you, you fucking dick?"

Where you *should be.*

Abbey paused at Faelith's comment.

"So I'm right. He has her."

Faelith said nothing, but Abbey swore she could hear her, sipping tea from that skull.

There were pictures of Gloria in her twenties, plenty of friends and men, but no one that looked like a lover. Abbey did the math in her head, trying to figure out what year Gloria would have gotten pregnant. She flipped to the photos around that time, evaluating each guy, trying to spot a resemblance to Suzy.

Then a photo, a single snapshot on its own page. The guy wasn't in any other photo. Abbey stared at it, her heart aching and tears filling her eyes. She peeled the photo off the page and sat at the desk. Her hands shaking, she fired up the desktop computer and launched into a search. Took some digging, and some willful attempt to calm herself enough to do so, but she found what she was looking for. What she didn't want to find.

The questions she never wanted to ask. The ones never considered the answers to. The ones she blocked from her mind.

Year. Crime. Conviction.

Anton, manslaughter.

Self-Defense, the lawyer argued.

Self-Defense, the jury decided.

Couple years of jail time.

Out for good behaviour, around the time Gloria conceived Suzy.

Abbey fingered the picture, a young Gloria, red curls draped over freckled shoulders, Anton standing behind her.

Charged for rape, battery, and assaulting a police officer on arrest.

Life sentence.

Abbey threw up in a nearby garbage can, crumpling the photo in her hand as she heaved.

You know, Faelith said.

"I know," Abbey replied.

28

―――――――

The drive was long, but not long enough. Abbey needed to get there, but didn't want to. Everything in her life had been leading her there—no—*pulling* her there, demanding her attention and presence. The darkness was at its peak, the moon high in the sky but shrouded by cloud cover, and the lights few and far between on that lonely stretch of highway.

It was the middle of the night when she arrived, nearly 3am on the dot. She travelled the last few kilometers slower than all the ones before that, the familiarity of the scenery and emotion lightening her foot on the pedal. She recognized everything—every tree, every mailbox, her school as she rolled by, the alleyway where she and Gloria had shared laughs and root beers that had earned her a severe lashing.

The driveway spotlight was on, spilling a yellow carpet to greet her as she pulled the car off the country lane and up to the old two story house. It was quite different from what she remembered, vines and mold growing up and out of every brick and crevice on the exterior wall. Nature had conquered the property, the grass blanketing the driveway, roots grabbing hold beneath the gravel. The garage had rotted and collapsed, the red paint weathered to naked wood and the exposed rafters turned home to all manner of rodents and birds.

Abbey parked the car across the end of the drive, hopefully blocking Anton if he decided to flee.

And then what will I do? she thought, but that thought didn't stall her. She marched up to the front door, taking care not to fall through the holes in the rotten deck. Father's porch swing was lopsided, hanging by one rusted chain, the wind blowing it against the side of the house, a war drum warning her arrival. Father's mason jar full of cigarette butts was still beside the swing, the butts long since decayed into a brown sludge of tar and rot.

She could taste Father's breath still hanging there on that porch.

The inside of the house was akin to the outside, weeds and green growth occupying surfaces previously uninhabitable, the counters, floor, and carpet a veritable garden. The whole house smelled of earth, damp and loamy. The television still hung on the wall, the remote still sat on the couch where Anton had left it when they went to witness Uncle Herman's final stand.

Abbey walked up the stairs, rotting wood splintered through carpet soggy from rain. She remembered the many times she had walked up those stairs, wishing she would never wake up to walk down them again.

Anton's room was a mess, as were all the rooms on the top floor. There were massive holes in the ceiling, exposing the upper floor to the elements of the last decade and then some. There were old, broken shingles that had fallen through, littering her bed with black crumbles that marred her floral blanket. Abbey stood in her room, feeling the heat of Uncle Herman's body behind her.

She walked down the stairs, then down again into the murky, muddy depths of the basement. With no one around to pump out the water when it flooded, the basement had become a swamp, ankle-high water reeking to high heaven of all manner of sewage, rotten food, and dead rodents. The washer and dryer had been gutted, becoming home to some sort of woodland creature that had made cosy nests in both, twigs and garbage and old fabric tightly packed into neat little beds.

"You fucking pussy."

Abbey didn't turn to the sound of Anton's voice. She knew he was there and where he was. She had smelled his evil from the end of the drive.

"Where is she?"

"Who? Your pretty little girlfriend?"

His voice was shaking, unsure.

Abbey turned and saw the quivering mess that had once been her brother. He was still that, but now even less. A pathetic excuse for a human or animal.

"Anton, you are sick."

"No, Abbey, you're the one who's sick. A fucking witch, Abbey? You believe that shit? C'mon, you aren't a little girl anymore!"

"I never was," Abbey said, taking a step towards him, fists clenched. "I was never allowed to be. I was never allowed to be anything at all."

"Fuck you, you whore! You were a little shit then, and you are a useless waste of skin now!"

Abbey watched Anton's movements, panicked and defensive, a weapon of some sort clutched in his hand. It was too dark to see anything but the glow from his eyes, but Abbey thought she could make out the handle of a bat. The low rumble of Faelith's growl ignited, but not in her ear or her head this time. This time it came from beneath the stairs.

"Gloria," Abbey said, trying to keep it simple for the devolved mess in front of her.

"Mine," he spat. "My Gloria."

"She's no one's Gloria. She's Gloria's Gloria. Suzy's mom."

"My Suzy." She heard his voice break. "She's mine, and you were gonna steal her from me, you fucking bitches!"

"She's not yours, Anton."

"She *is*," Anton said. "I made her. I put my dick in that bitch when I finished my time for murders I didn't commit. I thought I'd teach you a lesson, cozy up to your best friend, but she wasn't a smart girl, was she? She turned me down. *Me*. Well I took what I wanted, of course."

Abbey could hear muffled crying, somewhere close, like pleading into a gag.

"The cunt never told me how potent I was. One round and I knocked her up. Never got a chance to see my baby girl, though. Didn't even know she existed until I came to find you."

Abbey felt a scream expand in her belly, a balloon of rage and guilt and sadness filling her to the brim, ready to burst.

"I had it all figured out, but had no reason to make the effort to escape prison. Not until I saw you, at least. Thought I'd never find you, to make you pay. But hey, you found me."

Abbey kept staring at the swaying, glowing eyes, trying desperately to locate a weapon in her peripheral, a fire extinguisher, garden tool, anything at all.

"And when I came to visit you? There she was, that little blonde brat in her arms, her hand on yours. And Gloria's lips…"

Abbey saw movement, a white mass at her right, low to the ground, slithering through the water.

"Life's been pretty sweet for lucky Abbey."

Thick and wet and slippery, Faelith groped through the water, blindly finding her way around Abbey, brushing against her as she passed.

"No," Abbey said, voice strong and sure, directed at Faelith. "Let me. This is mine."

Faelith paused, the water rippling in her wake, then retreated, slithering back into the nook beneath the stairs.

"You were nothing, Abbey, and yet you ended up with everything," Anton said. "You lived, they died. You were free, I was locked up like an animal."

The muffled cries became panicked, wet pleas and sludge-coated screams.

She's drowning.

"You fucking idiot," Abbey said, her voice low and solid.

Anton stopped. He stopped speaking, stopped moving. It even sounded like he stopped breathing.

"What the fuck did you say to me?"

"You heard me," Abbey said, taking a step forward. "You're the one who's nothing. All of you. You always were."

Anton took a step forward, but Abbey did not stop. She kept moving, and her words kept flowing.

"I was a little girl, Anton. A human being. You sat idly by while I was berated and abused, doling out a healthy dose of it yourself."

Abbey's word came rushing out on tears, her body convulsing with rage and relief.

"I thought I hated myself, Anton. My fear, my weakness, my stupidity. I couldn't do anything, and I loathed my lack of power. Or so I thought."

Abbey reached Anton, standing toe to toe with him. He straightened up, posturing to intimidate her. But though he was a few centimeters taller, she stood higher. Stronger.

"I didn't hate myself, Anton." She moved in close, her lips nearly touching his, and looked right into his eyes. "I hated *you*. All of you. The fear was yours, that you felt compelled to quash my strength. The stupidity, yours, for not thinking you were creating a monster. The weakness, yours, for being less of a person than me. And the power?"

Abbey braced herself, widening her stance. She leaned in, pressing her cheek against Anton's and whispering in his ear.

"The power was always mine. I just didn't know I had it. Until now."

Abbey's knee snapped up, the strike of a cobra, making contact and burying Anton's testicles deep in his body. He fell down into the muck, and Abbey swung all her weight, kicking him square in the jaw and spinning him clear around onto his back. He sputtered, water filling his mouth as he howled in pain and grabbed at his bruised balls, and she landed a heel on his ribcage. She felt the bone splinter through her leather boot.

Blood spread like oil through the rancid water, the bleeding from Anton's gushing face visible even in the dark of the basement. Abbey waded around her brother, feeling around the floor for any part of Gloria she could find. She couldn't hear her voice over the sound of Anton's howls, so she searched the basement as fast as she could, running her hand over every corner of the waterlogged floor. She finished under the stairs, where Faelith sat patiently, drinking her tea.

"Help me," Abbey whispered, wondering why she cared if Anton heard her talking to the witch.

Faelith said nothing, but grabbed Abbey's forearm. Abbey pulled away from the pain as cold and intense as dry ice.

"Fuck, Faelith! How…"

Cold.

Abbey stumbled through the water, giving Anton's convulsing form a wide berth as she hurried to the cold storage room. She flung open the door and plunged inside, losing her footing and landing on top of Gloria. Abbey scrambled to her feet, then grabbed Gloria's wrists, bound behind her back, and pulled her out of the water. She tore the soggy gag out of Gloria's mouth and untied her wrists. Gloria sucked in air, hungrily gulping life back into her lungs.

Abbey planted kisses all over Gloria's face and Gloria kissed her on the mouth, laughing and crying at the same time. Then Gloria quit breathing, only for a moment before she started screaming.

"Suzy, Abbey! Get Suzy!"

"Where is she?" Abbey screamed back, fumbling around the floor.

"Not here," Gloria said, ripping off the rope around her ankles.

Abbey leapt out of the cold storage room, back into the main room. Gloria was right behind her, slamming into her when she stopped.

"He's gone," Abbey said.

The water was still, except for the ripples from their own legs. Abbey swished through the water, feeling for the brother that wasn't there. She looked up the stairs, at the light from the undressed moon shining through the kitchen ceiling, and saw wet hand and footprints all over the stairs.

They ran, almost stampeding each other, up the stairs and out the back door, following the wet tracks Anton had left behind. Abbey could see him, moving through the tall grass towards the woods, and she followed as fast as her legs would carry her. She heard Gloria panting behind her, struggling against her injuries, but Abbey persisted, knowing the danger was ahead, not behind.

She broke through the trees, running and dodging, taking branches to the face and brambles to the shins, muscle memory of her childhood guiding her down a path she could not see. It was dark, so dark, and the birds and frogs offered no song to aid in her travels.

Within a breath—whether one or one hundred, she could never tell—Abbey was released by the forest to the warmth of the clearing.

"Gloria!"

Abbey knew she wasn't there. She looked behind her into the woods, but realized that she had gone somewhere that Gloria could not follow.

Abbey walked up to the cottage, alive and immaculate as the day she had first seen it, the faeries swimming in their pond, throwing silver light to the sky. The plants were fragrant and gorgeous, and the fire crackled inside.

It was beautiful.

"Abbey."

Suzy's voice was weak and scared, and, worse, defeated. Anton was there, standing on the porch, Suzy's body limp in his arms, her eyes barely open.

"It's okay, Suzy."

"Abbey, I'm scared."

"You should be, brat," Anton hissed. "A monster lives here."

"No Suzy," Abbey said. "Love lives here. A monster has you in his arms."

The energy in the clearing changed, like a bolt of lightning had hit the cottage, igniting in with a silver frenzy. The faeries swarmed like angry wasps, attacking Anton and lifting Suzy out of his arms. He swung at the air, tentacles stuffing his mouth and ears as the faeries held him and carried Suzy to Abbey. Abbey lowered Suzy to the ground, checking her for injuries. A little scrape here and there, and a swollen ankle, but she'd be all right.

"It's okay," Abbey said, stroking her cheek. "You're going to be fine."

"But you won't."

Abbey turned just in time to see Anton rushing towards her, shaking faeries off left and right, a splintered piece of a post from the porch in his hand. She felt it as it pierced her skin, finding the sweet spot between her ribs and spearing her heart and lungs. Warm copper filled her mouth and bile bubbled up her throat, thick and suffocating. Pain radiated through her body, throbbing from the top of her head to the tips of her toes.

Anton lowered Abbey to ground, jamming the stake in a few times for good measure, then sat back on his haunches to admire his handiwork.

Abbey felt it, starting at her lower back and traveling like electricity up her spine, settling at the base of her skull. She looked down at her body, at the large stake in her chest. Breathing was hard, a car parked right on her chest, and she felt her pulse slower, slower, softer...

Abbey.

"Faelith," Abbey said, words gurgling through blood.

Abbey felt her chest heave and saw Faelith's grey hands come up and wrap around the stake.

Pull.

Abbey pulled, freeing the stake from her body.

Stand.

Abbey stood, stake in hand, and looked behind her at the ground where she had laid dying.

Faelith was there, naked, sprawled out on the ground and gasping for breath, gaping hole in the middle of her chest. She lifted a long finger and red talon, pointing it at Abbey as black blood dribbled from her mouth.

You.

Abbey turned, grasping the wood in her hand. It was smoother and heavier now. She looked down. It was the hatchet, ornate carvings on the handle and engravings on the blade. She didn't hesitate. She stepped towards Anton, who was a speechless statue, looking at Faelith and wavering on his haunches. Abbey lifted the hatchet up in the air and brought it down with both hands, slicing through Anton's skull until the blade jammed into the top of his spine. He stayed erect a moment, eyes vacant and bloody, then crumpled to the ground, his life seeping into the dirt.

Abbey screamed at his body, over and over, spitting and kicking dirt over it. She would have kept it up, had she not heard Faelith sputtering on the ground.

Abbey dropped to her hands and knees and crawled to Faelith, embracing her and cradling her head on her lap. Faelith looked up at Abbey and reached out her hand, cupping Abbey's face and stroking her cheek.

"Abbey," she said, blood leaking from her corners of her mouth.

"Faelith," Abbey said.

Abbey put her hand across the hole in Faelith's chest in a feeble attempt to stall the flow of blood. But she knew it was over.

"Abbey strong," Faelith said, squeezing her hand. "You know now."

"Yes," Abbey said, tears raining down onto Faelith's body. "I know."

Faelith grunted, shifting her weight forward, trying to get to her feet.

"No, Faelith," Abbey said. "Don't move. I'll stay with you."

"Yes, please," Faelith said, "But out there."

Faelith pointed at the woods. Abbey looked towards the cottage, and saw the faeries lining the porch, sobbing into other's shoulders.

"But this is your home," Abbey said, looking at the cottage, the stones, the ponds, the serenity.

"Was," Faelith said.

She struggled and huffed, heaving and hoisting herself up unto her buttocks. She put Abbey's face in her hands and gave her a soft kiss on the forehead.

"Yours now."

Faelith groaned, rocked twice, and stood, black blood flowing down her pale body, staining her torso and legs and pooling on the ground beneath her. She swooned, and Abbey caught her before she fluttered to the ground. Abbey winced at the feeling of her skin, hard and rough, flaking and abrasive.

"Faelith? Please," Abbey pleaded. Her chest hurt, heavy with impending loss, a flood of tears choking off her breath.

"Child," Faelith said, smiling wide one last time. "I always with you. I love you."

"I love you," Abbey said.

"Now go."

They went. Into the woods, through forest too thick to traverse, yet they made it through somehow. In what seemed like a mere handful of seconds, they were on the other side of the tree line, with Abbey's yard and house in view. They struggled over to the old tree where Abbey eased Faelith to the ground, taking care not to scrape her skin across the bark.

Faelith touched the tree, hands spread wide, and caressed it's flaking bark. Her skin sloughed off in response, rough and peeling, dark crimson seeping from the lacerations on her flesh. Abbey touched Faelith. Her body was stiff and dehydrated—petrified, even.

The witch relaxed, her every muscle and tension relaxing into the tree as she embraced it, wrapping her arms clear around it and holding it tight.

"Mother," Faelith cried, her voice that of a child, but one at peace.

Faelith's body seized, throwing Abbey back on the ground. Abbey watched in amazement and horror as the tree grew into Faelith, branches stabbing through her skin and bark piercing her eyes from the inside. Blood flowed from her every orifice and wound, thick and slow. Abbey leaned forward, touched Faelith's blood, and found that it was tacky. Sticky.

Sap.

Abbey sat back as her tree lit up, silver veins of sap shining from the glow of the faeries flitting about, kissing and stroking the bark, the leaves, the moss. The tree glowed, silver foliage raining down in sparks. More faeries appeared, carrying Suzy on interlocked arms to Abbey's side. Abbey put her arm around the girl as she opened her eyes, looking in wonder at the stars and faeries dancing in the sky and on the tree.

And Abbey smiled through silver tears.

EPILOGUE

The children squealed and played, sandy blonde hair blowing in the breeze. It was summer again, and Abbey wondered where the time had gone. The years had sprinted by in a flash, a blur of beauty, of tastes, of music. Hundreds of pitchers of strawberry lemonade had been consumed on that porch, hundreds of songs sung around the campfire in the pit in the yard.

Abbey's house had been rebuilt, then renovated, then renovated again, and was now a simple but modern home, big enough to hold the family of three, two dogs, a cat named Mortimer, and a siamese fighting fish named Ursula. Many meals had come and gone in her dining room, and barbecues in the backyard. Suzy had learned to ride her bike on the long gravel drive, planted Saskatoon bushes along the edge of the yard, boarded and hopped off the bus at the end of the lane as the grades melted away.

Suzy became an adult, with a life and family of her own. She married, and had a son and a daughter who had families and children of their own.

Abbey and Gloria watched as their family grew before their eyes, living and loving every moment. The old house that had been rooted in torment for Abbey became a place of wonder and magic, a weekend getaway where everyone would meet and laugh and eat and drink. She and Gloria couldn't get around as much as they used to, but they were content to sit and watch their roots flourish with new growth. More than content. They were truly happy.

And Gloria was just as magical as she had been many years before.

Abbey gave Gloria's hand a squeeze and kissed her cheek.

"What was that for?" Gloria said.

"Love," Abbey said.

Gloria was beautiful, her lips still peach and plump, her golden-gray hair a soft, shining ripple in the sun. Her green eyes glowed within her white skin, deep crows feet adorable little sketches of art every time she smiled.

"Love," Gloria said, kissing Abbey on the mouth.

They sat on the patio sofa, hand in hand, watching their grandchildren play. The picnic table in the yard was heaping with bowls of fruits and breads, and condiments for the burgers cooking on the grill.

"Mom?"

Suzy walked up the steps, glasses of lemonade in hand. Abbey still couldn't believe what a beautiful creature she had become. White hair shimmering in the sun, icy-blue eyes like crystals placed in a porcelain face, tall and lean and long and simply perfect.

"Fresh, just like you ladies taught me," Suzy said, smiling wide and bright.

Suzy placed the glasses on the end table beside the couch and embraced her mothers, holding them close before returning to her family. She leaned on her husband as they looked lovingly at their children and grandchildren playing football in the yard. Gloria laughed and Abbey smiled, happiness blanketing everything around them. Abbey's eyes wandered to the tree, and the swing hanging from her heavy branch. Bridget, Suzy's youngest grandchild, swayed on the swing, lost in her own world.

With great effort, Abbey stood from the sofa and grabbed her cane.

"Where are you going?" Gloria asked, refusing to let go of her hand.

"To chat with Bridget for a spell," Abbey said, smiling.

"Odd duck, that one," Gloria said, releasing Abbey's hand.

"Indeed," Abbey said under her breath. "Everyone's got a story."

Abbey worked her way down the steps into the yard and hobbled to the tree. Bridget lifted her eyes and gave her a huge smile.

"Great Grandma!"

"My wee love," Abbey said, embracing the girl as she leapt from the swing. "Come. Sit with me."

"You want a chair, Gran?"

"No thank you, dear. I like my spot."

Bridget helped Abbey down to her knees then onto her buttocks, leaning her back against the massive tree. Abbey closed her eyes, feeling hands first on her shoulders, then wrapping around her body, embracing her tight. She let out a huge heave of air, releasing all of her tension, stiffness, age.

"Great Granny, you love your tree."

"I do, my love."

"You know what I think?" Bridget said. "I think it loves you, too. I do believe it grows a little every time you sit against it."

Bridget jumped up and batted at the leaves, giggling and chattering to the tree like it was an old friend.

"I believe you're right," Abbey said, looking up at the massive tree. Its great green leaves shimmered in the sunlight, its girth so plentiful even Suzy's husband could not wrap his arms around it and touch his fingers together. Not even close.

And the bark was strong and thick, with fine lines of silvery sap peeking through the striations in the wood. Abbey breathed in deep, smelling the musty fragrance of her old friend.

"I love you," Abbey said.

I love you too.

"Where are you going?"

Dinner had been divine, and Abbey was stuffed, full of food and happiness. She looked at her wife, her emerald eyes glowing in the night, then looked into the trees.

"For my nightly walk," Abbey said.

"It's so late," Gloria said.

"In so many ways," Abbey said.

"It's dark."

"It always has been."

Gloria paused, lingering on the same question she had been asking for years.

"Where do you go?"

Abbey didn't say. She never did.

"I love you," Gloria said, kissing Abbey on the cheek before heading back to the house.

Abbey smiled and watched her go. She was more in love with her every day. More in love with life.

She braced herself with her cane and gave the old tree a pat on the way by.

THE WIND CHIMES SANG OUT, A DARK MELODY IN A MINOR KEY, haunting and beautiful. Abbey stood on the porch, looking over the beauty of the clearing, watching the faeries dance and twirl in the moonlight. They were as silver and bright and beautiful as ever, glistening and radiating joy with every movement and every sound. One landed on Abbey's shoulder, pecking her leathery cheek with tiny lips, then flew off, taking a nose-dive straight into the pond to wrestle with the koi.

Abbey sighed. Her world was beautiful. She was beautiful. She was strong.

She walked into the cottage, embracing the warmth from the wood stove and the raging fire burning within. She lingered in the living room for a spell, looking over the shelves and bookcases at the many trinkets she had collected through the years.

A sprig of flowers she had pulled from the Bow River the day she and Gloria had married. It had been beautiful that day, sunny and crisp, the Three Sisters mountains towering over the ceremony.

Vials of sand collected from the many beaches around the world that she and Gloria and Suzy had visited.

A rock from Mount Edith Cavell she had taken on their first solo vacation after Suzy had moved away from home.

Dried flowers she picked from Marie and Chuck's graves behind the old motel in Lamarque. They died within a month of each other, having lived to almost a hundred years old together. They were always happy to take Abbey and her family in, a monthly visit that included swimming, chatting, and hefty helpings of greasy food.

The dancer. The little ballerina that spun in her mirrored box.

The hatchet, hanging on the wall, its engravings glowing silver, pulsating with every beat of Abbey's heart.

And the red journal.

Abbey took the red book off the shelf and settled in by the fire. A faerie fluttered in through the open window and landed on her lap, spinning three time before wrapping itself in its wings and curling up on its tentacles for a sleep. Abbey stroked it as she flipped through the pages, looking at sketches both old and new. The book was the same size, but somehow endless, thousands upon thousands of pages with a lifetime of sketches inside

And there were many more blank pages waiting to be filled.

Abbey flipped to the final sketch, a colourful drawing of the woods at night, and a row of trees, branches reaching, intertwined, like lovers holding hands. The trees were mesmerizing, coppery browns with veins of silver that lit up the page, the leaves rustling, glowing emeralds in the purple night sky.

Abbey closed the journal and scratched her head. When she

brought her hand down, there was a clump of white hair in her hand. She barely regarded it as she tossed it into the wood stove before moving to the mirror that hung on the wall.

She was an old woman now, older than possible, grey and white but not withered. She was stronger than ever. Her hair was almost gone, her head a shining white orb, her eyes black and fiery.

She opened her mouth, her joy and strength pushing to escape.

And she let loose a low, growling cackle that found its way out of the cottage, through the woods, and into the night.

ACKNOWLEDGMENTS

Here's the part where I thank the people. You usually read this kind of thing at the beginning of the book, but I had to leave it to the end, as none of you had met Faelith yet, and therefore my acknowledgements contain spoilers. Also, they would make no sense.

This book is for all the strong women in my life. There are so many of you, but there are a specific few whose silver light has shone especially bright during the telling of this tale.

For Amber Z., who was an ear when I needed one, when things seemed their worst. You let me vent and drone on and bitch and moan and complain, and then had just the right thing to say to get me back on track. Your critiques and guidance have made me a much stronger writer. You, Amber, are my Faelith.

For Des B., who did more for me than she'll ever know. My very own "Annie" that I never dreamed I would have. Des, you have made all my blood, sweat, and tears feel worth it, simply by reading and supporting my work. Funny thing, that behind the support and love of reading was a talented author hiding behind unseen words. Des, I look forward to seeing you on the shelves one day, and on the bestseller lists. Des, you are my Faelith.

For Jessica R., who is the most inspiring woman I've met. Jess, your fearless approach to writing, reading, biking, relationships, politics, animals, pop culture, derpy humans, and life in general has made you my muse. You are someone I aspire to be. Aside from all that mushy bullshit, you were instrumental in the completion of Crone. Thursday nights at Denny's will always be my favourite night of the week. Jess, you are my Faelith.

And Mom. For birthing me, raising me, tolerating me as a bratty teenager, and offering your unconditional love and support in my years as an "adult", I adore and appreciate you. From instilling in me a love of reading and a strong command of the English language, I am forever grateful. You are a perfect example of a strong woman and good human, and inspire me in everything I do, every day. I love you, Mom. You are my Faelith.

Have a Faelith. And be somebody's Faelith.

Jae

ABOUT THE AUTHOR

Jae Mazer is a Canadian who was born in Victoria, British Columbia, and grew up in the prairies of Northern Alberta. After spending the majority of her life battling sasquatches in the Great White North, she migrated south to Texas to have a go at the armadillos. Now she enjoys life as a mom, a musician, and a connoisseur and creator of horror, science fiction, and fantasy. Many moons ago, a rampant love of reading led her to believe she could weave a good tale herself, and she now has seven novels under her belt, as well as short stories published in various anthologies.

ALSO BY JAE MAZER

Landing in Eden

Delivery

Pal Tailor

Gahl's Door

Chrysalis and Clan

Also written by Jae, under the Pen Name J.M. Adler

Notch

Jae Mazer has short stories included in the following anthologies:

Eclectically Heroic, by Inklings Publishing

Hair Raising Tales of Villainous Confessions, by Mad Girl's Publishing